W9-BMJ-942

The Man Who Thought
He Was Messiah

OTHER NOVELS BY CURT LEVIANT

The Yemenite Girl
Passion in the Desert

The Man Who Thought He Was Messiah

a novel by

Curt Leviant

The Jewish Publication Society

Philadelphia • New York

5751 • 1990

First edition
Manufactured in the United States of America

Library of Congress Cataloging-in-Publication Data
Leviant, Curt.
The man who thought he was Messiah : being a fantastical fable of Reb Nachman of Bratslav, his temptation, love, and worldwide adventures in realms known and unknown / by Curt Leviant.—1st ed.
p. cm.
ISBN 0-8276-0371-1
1. Naḥman, of Bratslav, 1772–1811—Fiction. I. Title.
PS3562.E8883M36 1990
813'.54—dc20 90-5261
CIP

A portion of this book appeared in slightly different form in *The Missouri Review*.

The author wishes to thank the New Jersey State Council on the Arts, the Jerusalem Foundation's Mishkenot Sha'ananim Artist Colony, and the Rutgers Research Council for grants that assisted in the completion of this novel.

Designed by Jonathan Kremer

This book is dedicated
to the memory of
my parents
Fenia Dusawicki Leviant
פּײגע בת צדוק וחסיה דוסאװיצקי
and
Jacques Leviant
יעקב בן משה וסלבה־זלדה לביאנט
and
to the memory of
our Opi
Leo Pfeifer
יהודה בן חיים וברטה פּײפר

AUTHOR'S NOTE

Those who look here for a mirror of facts, for fidelity to real events—historical, biographical, musical—seek in vain.

Know that this is a work of fiction, a series of invented remembrances, of may-have-happeneds, of might-have-happeneds.

For even the presumed real life of a man may be legend.

Illustration by Curt Leviant

BS"D

God's whisper

After God whispered to Nachman that he was within the Messianic line, his life was never the same. For months now a haze had enveloped everything. A fine layer of the thinnest glass, so diaphanous and pliable it could be bent and molded like clay, was draped not over him but over people and places, over melodies and dance. He felt removed. He had thought that this whisper would be a blessing, but it was a—he clapped his hand over his mouth to drown the thought. Could God have whispered untruth that plain Tuesday morning as Nachman walked back from his early morning river swim? No. For that would be a theological contradiction. Still, that enchanting whisper was no magic elixir, it did not relieve him of earth-bound woes: He struggled to climb the ladder, he coughed as usual, and the smell of a woman's hair still drove him wild.

Book One

This is how it begins:
Remember this beginning,
for it can be like a mirror that,
when darkness comes,
sheds light like a thousand candles.

During that mystery-laden time of day when, in the words of the passover song, it was "neither day nor night," and the milk white no-light might have been dawn or dusk, so tenuous, so precarious, was the silver balance between light and darkness, Nachman of Bratslav, the great-grandson of the holy Baal Shem Tov, walked to the river, alone in the world. He walked to the river, alone in the world, and that was his undoing; he walked to the river, alone in the world, and that was his uniqueness; he always walked alone in the world, for that, he knew, was his choice, his destiny. He walked alone with his thoughts, humming songs of his own creation as he looked at firs and up at tops of swaying hills, rounded like carefully scribed Hebrew letters. He marvelled at the wonders of God, who daily renews His acts of creation and garbs Himself in light as in a mantle.

Nachman recited, sang with the birds, the morning prayers. He prayed slowly, syllable by syllable, almost letter by letter. For he knew what infinite power the letters possessed. He taught his followers, the Bratslav Hasidim, that each letter was holy. Worlds upon worlds, life itself was dependent upon these Hebrew letters. And hence prayers, holy in themselves and built upon the holy alphabet, had to be recited with devotion, earnestness, and joy. What wonders lay hidden in each letter. Each had a personality, a music, a life of its own.

The year, by the reckoning of the gentiles, was 1800. A perfect number, a perfect year, for even the numbers of the gentiles may be laden with Jewish meaning. 1800 is 100 times 18. 18, the Hebrew number for *chai*, which means "life." One hundred times life, and it was also 100 years since the birth of his great-grandfather, Israel ben Eliezer, the holy Baal Shem Tov, the founder of Hasidism. Had Nachman been born ten years later, he would have been eighteen years old this year, thus making a perfect cluster of three. Ah, the wonder of numbers, of time and of space. At this moment, while I, Nachman the son of Feige and Simcha, may their memory be blessed, send my songs of joy flying like birds toward the Holy One Blessed Be He, at this moment, miles away in distance, centuries away in culture, Goethe is composing verse, Napoleon is planning conquests, and Beethoven's hand moves over a sheet of music. 1800, one hundred times *chai*. A year for life. For marvelous deeds.

Around him, silence. A song coursed through Nachman's body. Like angels, these melodies lived no longer than their mission; they survived only the act of creation and, by the time he came home, were forgotten. But there was always another melody waiting. Songs in him were an everflowing spring. God had created the world not with words but with melody; and when He whispered, music flowed. What secret alphabet, Nachman wondered, would preserve those songs?

The path Nachman followed grew lighter as he approached the river. First his head moved, then his shoulders. He began to dance. Once, as a child in Mezhibezh, the town of his birth, he had enchanted dozens of Hasidim with a wordless melody. Many of the older men had known the Baal Shem Tov. In the dance that followed, a Hasid, grateful for the boy's gift of melody, placed the Baal Shem Tov's fur cap on Nachman's head. Everyone smiled. How sweet the boy looked wearing the holy man's *shtreyml*. But Nachman felt as if his great-grandfather's spirit had entered him. An implosion of light. A sluice, a sliver of ecstasy, icicle-shaped, swift as lightning, hot as wax, speared him and burst. Nachman floated, alone in the woods, eyes closed, eyes open, dancing, alone.

The hills revolved slowly in the morning mist. With the first light, the dew glistened on the rushes, and cobwebs on low-lying bushes quivered with light. All creation was stirring. Blue jays, starlings, grackles sang as Nachman watched the rose light dance on slim birch trunks. On a beech twig a robin's loud song drowned out Nachman's thoughts. A little ditch formed by the rains stopped him. He smiled to himself, recalled a story told about the Baal Shem Tov, known to all as the Besht. Once, strolling in the Carpathian mountains, the Besht unwittingly stepped off a mountain top. Instantly, another mountain rushed forward to close the gap and save his life. But I, Nachman thought, I have to jump—and he did—over a little ditch. For him, in his day, no miracles. Well, one perhaps. Nachman was his parents' only son. For years Feige and Simcha could not have children. When, finally, Nachman was born, people whispered that he was a stray, a foundling, an adopted child. What did God do? He changed Nachman's face to look like the Baal Shem Tov's, so that everyone would know he was the Master's scion. Although his great-grandfather had died in 1760, a dozen years before Nachman's birth, Nachman always referred to the Besht as zayde, grandpa.

From zayde came his love of music, love of dance. Where others heard only a chirping insect, Nachman sensed melody. He saw music in bending wheat, heard it in a falling star, felt it in a person's soul. At a glance he could measure a man's character by the light, half-light, coarse light, or no light radiating from his eyes. The way a man held his head, pursed his lips, and moved his hands, the motion of his eyes, the cut of nostrils, were mirrors into a man's inner being.

The sun was coming up now. He sniffed. What was that? A faint perfume—not of any plant, tree, or flower he knew—wafted in the air. He inhaled deeply. How delicious. He had never smelled a fragrance like it before. Getting closer. First came the unusual perfume and then—he could not remember whether he first heard her footsteps or saw the tumble of blonde hair. A well-formed peasant girl of nineteen or twenty. Nachman stopped. Breathed. The fragrance like a weight in the air. Oblivious to Nachman, she cut a path at right angles to his through the rushes, then vanished. He tried to seize the trail of flowers she had left behind. He felt a heat surging in his loins. The blood throbbed in his head. He shook his head. His meditations were broken. He attempted a chant, sang louder. Turned and looked down the path the girl had taken. Wondered if she would look back at him. But she was gone, hidden by the tall rushes, the wild grass, the dips in the fields.

From Nathan's Diary

I, Reb Nachman's assistant, dance in the outer circle, Reb Nachman in the inner. The white velvet skullcaps we all wear paint white circles in the air. What awesome mystical powers, the Rebbe once said, are contained in two rings of dancers moving in opposite directions. It mirrors the very essence of the universe. The Master's eyes are closed in ecstasy. He transports himself in sacred dance to worlds beyond. And yet, when the dance is over, the prayers done, he becomes a man like the rest of us. It is not beneath him to raise vegetables, dig for potatoes, and tend the beautiful cauliflowers he grows. Every Jew must earn his bread, he says. Unlike other Hasidic rebbes I've seen, Reb Nachman is self-supporting. He does not ask others to solicit for donations. Weekdays he works, studies, and writes; Sabbaths and holidays he gives us melodies and stories that he hopes will infuse joy, change hearts, and bring goodness and purity to the world.

Other Hasidic leaders consider him strange. He has no use for miracles, claims no curative powers, disdains the wonder-working rebbes. Barren women do not come to him for a blessing. The ailing do not ask his intercession with the heavenly Father. Pray, he preaches. Every Jew has this gift. Of other rebbes stories are told. Nachman creates his own stories. And this is something other Hasidic leaders cannot comprehend.

After the Evening Service, they formed, as usual, two circles. Nachman inside with all the children moving in one direction, the Hasidim outside dancing in the opposite direction. To symbolize that, though the world went one way, a Jew could go the other and still prevail. Nachman held hands with the children, but still felt far away—on the other side of a glass wall. Can one whiff of perfume put a wall between me and them? he wondered. He looked up at his Bratslav motto on the flying wall: "Jews, do not despair." Was the glass wall despair? But how could it be, when he taught his Hasidim not to despair? Nachman stared at the glass until a silver coating came over it and he saw his own reflection.

Later, he sat in his room adjoining the bes medresh, the synagogue and study room. A May breeze from the mountains chilled the air. He started a small coal fire. Then the fragrance returned to him. Delicious afternoon scent. The blonde peasant girl. He went to the stove. But even the coal smell could not drive away her hay and rose perfume. That. That. That was the worm that stood in the way of his quest for holiness. That *yetzer ho-reh,* that wormy evil inclination, was all that stood between him and God's whisper. If he could wring the neck of that passion, he would be an angel, a saint. He would fly with lead in his shoes. He laughed, remembering the Hasid who had come to him and suddenly bent to the ground. Nachman thought he was going to kiss his feet like a peasant bowing to a Russian Orthodox bishop. But the man quickly pushed up Nachman's trouser cuffs, grasped his ankles, and lifted his feet. "Forgive me, rebbe," the visitor explained, "but I had to see for myself. People say you are an angel; only the lead in your shoes keeps you on the ground. But your shoes are so light!"

Was it he whom his community of Hasidim revered? he often wondered. Was it his stories and teachings they admired, or was it only the Besht's radiance they grafted onto him? Because for Hasidim the Baal Shem Tov was as great as Abraham and Moses, and anyone linked with the great Master inherited the light.

Nachman took a deep breath. The room was too hot. Oppressed, he stepped outside. The night air was crisp. Perhaps it would drive the other perfume away. He smelled the cabbages. The cucumbers were ripe. An unseen fog encompassed him. He coughed. There is a Jewish remedy, he thought: honeyed warm milk and eggs. But the old housekeeper was gone. He'd been without one for months. Perhaps his assistant, Nathan, was right. It was time to find a new one.

The garden air was pungent with the taste of green. Nachman heard the crickets. Was that perfume still there? We have to begin again. Like the spider who spins the web anew, like the ant who takes the dropped grain and climbs the hill once more, like the sun that has set and must rise again each day. Out in the darkness Nachman walked, breathing air that he himself imbued with a light from within.

When he woke, there was light and yet no light. The light of dusk, the light of dawn. Blue was the stream. Blue on the side of grey. And the sky, as if seen on glass, was like the lake. God said, Let there be light, and there was light. There was light. But this light-no-light was not like the light of the sun, not like the light of the moon; it was as if light had not yet been born, but was just thought of as light, a pre-sun-like light, a post-moon-like light, a light made when rain and clouds clashed and light came from the clouds. How fine and nice was that light. But such milk light did not last long. It played its brief song, then left the sky.

As light and darkness were blending, Nachman walked to the water. Lake or river. Some called it a lake because of its shape; others, a river, because the lake was really an outlet of the river and derived its water from it.

That smell again. The hair of a woman. He could swear it was the hair of a woman, a special fragrance exuding heat and desire. Not a passive scent, like yesterday's, but an aggressive one, a fragrance that like a voice wanted a response. As the Yiddish had it—the scent made itself heard. Indeed, it vibrated like a stringed instrument.

Now she was coming toward him. Again he saw the tumble of blonde hair. She was drying herself with a cloth. Who smiled and said good morning? He? She? But though he whispered, "I will not notice her," he knew that he had sensed her even before she appeared. That her presence was palpable even before she passed (too fleeting, that moment when they passed each other like two swallows in flight). That he was aware of the vacuum she left. From the moment he met her, a hollow form walked beside him, hung heavily within him, until he came to the river. How could he, who knew every syllable, each note, all the images of the Song of Songs, *not* notice? He did not turn around, but she did, he knew. The hair on the nape of his neck bristled.

At the water's edge, Nachman waded to a thicket, pulled out his raft, and lay down to float. With a few strokes of his palms he was carried away from shore. He looked up at the sky, saw the ring of trees, beech and elm, willow and birch. He lifted his voice and sang a song of the trees. In the distance, the grey green hills and flaxen clouds were set against a deep blue sky. The current turned the raft slowly. No need to paddle. The world spun for him, as if he were the earth and a sun of hills and trees revolved around him. Memories came between blinks of eyelids. He saw himself as a lad of six or seven, floating on a raft in the lake near Mezhibezh where his zayde lived. And in the winter, without his parents' knowing, he rolled in the snow and prostrated himself on the Baal Shem Tov's grave, soaking the cold into his chest and bones in his desire to banish sin and infuse purity. It hadn't helped; all it gave him was a chronic cough. Nachman looked up at the sky, as he did as a lad, eyeing heaven, hoping he could grow up to be a *zaddik,* a holy, righteous, saintly man. Now he was grown up—but was he a zaddik? That everyone considered him one didn't really matter. People's impressions only changed the outer shape of reality, as a potter shaped clay—they didn't change the inner essence. Clay remained clay, no matter who the master potter. No amount of shaping could make gems of clay.

Nachman relaxed on the raft. How tranquil to rise and descend with the gentle, breathing waves. A wind whispered through the trees. He remembered God's whisper. But wasn't that heresy? True, he *was* a descendant of the House of David, and from that line the Messiah was destined to come; but if God's hint was right, what was he doing in the middle of the river, flat on his back like a lazy peasant? Nachman chuckled to himself. Thank God for laughter; it brought the mighty down from their fantasy-filled heights.

He took a deep breath, hoping to sense that hay blonde fragrance again. To have it float over the water to his raft. If he smelled it, it would not oppress him; he would be able to concentrate on his prayers, on melodies, on the beautiful Hebrew letters. For there was nothing more beautiful than an *aleph* and a *beys*. Nachman knew he would have to sharpen his concentration; for lately, when he prayed, a woman's leg would intrude, long, slim, naked to the thigh, about to step out of the ritual bath. It destroyed the petals of prayer he had created, the butterfly wings formed of scores of beloved letters, spoken in colors of rainbow. Then Nachman would begin to hum, to drown out the image of the naked leg, to conjure away image with music. His song prevailed. He stared at the leg until it lost its potency, became a leg of wood. The essence, the tempting nakedness, was driven away.

Nachman sat up on the raft. No, today he was not refreshed. The water, the floating between heaven and earth, had brought no repose. His nerves hummed. A restlessness like a vibrating string thrummed through him. He paddled back to shore, tied the raft to a root in the cove, splashed water on his face, and walked back home.

From Nathan's Diary

Our master taught:

"Try to purify your evil thoughts by day. What a person thinks of during the day torments him at night. Every day man thanks God for His daily renewal of creation. And every day man prays for the strength to conquer the yetzer ho-reh in him. For the yetzer ho-reh reawakens

> daily. What satisfied him Sunday won't suffice him Monday. Remember, what a person thinks of during the day torments him at night."

The next morning, Nachman made his way to the river again. Despite the early hour, a warm mist rose from the ground. The sun was up. A robin hopped alongside of him. The quiet path to the river, bordered on both sides by tall, flowering rushes, insured privacy, prompted dreams. Sunshine gleamed on the sand. Near the river he saw a colony of ducks. Nachman heard the occasional lap of a little bend in the water against a cove.

Nachman sat with his back pressed against a tree trunk. Would he see her again, he wondered. He rubbed the back of his neck. Looked at the nearby path. Heard the lap of water. A large brown and black butterfly, larger than he had ever seen before, swooped before him. He looked up; memories snapped. Ah. There again, yesterday's scent, a mixture of cut hay, roses, and spices. She trotted toward him, stared at him. Nachman avoided her eyes. He put his hand to his forehead. He was hot. The sun burned, like the heavy waves of a headache. A woodpecker clacked peck peck peck against a dead branch. Two magpies echoed each other's calls. Nachman, usually good at imitating bird sounds, failed this time. A warm flush rises from his loins to his chest and throat, choking him. The red spills over into his cheeks. He blinked; she was no longer there.

As Nachman undressed by the reeds, he saw the girl emerging from the water. No, that could not be. He had just seen her running the other way. He closed his eyes, reopened them. Perhaps a play of shadows, twigs. He knew, old woe, the scent of woman's hair drove him wild; he didn't know it would make him mad.

As he walked home, he thought: What good perfection and holiness, if what he longed for most was missing? What good were sun and sand, rain and trees, without a beautiful woman? God gave Adam a woman as helpmeet—but, as the Bible says, "a helpmeet against him." So a woman is also a test. Test and temptation. God gave Adam Eve. He gave Eve the snake. Both were tested; both failed. But he, Nachman, would not fail.

The true test of a Jew, Nachman thought, is to be able to overcome temptation. And what is the greatest temptation for a man? Woman's sexuality. Hence, he resolved, he would battle this enemy by meeting it head-on. He would seek out temptation. We have to take risks, face up to temptation in order to subdue it. In fact, sap the adversary's strength by *seeming* to give in to the yetzer's impulse.

Why hadn't he married? Had he been married, he wouldn't have had to worry about temptation. There was a time, several years ago, when matchmakers ran from town to town on his behalf. At first, Nachman rejected the prospective brides offered by other Hasidic leaders, for he didn't want marriage based on family connection. If every act of his, every teaching, would have to be weighed against what his father-in-law would say, then Nachman would lose his independence. He would not be able to go his own way. Also, each time a match was proposed, an empty feeling—a warning signal—went through him. He would find fault, carp, turn away. Soon, emissaries and matchmakers stopped coming to him. And then, when he heard God's whisper, he realized he couldn't burden a wife with that spiritual weight he carried on his back. When his destined bride would come, Nachman thought, he would sense it.

At evening prayers he held the Siddur in his hands but directed his glance into space. His Hasidim thought his eyes were closed in ecstasy. There, that naked leg again. Out of the doorway of the mikva, the ritual bath. Long, slim, golden hairs sparkling like tiny rainbows. Then, for the first time, the rest of her emerged: the peasant girl.

He felt a movement in his body, as if a stone had landed in the pit of his stomach. A force within rejected the image of the girl and sought to pull him back to his prayers. He saw the lovely Hebrew letters, each with its own special shape and form. The letters grew; they bent like young birches. Leaped up in dance with long, slim, naked legs. He wrestled with the letters, brought them down to size. And prayed God to set temptation before him so he could struggle and prevail.

The next morning his prayer was answered.

Nachman did not know whether it was a divine sending or a mirror image of his prayer, an anti-prayer adumbrating misfortune. Was he supposed to pass her by, look away as pious men did in Kabbalistic tales, lest they be ensnared by demons? Was she a Lilith introduced by the anti-heavenly forces to drown out God's whisper? Or a Godsend? He looked; she approached with a slow, confident stride, exuberant and gay. A body straight out of the Song of Songs. She carried a bundle of wet wash. As she walked, her breasts quivered under her loose blouse, as if animated by this lovely day. A column of heat, a fiery horseshoe invaded his chest and neck as she passed him. She smiled softly to herself. Nachman said nothing. For the next three or four strides he breathed in the pungent hair fragrance she left behind, a hay blonde essence. What did Nachman feel at that moment? Adam seeing, recognizing, finally knowing Eve? Did he feel as if the world had begun again? He was Joseph with Potiphar's wife, David gazing down from his palace window at Bathsheba bathing on her rooftop, Amnon lusting for Tamar, Samson for Delilah. Suddenly, Nachman understood them. He stood at the threshold of creation. The Zohar speaks of the union of Israel with God. Kabbala is full of erotic images. All theoretical. Here before him is the peak of understanding. A woman's body. Perfect. The beloved in the Song of Songs. Neck like a tower, breasts like twin gazelles.

She was tall, with long legs and long blonde hair. She wore only a skirt and blouse, and her breasts swung like the grape clusters on the huge branches that the scouts sent by Moses brought back from the Land of Israel. Perhaps she was going to her lover. Scents of mint and camomile spiked his senses. A sparrow twittered, two sparrows, a couple calling each other in love.

As she passed him, Nachman was tempted to turn. Two unseen fingers clasped his face, urging him to turn, to see if perhaps she would too. If both turned it would be a sign. In his mind Nachman turned as he moved forward to the water. With closed eyes he came to her, singing one of his beautiful melodies. He approached her unashamed, speaking her language until she spread her arms.

Suddenly, the girl changed direction, and with a little laugh, headed for the water. Nachman went to his little bower, placed his hat and skullcap on a stone, his clothes on a low limb. He heard her dive into the water.

As he swam he recalled her fragrance. A gleaming arm surfaced, then another, as if necks of swans dipped and played in the water. Nachman felt his heart shift in his chest. He swam to shore and stood rooted, watching her. Beauty is part of the divine order. Nothing is removed from God's plan.

About to move forward. Indeed, in his mind's eye, he saw his knee jerk forward, to go, find, seize the girl. Lustful thoughts, the Talmud teaches, are worse than submitting to temptation. What kind of prayer should he utter now? He felt his lips moving, but no sounds came. Bit his lip until he tasted blood. Dug his nails into his palms. He saw her clothes on a flat stone. Nachman turned sharply and followed his heart home.

Victorious again, he smiled. My heart, my mind, are whole, he thought. He recalled his father quoting the Baal Shem Tov's bitter opponent, the Vilna Gaon: "A man's mind is his holy temple." And his father added, "Even that little temple should not be defiled."

He stayed away from the lake two days. He sensed that she too had stayed away. His absence and hers, then, were related events, like substance and shadow. The hand moves in light, the shadow follows. Can a shadow move without the hand? A hand in sunlight without shadow?

The next day, Nachman went to the river again. Buoyant, confident. Master of prayer. Subduer of temptation. Like Joshua, he could make the sun stop, halt the moon floating through the clouds. This time she was ahead of him. As he walked softly behind her, she did not turn, perhaps unaware that he followed. He breathed in her pungent hay blonde essence. He dug his nails into his palms. His teeth sought his lips. He tried to cajole his arms, to speak to his legs, as Moses had spoken to the rock. Nachman could never afterward remember if he was still watching the naked girl swim, or if he had already turned to go back home, when he heard what he heard: a splash of water, less steady, more furious than before; a cry. Stirred, he looked out. The girl was struggling in the river.

"Help, please help!"

The sound echoed in his head. Perhaps she had been calling for some time and he, struggling with his heart, had not heard. At once, he tore off his shirt and trousers, stepped out of his sandals and ran into the water, swimming toward her.

"Coming," he cried. "Coming. I'm coming."

He swam furiously, shaking the water from his eyes, churning toward her. As he approached, he saw her head go under. Heart bursting, he swam with all his strength, groped, found, seized her hand and then her hair. We have to take risks, he said. We have to take risks. Swimming with one hand, he pulled her hair and raised her head. With even strokes he moved toward the shore, felt the sand under his feet. The power, the power, he thought. The best way to subdue the power of lust is to use a ruse. Fool the evil angel. Pretend one is succumbing to, enjoying lust, but in reality . . . In reality what? In reality, he realized, one fools oneself into thinking one is a saint.

"My feet," she said weakly, "my feet . . . caught . . . weeds."

Just then his own feet stumbled and he fell exhausted into the water, dragging the girl with him. In the tumble his hands went around her and hers around him. Though her body was cold and wet—I can't; I must be pure in mind and body for God's whisper—a delicious warmth surged out of it and he did not let go, hearing other whispers as she wrapped her lips around each fingertip, then kissed his lips.

From Nathan's Diary

> In the evening, the Rebbe spoke of the mitzva of saving lives. He who saves one life, he quoted the Talmud, has saved an entire world. And he who destroys one human being is like one who has destroyed an entire world. But he who saves one life stands at the threshold of creation and is worthy of union with the Divine.

"You saved me," she murmured afterward.

They lay in the shallow water by the reeds, not far from the cove where Nachman kept his raft. The girl drew her head back and looked at him, as if seeing him for the first time. "You're the one who passed me twice. The first day you didn't turn around, but you wanted to . . ."

"How do you know?"

"Because I didn't turn around though I wanted to."

He looked at her, still held her in his arms. Indeed, she was beautiful. As lovely as . . .

"And the second time?" Nachman asked.

"The second time," she said, "you were even more stubborn. I turned but you didn't . . ."

She rose out of the water, laughing. Nachman watched her dress. Yes, she was as lovely as an *aleph* or a *tov*.

"How many times have you seen me?" she asked.

"Once. Twice. Perhaps three times."

She smiled. "Then how come I've seen you six, seven, or ten? How come I've seen you more than you've seen me?"

"This must be a riddle," Nachman said. The riddle of the shadow and the hand. Substance and sunlight. "I don't know. Tell me."

She pointed to a tree near the water. "Last week I hid up in a tree every day and watched you bathe. I saw you dance. You dance beautifully, you know. I like the way you sing. It vibrates right into me." She pointed to her breast, as lovely as the breasts of the beloved in the Song of Songs.

Nachman stared at the girl.

"That means you . . . you pretended to be in trouble." A thought flitted. She's a demon. A Lilith. Sent to draw me under. Into the nether depths. To Sheol. Gehenna. Hell.

"Oh no! I really was in trouble. I could have drowned." She put her hand to her heart. "Promise. Really."

Nachman felt his heart surging. But he could not tell what kind of discomfort it was. You are an *aleph.* You are a *tov.* Indeed, you are as lovely as the letters.

"Look! Your foot is bleeding," he said.

She washed the slight cut in the water but the red soon surfaced again. Nachman ran to a tree, dug by the roots and gathered some moss and weeds and pressed them into the wound. "This will stop the bleeding."

"Where did you learn this?"

"When I was a boy I learned that roots and grasses can heal."

She sat with her hands wrapped around her knees. Looked fondly at him. Her eyes glowed.

"I can't imagine you as a little boy."

Nachman laughed. "What's your name?"

She took a twig and spelled her name in the sand: Lizabeta.

"And yours?"

He hesitated. Should he tell her his real name? But what difference would it make? It was Nachman who had done what he had done. He said his name softly; perhaps she had not heard.

"Will you save me again tomorrow? At the same time?"

He thought of his arms around her, his face nuzzled next to hers, the joys of lust and satisfaction. Yes, you are more beautiful than the alphabet, he wanted to say. You are *ayin* and *beys, zayin* and *ches, daled* and *lamed,* you are *hey* and *pey.* You are all the letters. But he said nothing. On the ground a butterfly was struggling, wings beating feebly against an unseen adversary. And Nachman was on the raft. A ring of slate clouds pressed tightly against his skull. He was floating. Away from people, from trouble, away from sorrow and temptation.

"If you don't save me tomorrow, you'll save me again soon enough.

I'm a cat. A cat has nine lives. It has to be saved. Again and again. And I like to be saved. When I was thirteen or fourteen, the local priest saved me."

Nachman swallowed, almost choked on his saliva. "Like this . . . from drowning?"

"On no. He saved me religiously. From the Kingdom of Satan."

Nachman was about to say something, to put words together, words that tasted like brambles; but Lizabeta bent down, picked something up, and skipped off, laughing.

"So? Will you save me again?" she called to him. "Being saved in water is wonderful. It helps put out the fire that Yadwiga the witch set in me."

Nachman put his hand to his heart to still it. Where was that fullness he had felt moments ago? He saw his face in the water, turned away. I have sinned. Now God will take everything from me. Whisper. Songs. Everything. I deserve nothing. I will have nothing left. Nachman stood and put on his shirt. Like dawn, in fine balance between light and darkness, he too stood in mid-point. He felt like a shell of a house, a flower without petals, a song without notes.

She stood four strides away from him. He couldn't believe his eyes. His white skullcap was perched on top of her head.

"Give that back to me." He ran to her but she skipped away into the reeds, laughing. "You can't catch me!" Her laughter tickled him, pleased him; yet, there was bite to it, a nasty echo, as if pointy teeth were nipping at his throat. He pressed his forehead into the bark of a maple, enjoyed the discomfort of the rough ridges. But his fingers still tingled with her kisses.

Perhaps, Nachman thought, God wanted this to be. Perhaps He sent me this girl as a gift, a miracle especially for me—for no ordinary man would He tempt in such fashion. For an ordinary man this would be temptation—but not for me. God wants me to luxuriate in my senses so that I can ascend even higher in my quest for closeness to Him. To realize that such pleasure was only fleeting. To take away my sinful, lustful thoughts. Why, then, consider it a fall? Surely God does not consider me sinful, for if He did, He would have punished me at once. In the water. But He did not—a sign of His favor. Indeed, a miracle.

From Nathan's Diary

Reb Nachman told a story, which I wrote down for him—his thirteenth tale.

Once upon a time there was a young king who loved a young woman. But since she was not of royal blood, she was forbidden to him. According to the law of the land, the king had to marry a woman of whom the High Court approved. And because he believed in God, he obeyed the law. But because of his love for the commoner, he came to her secretly, disguised as a workman.

Even as he did this the king told himself: The best way to subdue the power of lust is to use a ruse. One must fight the enemy with all kinds of tricks. In war, the enemy must be destroyed.

However, the king continued to see her; yet he was angry at himself for deceiving his royal kin and his High Court. First he pretended he did not enjoy meeting his love. But this did not work. The truth was that he loved to see the girl. The king felt that since he was not caught by the High Court, heaven decreed that he had not sinned. He was waging a holy war against lust by offering himself as victim. And he was ready, the king told himself, to undergo these humiliations for the sake of the law. The only way to destroy the yetzer ho-reh within him was to conquer it from within. He also sought salvation because of God's whisper: "You are in the Messianic line." But to attain Messianic purity the king would have to control his passion. All other earthly desires he had conquered. If he could conquer lust, he could reveal himself as king among kings, the righteous saint of his generation.

Moreover, the young king recalled the teaching that sinful thoughts are worse than sinful acts. Daydreams increase sinful musings; better, then, to sin and feel what other people feel. And then he could repent and go higher and higher. The next time he saw her, the girl tripped and hurt her foot. But as he tended her wound, she took his scepter and ran away. She laughed: "The king has no scepter, the king has no scepter."

After the Master had finished his tale, we walked home and discussed the symbolism, for in every one of Reb Nachman's tales there is meaning. The king is God, the woman Israel. God loved Israel, no matter what the circumstances. The High Court is the Torah, by which even God abides; and only through the Torah can God and Israel approach in mystic union.

At home, the full force of that morning swept over Nachman, like a wave of bad tidings. Gone the good feeling that it was no sin. He looked in the mirror. Is this the face God whispered to? Hinting that he among all men might bring salvation to the world? He pressed his hands to his face. Another punishment. She ran off with my yarmulke. Every time I succeed in climbing higher, Nachman thought, I'm cast down. Still, one must start again. Perhaps from unholiness, holiness can shine through. He clenched his fist, prayed and wept, asked pardon for his sin. Then he ate and drank, consuming food with gusto, in the hope of drowning the other passion.

In the bes medresh, where it was Bratslav custom always to wear white velvet skullcaps and prayer shawls, Nachman wore a black hat. It was not a sin to admire her body, he thought. She had translucent skin, like the fleece of sheep seen in distance, or the milk mist of morning fog. It radiated light. God had made her too, as he had created the twenty-two infinite letters, and she was a testimony to His grand handiwork. Lizabeta went through the reeds, ran along a path beside the river, hidden by the tall beige rushes. Nachman closed his eyes. Let her take off her clothes. That was not too much to wish for. Abimelech looked out his window and saw Isaac sporting with Rebecca. David had admired Bathsheba's naked body. The Bible did not censor these scenes, was not ashamed of them. Nachman would show the evil *yetzer* within him the power of his restraint. If I don't have her, he thought, I'm going to scream. If I don't have her, I'm going to scream. He would not dive in after her. Yes. Look. There. She was crisscrossing her hands to her blouse and lifting it. His eyes were blinded. It snowed, flakes of white marble, chips of ivory. They coalesced, those marble flakes, those bits of ivory, to form a lovely pair of breasts, as alike as a pair of gazelles that feed among the lilies. Lips a thread of scarlet, your neck a tower. The nipples were erect, awaiting the cold water. We teach joy joy joy. Joy from within ourselves. Was this not joy? Or was joy only in dance and song? She splashed water on herself. Jewish girls, even under layers of long drab clothing, did not have bodies like that. Such gifts were given to the other nations of the world. *We* were given gifts of spirit, mind, and soul. She swims out now, and Nachman is drawn to the water, like a fish at spawning time. The water is not cold, not warm. It refreshes the body, refreshes the soul; its sound is music, hand in, hand out, legs kicking, a rhythm that pleases, excites. She is near, misses a stroke, coughs, cries out. At once Nachman reacts, swims out, finds and seizes her. One hand is around her waist, another on her hair, assuring her. But she struggles, pulls him down. He pushes the water away, stroking, touching flesh. Her breasts float bouyantly in the palms of his hands, light, heavy, a water weight of sweet flesh—I'm human, he thought, I'm human. Letting oneself go is such a sweet feeling. A bitter-sweet burning sensation. A water feeding fire. She steps into the water, he parts the bushes; she runs and dives. Nachman turns. A pool of water before him. The prayer leader shouted the word "Joy" from the prayers and repeated, "Ay ay ay, joy!" He bends down and rubs water over his forehead. Dips his hands in up to the wrists to cool himself. Then she smiles at him, a friendly smile, a wifely smile. Not provocative but enigmatic, as if a Jewish soul were ensconced somewhere within her. And put each of Nachman's fingertips into her rounded lips, one by one.

The congregation stood. Nachman attempted to return from the fields. What if she were Jewish after all? Perhaps there would be a miracle, as in his tale, "The Lost Princess," one of the Hasidim's favorite stories. Once upon a time there was a king who fell in love with a beautiful commoner. As usual, there were problems of lineage. But later she turned out to be of royal blood, the long lost daughter of a neighboring king. And Lizabeta? Perhaps during the persecutions a Jewish couple left their daughter with a farmer in order to save her. So she is Jewish after all.

Back to the floating prayers. His eyes skimmed the Siddur. Too quickly, too quickly. As a child he saw a candle held up behind a manuscript. The little flame illumined each word. Now too when the cantor prayed slowly, each word was suddenly illuminated, as though a candle were behind it. But when a prayer leader read quickly, galloping across the terrain of the page like a horse gone wild, the words jumbled, melted, darkened. The elbows of letters jostled each other and confused the meaning. The light within them was snuffed out.

Nachman closed his eyes, focused slowly on the phrase "our God" to sharpen the intensity of his prayer. Just then Nachman felt something strange. Light and dizzying, odd yet pleasant, as in fever. He felt deliciously warm. His head was in a light spin. As though a column of sunlight had dropped through his body from head to feet, and was now expanding, brighter and brighter, forcing him up, like the bottom of the sea pushing the diver up up up—the reverse of the falling dream he used to have as a child. He looked down. For a moment Nachman stared at the floor, unblinking. Then realized. His feet were off the ground. He was standing in air. For how long he didn't know. Five seconds, ten. Half a minute. Deep in devotion, up in the air, some three inches off the ground, and only now, as he interrupted his concentration, did he descend. Then he remembered; once, as a youngster, he had jumped up three times for the *kodosh kodosh kodosh* of the *Kedusha* prayer, the "holy holy holy" during the cantor's repetition of the Silent Devotion, and the third time he stayed up a fraction of a second longer than he should have. Indeed, he was a descendant of King David, for according to legend, David had also once risen in the air.

Nachman smiled to himself. Proof again, uncalled for, signaling that his quest was successful. That the angels he was sending up his ladder of dreams were descending with blessings, special signs for him. Siddur in hand, he sought to go off into a dream world, beyond the hills of letters, the fields of words. He tried to slow down. But the Hasidim behind him pushed forward. He wanted to float through tranquil dreamspace, but the letters of the next word tugged forward and locked him into time. No one stopped. Like stones rolling downhill ran the prayers of these men.

At the Torah reading Nachman heard a tumult by the door. A man, shouting and gesturing wildly, tried to enter. A knot of Hasidim pushed him back.

"Drunken peasant!"

"Boor!"

"Out of here!"

"Let me in. Let me in, I say," the man roared. "Stop the Torah!"

"What's going on?" Nachman asked. A wave of red heat surged in his neck. "Who is it? Let him in."

A wave, a whisper, rising and falling, moved toward the door: "The Rebbe says. Says let him in."

The man, his shirt now rumpled, held a peasant's cap pressed to his chest as he followed Nathan to Reb Nachman's tall, carved mahogany chair. Nathan held him by the arm. He chased off the curious children.

"Rebbe, this man—" Nathan said.

"Stop the Torah." The man wrenched himself free of Nathan's grasp. "Justice. I know your custom."

"But you have no right—" Nathan said.

"Are there any others with him?" Nachman asked in Hebrew.

"No, he's alone," Nathan replied.

"We've stopped the Torah reading," Nachman said softly. "What is your complaint?"

"Rabbi . . . Rabbi," the man said, breathing with difficulty. His eyes were red. Spittle ran down the left corner of his mouth. "I want justice . . . The peasants sometimes come to you. We know you're fair in judgment."

"Tell us."

"Rabbi . . . Someone has . . . you see . . . my daughter . . . . A Jew . . ."

"A Jew with his daughter!" Someone laughed.

"Throw him out."

"Lie in the earth and bake bagels."

"Grow like an onion with your head in the ground."

Nathan raised his hands and quieted the Hasidim.

"What is your name?" Nachman asked.

"Vlodek."

"And who is your daughter?"

"Lizabeta."

Nachman wished he were floating in the air again, wished that that shaft of bright light would return, quickly wished wished wished. Rising. Rising. He would float in air, bend forward, and, like a cloud, like an angel holding the letters of prayers with its wings, like a dove bearing the bough of benison, fly out the window, away from Bratslav.

He looked at Nathan. Nathan stepped forward. Almost instinctively, Vlodek moved back. As Nathan bent close, his hat and coat gave off an outdoors fragrance, as though they had been hanging all day on the laundry line. Again Nachman breathed her perfume. Had Nathan followed him that morning? Was that why the smell of roses and hay still clung to his assistant? But how could he have done that if every Bratslav Hasid knew that in the morning Nachman went out to meditate by the river. Alone.

Nachman took a deep breath, as if to infuse the girl's perfume into his soul. His heart raced. Vlodek's presence was an ill omen. Nachman's rhythms, his hopes were upset. Yes, God was angry.

Nachman looked at the peasant.

"Are you saying that one of our people has been with your daughter?"

"Yes. With my daughter."

"Did she tell you this?"

"No. But I can tell. My wife can tell. By her behavior."

Nachman took a deep breath. He looked around the room, as if to find the guilty one by searching the faces of the fifteen or twenty men. He pointed to the children. With a finger ordered them to go. But who are you fooling, Nachman? You can search the world till East meets West and you will not find the guilty man. All Nachman wanted was that silver-coated glass wall between himself and his Hasidim.

"What did you say your name is?"

"Vlodek."

"And you live where?"

"A mile from the bend in the river. The house with the white fence. A thick birch stands there."

Nachman waited for more. But the peasant would not speak unless he was asked.

"Are you a farmer?"

"Yes. I have a garden farm."

"Ah, so you are the famous Vlodek, the garden farmer whose magic hands make flowers grow where thorns stung fingers and grass spring up in place of dust. Vlodek!" Nachman dropped his voice. "But this is circumstantial evidence, isn't it? *You* can tell. Your *wife* can tell. We don't speak like that in a court of law. In a court of law we need proof."

While the farmer and Nachman spoke softly, the men drew nearer and returned to their places.

"But I do have proof, Rabbi."

"Yes? Tell us . . ."

Vlodek pulled out of his pocket a white velvet skullcap. Held it up triumphantly. "This. See? This. This I found in her room."

Nachman looked quickly at Nathan. Nathan shrugged his shoulders. On the wooden prayer stand Nachman tapped his fingers, first one, then the others. He looked at his fingernails. In each was reflected the white skullcap that Vlodek, hand held high, was waving about like a lulav, a banner.

How could he make the skullcap disappear? Nachman wondered. How could he make himself disappear? Could not one who rose in the air like an angel also make himself disappear? Could he sing for them one of his magical melodies and enchant them into forgetting what had just been said?

"Did anyone here lose a skullcap?" Nachman asked. His voice was weak. But his face, not red with shame, gave no public evidence like the adulterous woman's thighs that swelled after she tasted the Biblical waters of bitterness.

No one answered. Nachman looked at Nathan. Did Nathan fidget? Was he nervous? Concerned that someone here might bear the guilt? Or did the white skullcap belong to him? Yes, Nathan had indeed followed Nachman early in the morning. Despite the unwritten Bratslav rule that no Hasid would go bathing at dawn, Nathan had gone anyway. And lost his velvet yarmulke. Nachman shook his head to drive the fantasy away. Perhaps Lizabeta was scheming with her father. What does she want? Nachman wondered.

He felt himself sinking. As in a nightmare of pursuit, his legs were leaden. My whole life, he thought, my whole life has come to naught. God's whisper was but a tease. And then Nachman raised his eyes and saw the Bratslav motto, "Jews, do not despair." He took a breath and forced himself to stand.

Stood. Breathed deeply.

"You say, Vlodek, that you found this in her room. Did she give it to you?"

No, no, Nachman answered for him, she did not. No, Lizabeta, you couldn't, you wouldn't have done that. One does not betray after loving.

"No."

"Where did she find this?"

"I don't know."

"You mean to say you took it without asking her?"

"Yes."

"Without her permission?" Nachman raised his voice. "Without even asking for an explanation?"

"She's my daughter."

"Is it not possible that she found it outside, in a field?"

"Maybe. I don't know where she found it. *If* she found it. Maybe it belongs to the one who left it in her room."

"Your assumption is absolutely false. I'll tell you whose it is."

Nachman snatched the skullcap from Vlodek's hands and waved it in the air.

"Does this yarmulke belong to anyone here?" he shouted. The word "here" bounced from ceiling to wall, echoing in the room. "What? Isn't anyone claiming it?"

Nachman looked from face to face. At first, Nathan joined him in looking around, the second in command reviewing his troops. But after a sharp glance from Nachman, he backed off and became part of the Hasidim, the looked at instead of the looker.

Nachman jumped up on a bench. "If it were mine . . ." he shrieked, then dropped his voice and spoke with exaggerated slowness, as if in pain, "I would confess! Haven't we taught and preached and counselled and commanded total, absolute, uncompromising honesty?"

As Nachman spoke, all the Hasidim, including Nathan, withdrew to the doorway. Good, Nachman thought. Let Nathan stay there with the rest of the Hasidim. In the room an unseen wind blew. It pressed the men together, chilled their bones. They stood on one side of the tornado, Nachman on the other. In the eye stood Vlodek alone.

"What if . . ." Nachman said. "What if I were to confess it was *I* . . . I . . . I . . . and tell you that even a zaddik, yes, even a zaddik must sin, for from the descent the ascent is swifter? We've learned that it is easier for a repentant sinner to go to heaven than an unblemished high priest, a high priest who never sinned at all."

Then Nachman began trembling. First his hands, and then the rest of his body. The holy trembling passed to the Hasidim and Nachman saw the trembling hands and limbs of the men who stood pressed at the doorway.

Nachman turned swiftly and faced the wall. The nervous energy coursing through his body, his limbs, his fingers, vanished. Composed, he turned back and said softly:

"Do you know whose skullcap this is?" Again Nachman waved it in the air.

A loose page of a Siddur fluttered to the floor. It landed on its edge; the sound was heard in all corners of the room. No one moved. The Hasidim, crushed together at the doorway, were paralyzed. Nachman strode over, picked up the page, kissed it, and placed it on a lectern.

"Well, do you?"

To whom was the question directed, Vlodek or the congregation?

To neither. The question was directed at Nachman.

"It is *my* skullcap," said Nachman. And as soon as he said it, he thought: No one will believe it, no one will believe it. The words pressed on his mind. No one will ever believe it, no matter what I say.

A murmur of astonishment hung in the air. Nachman sent a fiery glance to the cluster of Hasidim still immobile at the doorway. They looked at him. They opened their mouths but could not speak. Then Nachman lifted his black hat to show his skullcap was missing.

"I lost it either today or yesterday, during my morning stroll to bathe in the river," he told Vlodek. "Now go home, my man. No harm has been done to your daughter. She merely found an object that was lost, and you returned it to its rightful owner. Thank you."

Nachman took Vlodek by the arm and, brushing off the man's shirt and back to pacify him, walked him to the door. Everyone made way for the rabbi. Nachman crossed the threshold with him and said, "Thank you. Thank you very much, Vlodek . . . You said you were a gardener . . . If you have the time, we could use—"

With a rough gesture, the peasant shook off Nachman's hand.

"Don't think you can buy me off with gardening." He wagged a warning finger at Nachman. "I don't like this whole business. I'm going to ask my daughter some questions. And I'll be back. Yes, I'll be back."

As Vlodek walked out, Nachman ordered the stunned congregation: "Resume the Torah reading."

Nathan came up to Nachman and asked softly, "Rebbe, why did you say it was yours? It could have been any of ours."

"Indeed it could. Yours perhaps?"

A momentary distress flashed in Nathan's eyes. But instead of responding, he pointed to his own white velvet yarmulke.

"Then I guess it *was* mine," Nachman said.

From Nathan's Diary

Why did he do that? When he said, "Isn't anyone claiming the yarmulke?" and I looked at the Hasidim, he singed my skin with eyes of fire and made me take my place alongside of them. Put me in my place. Later, he couldn't resist a little jibe at my expense. "Yours perhaps?" He knew very well I didn't lose my yarmulke.

Later, in a different mood, the Rebbe invited us to sit around the long, cloth-covered table in the bes medresh.

He said:

"Once, in a village, the yetzer ho-reh ran through the street shouting to youngsters who were studying the holy Torah: 'Come, follow me, I have something in my hand I want to show you.' They ran out of the study house. Across the road that led from town they followed him, into the paths by the river and trees, where all is still and calm. Far from the marketplace the evil yetzer led them. Then he stopped in a beautiful glade. There the music of the willows was heard, and the waves of the river beat lightly against the shore. And then the yetzer ho-reh, who had tricked the lads into leaving their holy studies to follow him, opened his hand and showed them an empty palm."

The Rebbe stopped, looked at his hands for a moment, as if he too had something hidden there, and added:

"In this tale, you have a perfect picture of the yetzer ho-reh. He fools the world, tricking it into following him; he seduces man away from his responsibilities, luring him to the glade, to the river. Why do the boys chase after the evil impulse with the closed fist? Because they all think that the closed palm contains what they lust for. And, when he finally opens his fist"—here Reb Nachman opened both palms wide; the light bounced off his smooth clean hands—"it is empty. No desire is ever fulfilled. Worldly pleasures are like sunbeams in a dark room. They look solid; but he who tries to grasp a sunbeam finds nothing in his hand."

The next morning Nachman awoke with a headache. His head felt split in two. But it was not a headache, he knew. It was a soulache. An image of Lizabeta clung to him, from his head to his toes. His kissed fingers still tingled. What was happening to him? Was the poison of Sabbetai Zevi—lust in place of piety—infecting him, one hundred years after that false Messiah's apostasy and demise? What should he do? Wander off in penance? Leave Bratslav, simply pick up his walking stick and go away?

Nachman went out to his garden. Inspecting his carrots and cauliflowers made his head feel better. As he bent down to weed, another shadow fell across his own. His heart jumped.

"Ah, good morning, Vlodek . . . Come, look at these cauliflowers. Beauties, eh? Large and firm and white as snow—"

"Not interested in your cauliflowers."

"You're angry at the way you were treated yesterday and you're absolutely right. I'm sorry. The Hasidim have been instructed to be more civil in the future."

Nachman looked at the man. He had a tight, weatherbeaten face. Could this man have fathered such a beauty? I know your daughter, Nachman wanted to say. She is lovelier than the letters of the alphabet.

"Rabbi, I have to tell you something," Nachman thought he heard him say. "My daughter, she's a Jewish child."

"Jewish? Lizabeta Jewish? Your daughter—Jewish?"

"Yes. Left with me during times of trouble. Now the time has come for her to return to her people."

"Jewish, you say? Is the girl really Jewish?"

"Didn't you hear what I said?" Vlodek said sharply.

"No."

"I said, I don't like what's happening. Lay off. Stay away," Vlodek growled. "Keep your distance. I'm warning you! My wife was afraid to tell me the other day. She saw how upset I was. But this morning she told me. Lucky for you Lizabeta doesn't have any brothers. Otherwise, they'd have broken your bones. My wife saw her kissing—"

A hook of fear curled through Nachman's stomach and up into his mouth. His heart beat faster. Had the mother seen? Stood off in the distance, watching? Was it all a trick? The whole family involved?

"Kissing? Kissing?"

"Yes. Yes. Yes. Kissing. Kissing," Vlodek raged. "Holding your skullcap in her hand and kissing it, like it was a pussycat, or a baby lamb. Cuddling and stroking and kissing it. The girl is in love with you."

"What? In love? With me?" Nachman laughed bitterly. "How can anyone love a person one doesn't know?"

"Who knows what spells you Jews can cast? Anyway, what do you know, what do you care, about a woman's heart?"

I care, Nachman thought.

"Are you married?"

"No, I'm not married."

"No wonder you got the itch. Take one of your own, then a good Christian girl wouldn't fall in love with you. All you people have wives and children by the dozen, but you . . ." he looked around . . . "you have cauliflowers!"

"That's true." Nachman looked down. "I have nothing . . . Only cauliflowers . . . But tell me," he said mildly, "how can you be in love with someone you don't know?"

"Don't ask me. Women have a logic of their own. Maybe she saw you from afar. I asked her, but she won't answer. She's probably lying, because"—he shook his fist—"if she tells the truth she knows I'll beat her black and blue."

"But again you're assuming, Vlodek. Fantasizing."

"Don't give me your fancy language. I'm just warning you to stay away. If you don't, either I'll go to the police, or I'll—"

That unsaid threat was even more ominous. The police chief could be persuaded by a gift. But rioting peasants—God save us from them, Nachman thought.

In his room, fatigue swept over him. He was soul-exhausted. A wave of chills, like icy kisses, ran up and down his back. The inside of his mouth dry and hot as coals. A pain floated: from his wrist, which twitched like an arm in sleep, to his chest; then it coiled across his forehead. He knew his body was well. But when one's inner balance is broken, the soul became ill and feverish. To cure the soul's fever, he turned to David's Psalms. The king too loved women, and Nachman was his descendant. A malaise passed down through the generations. But he couldn't chant the poems. His eyes blurred. The Hebrew letters danced beneath a film of water. From between the pages Lizabeta floated out. Nachman had not gone to swim today, but his thoughts were by the water. Distracted, he closed the Psalms.

He consoled himself with an old teaching. The soul seeks union with God in the heavenly spheres, said the mystics, just as man craves to unite with woman here on earth. In other words, it was natural, no sin.

But his eyes got another message.

A mist that was not a mist arose before his eyes. He became like a child again. He read slowly, letter by letter, from the Siddur. Thus one day followed another. On the fourth day the letters, standing on an endless plain, separated like stretched fingers. Once, in the huge space between the letters of God's name, Lizabeta beckoned, peeking out as if from behind a tree, a cluster of reeds, a row of tombstones. Another time, the letters curled into the shape of a woman.

At twilight, several days later, Nachman looked out the window. The magic moment when dusk turns to evening. Birds sing louder. Warm winds blow until the stars come out. Which way would his life turn? Which direction would it take? For a moment all creation hung suspended in the sad silence of a country dusk. A silence broken by a knock on the door. Its suddenness made his heart leap in fear. Had Vlodek returned? Before he could say "Come in," an old, kerchiefed woman, slightly hunched, entered. In a husky voice, in a mixture of

Russian and Ukrainian, she told him that she was alone in the world. She had heard he was a compassionate man.

"Would you like money for food? Would you like clothing? Ask." Nachman opened a drawer in his table.

She shook her head. "I've heard that Jews here treat beggars well. But I am not a beggar."

"What then would you like, woman?"

"A little louder, please!"

"What do you want to do?"

"To scrub floors. Clean house. Prepare meals. I worked for Jews and I know the laws."

The woman's face was dark, from sun or age.

"Isn't it time others worked for you?" he said.

"But I'm strong. Look." Nachman watched with amazement as with one hand she lifted up a wooden chair by its leg. "I've worked all my life. Will you let me work for you?"

"Where do you come from?"

"A village near Golubsk."

"That's weeks away by cart and foot . . . Who told you about me?"

"People. Everywhere. The rabbi of Bratslav. I do laundry. I can help. No, no charity. No pity. I have always worked. You have no one here to help you?"

"Not now. We had a widow here who had to leave when her son fell ill."

Hands at her side, the old woman gazed at Nachman.

"Do you have family?"

"No husband, no children. All alone in the world, sir."

"Do you have any goods, any personal belongings?"

She ran to the doorway and brought in a large packet wrapped in a huge cloth, knotted at the top.

"Do you know how to prepare honey, milk, and egg yolks?" he said, half in jest.

"For coughs? My specialty. I'll make it for you every night."

Nachman looked at her pathetic bundle.

"Then you'll take me?" she asked.

For a moment he thought he was interviewing a Hasid.

"There is a little room in the corner of the house. That was the widow's room. I'll tell the beadle to prepare it for your comfort. You won't have to cook for us—he'll outline your tasks."

"My name is Natalya," she said. "I don't mind cooking."

Nachman carried her bundle in.

When the old woman was settled in her room, Nachman smiled bitterly. Some things succeed without effort. Like finding a housekeeper. He recalled an old Hasidic proverb: Sometimes a man doesn't have to leave his house to find what he's looking for. Nachman pressed his head to the window, gazing out at the moonlit field behind the house.

From Nathan's Diary

The first time we met, when I sought to become a Bratslaver, the Rebbe asked me which is more important, deeds or Torah study.

"Good deeds," I said. "Your remark is known all over Russia."

"Which one?"

"Helping an old woman with her bundles is the best page of Talmud."

"So it has gone that far, that innocent remark of mine?"

"Many consider it a folk proverb," I said. "Strange how a few words can sum up a movement."

The Master smiled. "Deeds count, not self-indulgent bench-warming." Then he surprised me with: "How do you, who looks so much like me, stand with temptation?"

I told him and then, even before I thought of daring to ask, I asked, "And you? How do you stand with temptation?" And only then did my heart leap to my throat in fright.

A shadow came over Reb Nachman's face. His left eye twitched for a moment. "It can come to any man, the yetzer ho-reh. I once had a teacher who said, 'I'm eighty years old, and blind in one eye, and yet when I go out on the streets, I pray in the words of the *Shema*, "May we not follow our eyes . . ."' I am still struggling to—. But we spoke of honesty, didn't we? And of you, not me," he shouted, his voice suddenly sharp as an axe cleaving the air. "You must understand the nature of the rebbe and the role of the disciple!" He looked straight into my eyes. "The rebbe is the sun. The disciple is the mirror, the moon, shining in the reflection of the sun. When the disciple looks at the master, he sees great light, but he cannot look too long. When the master looks at the disciple, he sees himself."

One day, during the Morning Service, when he stood to recite the Kedusha, the words "holy holy holy" suddenly turned upside down, as if a misprint in the Siddur. Nachman turned the prayer book around; perversely, only the three words, *kodosh kodosh kodosh,* spun on their axis. Nachman held the Siddur upright again. The message was clear. Holiness reversed; holiness turned on its head; holiness upside down.

Nachman shut his eyes. Perhaps it would go away, he thought, knowing that it would not; rather, it would get worse, like his cough, which for years he had been hoping would vanish. Nevertheless, Nachman prayed that the illusion would pass. He opened his eyes. Still the words were upside down. Had anyone noticed his distress? No, the Hasidim were immersed in prayer. Contrary to his usual practice, Nachman now recited the prayers by heart. But the words came slowly, as if the soul of each word was fading.

He closed the Siddur and ran to his room. Hand to chest, he caught his breath. Relaxed. Opened the Siddur again: the letters as they should be. Smiling, Nachman returned to the bes medresh. God's whisper will not be denied.

That night he dreamed of letters. But they were not Hebrew. Greek, perhaps, or Chinese. Perhaps an alphabet not yet invented. The next morning, at services, when he opened the Siddur, he felt a little pinch in his heart. Afraid? Yes, he admitted. Terror-stricken. Full of dread.

As he scanned the words, the letters thickened. Clear ink turned to tar. The letters oozed. Each was a slope, a hill, a mountain he was forced to climb. He had to slowly clamber up the side of one, reach the peak, and gingerly make his way down the valley. In the back of his eyes something had tied loops around the words. The letters were foreign. He could not recognize them.

He waited a moment. Perhaps like yesterday, the aberration would vanish. But his eyes saw nothing. Chunks of forms, shadow and pitch, amounting to nothing.

His prayer was dead.

His lovely alphabet, like the Divine Presence, was in Exile.

The shock of looking at letters but not seeing them was like the shock of looking into a mirror and seeing nothing there. But Nachman consoled himself with the thought that each letter contained a miniature universe. And perhaps within the tiny world of each letter there was a philosophic system that also taught "Never despair!"

At first, his heart sank. With whom should he share his dismay?

Everyone else had a rebbe; whom did he have? Then, with a rush of happiness, as if the letters themselves had returned, glowing with extra-terrestrial light, Nachman remembered that his zayde, too, had once forgotten the letters. Like the Baal Shem Tov, he would not despair; he would start anew, learn the *aleph beys* again.

Nachman shut the prayer book. He knew he must recite the basic prayer, but he could not remember. Chills now rilled over him. He pressed his fists together and bounced up and down slowly on his toes. Recite the alphabet, he told himself, recite the alphabet.

Nachman's tongue moved. His head nodded, as if the motion would open his memory. A scream, silent, vibrant, tore through his head but did not escape his throat. I cannot begin.

Begin. Begin, he commanded himself. The strain of concentration created a point of pain, then a scythe of pain in his forehead. He could not recall the first letter. He felt dizzy. Count, count, he told himself. Do not despair. Count! God is one. His tablets, two. The patriarchs, three. He counted to ten. Calmed, he turned his thoughts to the letters.

He didn't cry. He was not depressed. Depression was too easy, he told himself. Depression is a kind of moral drunkenness, and Jews are not drunkards. He started over again. If one falls, one rises. If one is set back, the Besht taught, one must start again. Nachman set up a ladder in his mind, started at the first rung and began to climb.

That night he told his Hasidim:

"A story. You heard a different version some time ago. Once upon a time there was a king who taught his people everything. To see and sew and sing, to count and cook and hike. Now this king, who was lame, always dressed in white because he loved purity. One day God spoke to the king and told him that he might become the salvation of all of Israel. His heart was uplifted but still he limped. God's whisper is no magic cure.

"The king then fell in love, and illness followed. He could not speak. His lips were mute. The king who loved to speak and sing, his tongue was still. Doctors came, found nothing wrong. His counsellors said: Music brings the cure. They called musicians who played and taught the king to sing. Then a song welled up in him as nectar rises in the rose. A joyful song touched his lips and the lame king began to sing. Music was the sweet, magic elixir that chased depression away.

"The king was cured. Mute no longer, he taught his people everything. To see and sew and sing, to count and cook and hike. He dressed in white and sought salvation for his people and the world. And did he still limp, you ask? Yes, he limped; for music helps, but God's whisper is no magic cure."

The next morning—it was a Thursday, the day Ivan the vegetable peddler came to buy produce—Nachman played a little game. He made believe he wasn't Nachman and went casually to the Siddur to take it by surprise. If he pretended to be someone who could read, he thought, he would read. But this "other" could not read either. The flaw was transferred. He could not fool his defect.

But a Jew has hope. Even when there is no room for hope, he hopes. There was one more chance. From his bookcase Nachman took his zayde's Siddur, printed in 1700, the year of the Baal Shem Tov's birth. Exactly one hundred years ago. Fine old paper, each letter imprinted so carefully that a finger could slide into the black indentation. Perhaps the light that zayde cast on the letters would reflect back at him. Nachman opened the Siddur.

In vain.

Shortly after noon Vlodek burst into Nachman's room. The door opened so easily he stumbled in with the force of his rage. He looked wild-eyed, drunk, but he did not smell of vodka. Crouched over, he growled like an animal. Nachman closed the door so that the old woman working in the garden would not hear.

"What do you want? Why don't you knock before you enter?"

"She drowned."

"What?"

"Dead! Dead!" The father panted.

Oh no! Dear God! He closed his eyes. Fragments of black letters melted like wax. A leaden taste of death in his mouth. Nachman pressed his chest to stop the pain.

"She didn't come back . . . worked in the fields. We thought she went to visit her aunt. Didn't come back." Vlodek looked around the room. His brows twitched. He swept his glance from one corner to another.

Nachman began softly, "You still hope that . . ." then suddenly shouted, "You actually think she's hidden here?"

Startled, Vlodek repeated, "She's drowned, I tell you."

"Then why are you inspecting? Look!" Nachman opened his wardrobe, moved his bed, opened the door to the stove. "Look!"

"The child is dead, Jew, and you're making jokes."

Nachman seized Vlodek's arm. "My name is Rabbi Nachman."

Vlodek wrenched himself free.

"I? Making jokes? Don't you think this grieves me?" Nachman's voice trembled. "Oh God, God! When did this terrible thing happen?"

"Yesterday, the day before. She was out working in the fields. We thought she went away."

"When did they find the body?"

"Not found. Just a bundle of her clothes." Vlodek pulled Nachman forcibly by the hand. "By the river. Come. I'll show you."

"Stop pulling. You're hurting me."

In the garden Natalya, on her haunches, looked up from peeling potatoes. Her eyes shone.

"Does the rabbi want a glass of warm milk?"

"Not now. This evening, thank you."

"What?" She cupped her hand to her ear.

"This evening," Nachman said louder. "If Ivan comes for the vegetables, tell him I'll be back soon."

He and Vlodek walked the path that Nachman usually walked alone. At dawn there was a light mist, a play of rainbow colors at sunrise. Now the shadows were gone. A moist heat hung in the air, so heavy it pressed like a stone against his heart. She wasn't dead. She wasn't. She couldn't be. Vlodek's looking around the room was one hint. The missing body was another.

"Was it an accident?"

"No accident," Vlodek grumbled. "She killed herself." And then he wheeled and shouted into Nachman's face. "On account of you!"

"Again me? Will you leave me out of it?"

Vlodek stamped his foot. "No, I won't! You're responsible! It's because of you." He clamped his bony fingers into Nachman's shoulders and brought his face close. Nachman turned away from his yellow, dirty teeth. "She folded her clothes and jumped in the river."

"She had no reason to kill herself."

"A lot you know about women. You know nothing about women. You're worse than a Catholic monk. Why don't you fool around with your own Jewish girls?"

"I don't know your daughter and yet I know her better than you. That bundle is a ruse to trick you. She ran away from you. She just wanted to get away." Nachman was elated; he knew he was right but tried to subdue his tone. "Sure, she's run away. Perhaps you were pestering her. Perhaps you and your wife gave her no peace. Perhaps day and night you laced into her, saying, 'You were with the Jew. You were with the Jew. Admit it! Admit!' Day and night you tore her apart with insults, questions, accusations." Nachman mimicked the accent of the Ukrainian peasant. "You were with the Jew. You were with him by the water, weren't you? How else could you have got his little cap? You were with him by the water, weren't you, you slut, and when no one was looking, in the woods beside the water, you spread your legs. . . . That's what you told her, day and night, didn't you? Admit it! You said it again and again until you drove her crazy, drove her away. . . . Admit it! I would have run away, too."

"You're mad," Vlodek shouted. He parted a clump of reeds near the river shore. "Here. Look. This bundle. It's hers. You turned her head. Seduced her. And now for the shame of it she killed herself."

Nachman looked at the bundle: shoes, blouse, skirt, kerchief. Yes, Lizabeta's. Blouse, skirt, they belonged to her. As he gazed at the clothes, the shoes seemed to grow larger and heavier, until Nachman said:

"Why are her shoes here? Did she drown herself without shoes? People who drown themselves wear shoes to help them sink."

Vlodek picked up a stone, weighed it in his hand, then threw it furiously into the water. Nachman watched the growing circles.

"My child is dead," Vlodek keened, "and you're talking of shoes. You're some man of God. I feel sorry for your Hasidim."

As Nachman began to walk away, Vlodek said loudly, "You're not going anywhere. I'm taking you to the police. You'll rot in jail, you filthy Jew with your filthy mind."

"Who do you think you're talking to?"

Vlodek put his hands on his waist and smirked. "Nobody special, just a Jew. That's all you are. The police consider you just a Jew. The Czar considers you just a Jew."

"But no matter what, they still need evidence. On what flimsy evidence are you taking me to the police?" Nachman began to walk away, then wheeled and raised a warning finger. "If you make a scandal, it will end up badly for you."

"Ha! You won't turn the tables on me! Here's the evidence. The white cap," Vlodek shouted and dug his hands into his pockets. "Where is that damn thing?"

"On my head!" Nachman lifted his black hat. "We thanked you for returning it, remember? And how do I know you didn't place that neat bundle there yourself? False evidence! They'll throw *you* in jail."

Nachman turned and strode along the path.

Vlodek whistled twice.

From the reeds two men jumped out. One seized Nachman's arms; the other dragged him forward by his shirt. "What are you doing?" he yelled. "Are you cra—" A palm covered his mouth. Vlodek came and lifted Nachman's hat, snatched his white yarmulke, and stuffed it into his pocket.

Nachman shook his head from side to side until he freed his mouth. "Help! Help!"

"We'll give you help," said Vlodek. "At the police station . . . So you know everything I told my daughter, ha? Stood outside my window like a thief, listening in, ha?"

A cart waited by the side of the path. The horse was tethered to a tree. One of the men loosened the rope. "Up into the cart. Keep still. You haven't felt anything yet."

The cart rolled along the path to the police station on the outskirts of town. The three men were silent. Nachman looked left and right, saw no one. In the distance the heat shimmered. He repeated to himself: The entire world is a very narrow bridge. The main thing is not to fear. His heart pounded, creating its own heat. No deed is done in isolation, he thought. Everything has its public consequences. Even private lust. From his face he wiped away the aftertouch of the peasant's filthy hand. So this is holiness reversed. This is *kodosh kodosh kodosh* upside down. *That* was the message sent to me. The hint of things to come. Humbled, Nachman bowed his head. Kept it there until he heard a clomp of hooves coming down the road.

A wagon was approaching. If it was a Jew he could cry for help or summon others. When he saw the bareheaded wagoner, he realized it wasn't one of his own men. Then, to his joy, he recognized the driver.

"Ivan! Ivan! Help me!" Nachman jumped up and waved his hands.

Hearing Nachman's voice, the vegetable peddler moved his horse and wagon and blocked Vlodek's path. Ivan jumped off and demanded:

"What's going on? What are you doing to the rabbi?"

Nachman and the three men spoke at once. Ivan held his ears and shouted, "I can't hear all of you at the same time."

"They're dragging me to the police station," Nachman said.

"My daughter drowned. Here are her clothes." Vlodek lifted the bundle as proof.

"So what's the rabbi got to do with it?"

"He seduced her," Vlodek said. "Here's his cap."

"Ha!" Ivan laughed. "The rabbi is a holy man . . . Come with me, rabbi, I'll take you home."

"You didn't see a young woman on the road leading away from Bratslav, did you?" Nachman asked.

"Do you know how many people are tramping the roads at this season? No, I didn't see a young woman."

At that moment Nachman's confidence that Lizabeta's drowning was a ruse left him. He felt a stone descending over his heart.

Ivan whistled, pointed, and tried to grab the white yarmulke out of Vlodek's hands. Vlodek threw it to his friend. When Ivan lunged at the second man, he threw the yarmulke to the third.

"That's our proof!" Vlodek cried.

"He just took it off my head," Nachman said.

"You fool!" Ivan told Vlodek. "This man has thousands of followers all over the country. You harm one hair of his head and you're all doomed men."

"Jew-lover," one of the men taunted.

"I'm just telling you facts . . . Now off with you . . . Move your cart out of the way. Come, rabbi, I'll take you home."

Nachman lay down on his bed and stared at the ceiling. There, again and again, like a bizarre Purim play, the incident repeated itself. At prayers, he picked up his Siddur. Forgot he could no longer read. Later, he told Nathan what had happened with Vlodek.

"I'm afraid the matter won't end there," Nathan said.

"So then, what should I do?" Nachman raised his voice. "Put my own clothes at the river edge and spread the word that *I* drowned?"

Nathan licked his lips.

"I hear another message in your words. It says, go, disappear for a while."

"Why give them that joy? That's like admitting guilt."

"You always speak of the Land of Israel. What better time than now? Go for a few months until things quiet down."

"No. I'm not running away."

"He still has the yarmulke," Nathan retorted.

Nachman turned to his bookcase, chose a book, then wearily put it back. Now there were two stones on his heart. He began coughing.

"Tell the old woman . . . a big glass," he gasped, "hot milk . . . honey and eggs."

Soon Natalya brought him the drink. She bowed her head as she served him and Nachman told her not to do that again.

Several days passed. Nachman could not read, could not write, could not pray. He could not lead. Had he strayed into the territory forbidden to Hasidim—depression? He had once told them, "Depression can make you forget your name." He had not forgotten his name—" Nachman, Nachman, Nachman," he shouted—only the letters that comprised his name. Perhaps, then, he *had* sunk into gloom without knowing it. But one thing he did know: the reason for his punishment. The holy letters had risen up in jealousy. Alpha bet. Alpha beta. Lizabeta. More beautiful than the letters. There! There was the link. Eye for eye. Measure for measure.

April turned to May. The sun shone brighter every day. Warmer, longer, grew the days. But the cold shadows in Nachman's heart lengthened. Everything sang, but his soul was in disharmony. Tomorrow will be better, he thought. But tomorrow was not better. He could not stop thinking of Lizabeta. Many nights he dreamed of her. She came to him. Since Vlodek was quiet, perhaps she was alive after all. On the other hand, maybe Vlodek was frightened by Ivan's threat: "The Rabbi of Bratslav has thousands of followers. If you hurt him, you're all doomed men."

One Friday night after prayers, Nachman confessed to his Hasidim about his lost letters. At once they crowded around, embracing him with love.

Nachman felt the warm, wordless wave, like the close feeling in a crowded room when outside it thunders, the room darkens, and the rain begins.

"Brothers, there is a tension between man and God, and this tension is like the string of a violin. The tighter it is stretched, the better the melody. So, too, the tension between soul and body. But, good Jews, don't worry: I am not the first to lose the alphabet. It also happened to . . ." Nachman paused, raised his right index finger, and said, "to the Baal Shem Tov of blessed memory. The holy Besht overcame it. And with God's help, I will overcome it too."

"To make up for my lost letters, strengthen your own. I want all of you to read better. Slower. To pray slowly. Especially you youngsters. Savor the words. Feel their meaning. Some Jews rush through the *Ashrey* as if they are rushing to get out of a storm. True, Jews recite the *Ashrey* three times a day. But let God hear it as if you're saying it for the first time. I know, I know . . . you don't rush through that prayer here. I'm referring, of course, to the Jews in Paris, in Amsterdam." Nachman laughed. "Come, recite it with me."

They recited the Psalm slowly. He felt their devotion building, thickening, until holiness, like a dense cloud, hung in the room.

"A dance!" Nathan cried. "We must dance!"

Nachman nodded. His heart surged.

"Remember, I once told you I could dance an inward dance without moving a muscle, with movements so delicate, so subtle, no one could tell I was dancing? Now, I shall turn my inward dance outward," he said.

And Nachman began to dance. "The entire world is a very narrow bridge," he sang, "a very narrow bridge. And the main thing is not to fear, not to fear at all." He bent his head and stamped his foot and raised his hands and clapped his hands until he seemed to be a wave rising and dipping, dipping and rising, faster and faster. The Hasidim joined him; they picked up the thread of his melody. The room: they could have sworn it was sewn with sparks.

Yes, Nachman thought, losing the letters was punishment. But everything bad, says the Kabbala, contains a measure of good. From within his dancing Nachman looked at himself. Once again the hat of the holy Baal Shem Tov was being placed on his head. Nachman was happy; he was chosen. To the men's rhythmic clapping, he stamped his foot, raised his hands, arched his back. He closed his eyes. On his lids he saw a picture of himself dancing amid lovely letters. He melded with the Besht's spirit. Never say yes to gloom. Run around it and surprise it from the front. Create a ladder and climb up it, rung by rung. Though I walk in the valley of the shadow, I fear no evil. For you are with me.

In his room, Nachman stared at the blank walls until he had a wonderful idea:

One by one, he would ask each of twenty-two Hasidim to secretly make him one large letter of the alphabet. You, the first; you, the third . . . you, the tenth . . . and you, the twenty-second.

From Nathan's Diary

But I still felt that the Master should journey to our Holy Land. And I used Natalya's arrival in the following way:

The old woman knew how to cook and keep house. She was adept at tending the vegetable garden. It was as if the Almighty Himself had sent her. This was very important for the Rebbe, who provides for himself from its produce. Early in the morning, before dawn, he picks vegetables to be sold in the peasant markets. The money from this is his sole support. Once a week, on Thursdays, a vegetable peddler named Ivan comes from a neighboring village and buys the Rebbe's produce for a local nobleman who pays a better price. However, coins are round, not square. They roll away. The Rebbe gives to the poor whatever extra money he has. "Nachman is not a bank," he says.

"Rebbe," I told him, "as you yourself taught us, the Kabbala says that every earthly action has its mirror image in the holy sphere. Natalya may be a message for us. She has traveled a long distance to come to you. This represents the earthly aspect. The heavenly would be for you to take your long-delayed journey to the Holy Land."

This time the Master said nothing.

When the Hasidim had brought Nachman all the letters, he tacked them onto the walls. Wherever he looked, he saw the alphabet. Except in his letter-less mind. They screamed down at him, like mirrors on every wall. Larger and larger, black and blue, like the condemned in hell they screamed and stared, leaping out of the white space that surrounded them. Take me. Choose me. Read me. But Nachman could not decipher them, for they shouted in a foreign tongue.

Nachman lay on his bed, gazing at the alphabet with eyes not his own. Then rose and walked around the room, not taking his eyes off the huge letters. The size, Nachman reasoned, would outwit his loss, overwhelm his ignorance. But it was nonsense. Size did not matter. One cannot fool the Almighty.

The afternoon was waning. Another day gone. The Hasidim had come and left. He felt alone. The bluing light of evening brought gloom. Saving Lizabeta from drowning had not done any good. She had drowned anyway. A man's feet take him, says the Talmud, where he's destined to go. What else will God do to me? Nachman screamed at the estranged letters; perhaps they, too, screamed at him. Praying didn't help. He prayed he would not dream at night, would not relive nightly the meeting with Lizabeta by the water. But his prayer was not answered. Every night in his deep sleep he had the same vivid dream: a naked woman comes to him.

Nachman knew he had to pray to exorcise the Lilith, but how could he pray when he lacked the letters? As he moved from wall to wall, the letters, mocking him, seemed to change places, like when he riffled the pages of a Siddur and watched the quick alphabet dance. But now it was he who moved, changing place, while the letters hung immobile, pasted, hammered, tacked, and he in a demonic frenzy, dashing from one letter to another, from bed to wall, from wall to table, there, there catch it on the other side of the bed, walking up across the mattress and down to the wall to the elusive what-letter-was-it, there, there, eluding him, all with their circular shapes like holes he could fall through and enter, an endless abyss, grinning at him and teasing him, he could almost taste it at the tip of his brain, almost revealed, only to be lured, roped to another piece of paper, he dizzy with the dance, as if spinning with a Torah on Simchas Torah, only now there was no Torah in his hands but a blank spot in his mind, a blank spot as if a portrait of him had been done in colors and a part of a cheek, an eye had been left out, with only white canvas showing, a blank spot smeared with black and blue glyphs, he couldn't catch the letters.

Exhausted, shivering, Nachman fell down on the bed. His body shook. He dived under the covers, seeking warmth. He coughed dryly, as if he had swallowed sawdust. Breathing heavily, pressing his right hand to stop the trembling. Yes. A person is punished according to his love for things.

As he stared at the large letters, sometimes a faint memory teased. From a dark tunnel rolled a snowball of light. He waited for that fluffy ball of light to reveal itself. About to grasp it, the light faded, a candle snuffed.

The next day Nathan rearranged the letters in alphabetical order. Nachman gazed and gazed with Samson eyes, deprived of light. When he shut his eyes, the beautiful letters remained imprinted on his lids, like candlelight after eyes are closed. He knew which Hasid had made which letter, could point out all twenty-two of them. Old, white-bearded

Chaim had made the *mem* with the hand of a Torah scribe. Meyshe, stately and dignified, drew the *shin*. Yankev, the beautifully formed *yud* near the mezuza. Could one see Yankev's precision and good humor in his letter, the little *yud?* And the *ches* in blue was made by Yankev's son, Tzodik-Meyshe, who loved to put letters into words and words into sentences. Nachman did not see that the four letters in Hebrew spelled *meshiach*, Messiah. And then Nachman realized that beauty did not yield understanding. Ah, poor Lizabeta; beauty did not even guarantee life.

The next day, in a wave of frustration and rage, Nachman tore all the letters from the walls.

From Nathan's Diary

When I hung the letters for the Master, I offered to start him on the *aleph beys* again. But he refused; he rebuffed me. "He who took them from me will return them to me. God has taken and God will give. Blessed be the Righteous Judge."

Then I told him something was troubling me. I told the Master I was afraid. That I saw the silence in the Vlodek affair as a bad sign.

"And I see it as a good sign," the Master said. "It's forgotten."

"It's not. It's the silence before the storm. The danger isn't over. They don't forget so quickly, the goyim. He may still call the police. After all, his daughter—"

"How do you know? Have you heard in town? Did they find the body?"

"I assume not."

"Don't assume. Go to Vlodek's house. Say that the rabbi—"

"I think you're making a mistake, Rebbe. After what he did to you, why should you be interested in his daughter? Let's ask the neighbors."

"No good. The peasants will misinterpret it. How come the rabbi is still interested in the girl? It will reawaken old slander. You know what? If you ask him for my yarmulke, I'm sure you'll hear about his daughter."

Ask him for his yarmulke? After what he did to the Rebbe? I'd be crazy to do that. I was afraid to go to the peasant's house. He might beat me or set his dogs on me. But the next day, on the way to Vlodek's farm, I met a couple of peasants and engaged them in conversation. Then I casually asked about Vlodek.

"He's mourning his daughter," they said.

After a while I returned and told the Master:

"Vlodek refused to give it back. I had a feeling he'd refuse. And you should have seen the mouth he opened! How red his face got! 'What?' he raged. 'He killed my daughter and now he wants his little cap back? Tfui on him!' he spat."

"So she's dead," the Rebbe said.

"It's known all over."

"And his wife? Was his wife there? From a mother's reaction one can always—"

"I didn't see the mother. But I didn't like the look on his face. Rebbe, dear Master, listen to me. She's gone. They're mourning her. Take the journey. It's the perfect time. It would help cool the atmosphere. For you and for us too. Go where you always wanted to go, where your saintly zeyde wanted to go but never could. Go to the Land of Israel. There the letters will be returned to you."

"I told you I'm not running away." The Rebbe bit off the words. "Don't mention that to me again!"

Then I stepped close to Reb Nachman and whispered:

"All right, Rebbe. I didn't want to tell you. I haven't told anyone. No need for the Hasidim to get frightened. Even my wife I told it was an illness. But last night I found our milk goat strangled. They're warning us!"

Although Nachman mastered his days, his nights were beyond control. His intense dreams surged with fleshly delights. He would wake from a deep Adam's slumber, exhausted and satisfied. The smell of roses and hay clung to his pillowcase. One night, Nachman dreamt he was a woman lying and waiting in bed. Her desire was so strong, she felt she was changed into quicksand that in the wind created a pit, a crater, a suction that would bring her lover closer. Soon she sensed him coming. First she saw a little glow that reddened and grew more intense. She held her breath awaiting fire and sun, and everything in her sucked inward, waiting, burning wildly, metamorphosed into one big cavity. A wave of fear swept over her. The heat would burn, consume her, and only sand would be left. But she could not act. There was fire in her and fire approaching, and she feared the fire of destruction. Nachman woke, glad he was a man; but he didn't really wake—he just slid into another dream. Twice in two days he'd had the same dream, a respite from his carnal dream bouts. He lay in a field like Jacob, his head on a stone pillow, gazing up at the stars. As he dozed off, an angel whispered, "Go to Vienna, find a treasure." Twice Nachman heard the message; twice he was silent. Now the dream came a third time. Folk wisdom taught that thrice-repeated dreams were, or would come, true. Nachman knew he had to speak. "Where? Where in Vienna?" he shouted. But the angel, hovering on a moonbeam ladder above Nachman's head, was silent.

When he woke, he weighed the messages. The finger was pointing. The dreams said go. Nathan said go. The loss of letters was telling him go. And the strangled goat, it too warns: Go!

From Nathan's Diary

"Do you sleep well?" the Rebbe asked me.

"Fairly well." He surprised me with the question. Perhaps he wanted me to ask him how he slept.

"And you, Rebbe, how do you sleep?"

Our Master smiled, but a frown framed the smile.

"I sleep so deeply that I feel I travel to distant worlds. Everyone knows that sleep is a sixtieth part of death; at night the soul of man ascends to heaven and writes there what it has done by day. My soul, it seems to me, begins its lengthy journey as soon as I fall asleep. My soul journey during sleep is so intense, I am unaware of my body. At night, I live two separate existences. My body sleeping, and my soul ascending and descending. In the morning, when I thank God for returning my soul to me, I feel I've actually returned. My life is renewed and another day of life is before me. When I was a child, a large wild dog barked outside my window while I slept, and I didn't even hear it. Once, when I was five, there was a fire near my little bed and I slept through that. That's how deeply I sleep."

"Do you dream?"

"Nathan, I've answered more than I intended."

Late Saturday afternoon, in the sleepy dusk between the Afternoon and Evening Services, Nachman sat at the table with his Hasidim. He covered his eyes, hoping he would be inspired to tell a story. Oh, if he could only tell a tale! But how could he form a story without the letters?

In his room, an empty excitement, a negative feeling, soughed through him. Then a melody hummed in his veins. Prickles ran along his skin. His fingers tapped his sides nervously. A voice within him shouted "Vienna, Vienna, Vienna" so clearly that he clapped his hands over his ears and ran from his room into the shul, trying to drown out the voice by roaring, "Music, music! Niggun!" At the table, the Hasidim softly, timorously, began a melody. But they soon broke off because their master had not joined them.

"Niggun, niggun, niggun," Nachman cried passionately. "Louder!" His face throbbed, as though in pain.

"Rebbe," one of the Hasidim said. "You told us once about the king who studied music and was cured."

A strange weakness coursed through Nachman's limbs, as if he were about to fall. "Yes?"

"You should study music," another Hasid added.

Nachman looked up for a moment at the Bratslav motto. "But I'm not depressed."

"God forbid! Of course you're not. But music will help." And the Hasid quoted from one of Nachman's tales: "Music was the magic."

Another Hasid said:

"'Praise Him with horn and harp and lyre. Praise him with fife and strings,' says the Psalm. You see, Rebbe, even King David tells us that music is the answer. David cured King Saul of his depression with his harp."

"But there are no music teachers here in this tiny town."

"Then go abroad."

It's Nathan, Nachman thought. He put them up to it. But the Hasid was right. If David composed songs and Psalms and played the harp, and if the Messiah—God's whisper, God's whisper—is destined to come from David, it was only logical that Nachman should study music. That was the unsaid part of God's whisper.

"Where should I study? Where is the best place to go? What city is the capital of music?"

The Hasidim looked at each other.

"Paris," said a Hasid who was a miller. "At the mill I've heard wheat dealers say it's Paris."

"Not Paris," Nachman said. "Paris is where—remember, I once told you?—that's where they pray too quickly."

"Vienna," said a wagoner. "I heard passengers say it's Vienna."

My dream, Nachman thought, my dream!

"Maybe the Rebbe doesn't want to leave . . ." Nathan said innocently.

"I don't, but I will. I'll listen to my Hasidim and go."

"To Vienna?"

"No. To Israel. Where the music that music listens to is hidden."

"When?"

Nachman put his finger to his cheek and said quickly: "Tomorrow morning."

Around the long, white-decked table everyone jumped up.

"Wait, Rebbe, wait. We will choose two men to escort you."

"I'll go with you!" One of the youngsters ran up to Nachman.

"I'll take you," cried the wagoner. "On my wagon. Even on my back, to the Land of Israel."

Nachman smiled at the lad, patted his cheek. "You stay here and study in the morning, and help old men and widows in the afternoon . . . I'll go alone. For *tikkun,* for mending the soul, one must travel alone!"

"Master, are you running away from us?" a Hasid asked.

Nachman did not like the question, but he laughed. "No. I have no desire to flee from any of you. The opposite is probably true. You want to run away from your rebbe who can't even read."

"No, no, no." They all shook their heads. "God forbid, Rebbe."

Then Nachman called Nathan aside. Drew him close.

"Do you want to come with me?"

"Didn't you want to travel alone?"

"A question for a question?"

"Yes, yes. I want to come with you."

Nachman stepped back.

"Then who will take care, who will be in command, who will see that no money remains overnight in the charity box?"

For a moment Nathan imitated Nachman's finger-on-cheek thinking position.

"You're right, Rebbe, I can't go. I'll have to stay."

Nachman was surprised by how quickly Nathan agreed. Nathan held his head to the side modestly, but Nachman knew that Nathan was not a modest man. It was make-believe.

"Yes, you stay here and play the Rebbe . . ." He watched Nathan's face turn red.

"I'm sorry, Nathan," he said. "I didn't mean to hurt you."

Nathan blinked and nodded imperceptibly.

"You stay here, Nathan. I must climb the ladder alone."

"Where? Vienna? Paris? Or will you really go to Israel?"

"Are you being sarcastic? Don't you know that a spiritual journey can take place anywhere, even in those two cities? For the entire world is a rung and the ladder can be climbed anywhere."

Nathan did not say a word.

Nachman concluded: "A man's feet take him where he's destined to go."

From Nathan's Diary

To death? On a one-way journey? Is that what he meant? If not, then why did he quote the Jerusalem Talmud? Because I let him go alone? Did he sense that I deceived him? Still, there is no doubt in my mind that for his sake and ours, the Rebbe should leave. Perhaps on his journey he will compose the fourteenth tale. Despite his gloomy quote, where are we all really destined to go? To the Land of Israel. And that's what I told the Hasidim. I told them: "The holy Besht could not set foot in the Holy Land; when he set out, a storm drove him back; but his great-grandson will bring all of us closer to redemption." And that is why I was forced to make up the story of the strangled goat.

Book Two

He rose early in the morning, knew he was going but did not know where. He said goodbye to the table, he said goodbye to his books, goodbye to his papers, goodbye to his bed. As he stood with his shinbones pressed against the frame of the bed he had a strange feeling. This bed is the cause, the locus of my sorrows, he thought. He turned to the stove and bade it farewell. Objects have an inner life too. Stay well. Be well. Goodbye. He gazed at the silent letters on the wall. Goodbye to you too. He pressed his lips to the mezuzah of the outer door. Goodbye. And goodbye to old Natalya still sleeping in her room.

Pink blue morning air. Chilled and slightly damp. He inhaled and looked around to see if anyone was watching, or following. But no Hasid dared watch Nachman now, not even from behind a curtained window. He had said that he wished to leave unaccompanied; that he would have to tread his path alone.

Nachman began to walk. His Hasidim could assume he was going to Paris; they could assume he was going to the Land of Israel. Let them assume what they wished. He knew a trip to the Holy Land now would be premature. Before he attempted the sacred journey that had been denied his saintly zayde, he would have to rid himself of this-worldly dross. If the Besht, he thought, to whom I am as a shrub is to a Cedar of Lebanon, was turned back from his attempt, how shall I be worthy?

After he walked a short way, a farmer gave him a lift on his wagon. They passed the shops, the artisans' quarter, the gentile section. Soon, moving at a lively pace, they passed Vlodek's farm. Nachman's heart raced. I must forget. Yet whom did he want to see standing in the doorway? The woman who invaded his dreams, made a Garden of Eden of his nights. No. I must forget.

The farmer turned into a side road; Nachman alighted.

A perfect day for walking. The open road beckoned in all directions. Gone the pink sunrise. The air clear, blue, lustrous. Slopes and hills and clover in perfect focus. Scents of sunflowers, barley, and pines, like Lizabeta in the morning radiating frankincense and myrrh. I must forget. But that day was then, and this day is now. No two days are ever alike. God does not make mirrors of mornings.

Today, like a little hook in his mind, the dream of Vienna snagged his thoughts. A treasure in Vienna, the angel had said. Nachman realized it was not a treasure of gems or of gold. To him God would not grant such a trivial reward. Men dream of what they long for. His treasure was of another kind.

He set his feet westward. I must forget. She was punished by water, I by thirst. Thirst for my beloved letters.

He travelled in a battered coat, a workman's cap. On his feet he wore the thick boots common to poor Jews. Better clothing was packed in his straw suitcase. He told no one who he was, for everyone knew of Reb Nachman. His stories travelled to regions where he had never set foot.

Within a day's journey of Bratslav no one knew what he looked like. The first night, he stayed at a little country inn managed by a Jew. Alone for the first time, he opened the door to his room and was surprised that Nathan was not there to serve him. It was quiet; he did not hear the mixed chorus of Hasidim reciting Psalms or studying Mishna. The corridor was empty. Perhaps another step, another door, and he would see his candle-lit bes medresh, full of Jews.

Afraid to sleep, afraid of his weighty, sinful dreams, Nachman sat on his bed, looking out at the night. By a sliver of moon, he discerned tomorrow's road and an endless stretch of fields. Candlelight flickered in the houses of a neighboring village. Dogs barked. A horse neighed. It was too early for the cock to crow, although in his mind he heard—he wished he could hear—that pleasing harbinger of dawn. Afraid to sleep. Afraid to dream. Maybe soon the cock would crow and chase all dreams away. Maybe soon the cock would crow. He looked at the brass bed. Above it hung a little picture of a robin, a child's drawing. Why did the bed have six bars? Of course! I know. On each bar Nachman hung a reason for leaving Bratslav and taking up the wanderer's staff.

On the first:

To learn music. When I return, my dear Hasidim, I shall play and you shall dance.

Nachman's eyes moved to the second bar.

To strengthen my hearing. A blind man hears better. Since a man who can't see letters is partly blind, strengthening one sense will improve the other, and the beloved letters will come back to me.

On the third bar he saw the message:

To learn from the world.

And Nachman turned to the window and looked out at the world, into the black rectangle of the night, to see if he could learn anything from it. But with each heartbeat the dark pulsating silence drummed his aloneness into him. The black rectangle said nothing.

In his mind's eye Nachman's hands seized the fourth bar for support. To root himself in reality, in substance, so as not to be taken captive by the breathing, smoking Egyptian darkness.

Fourth bar, fourth reason:

To go into exile to atone for my sins. Just as Israel is in Exile and the Divine Presence is in Exile, so am I in exile. To forget. Forget.

Now Nachman breathed easier, as if the worst part of the trial were over. He looked at the fifth brass bar:

To refresh my spirit.

Yes, to refresh my spirit. How can anyone sit in one place without moving? It makes one a tree. No wonder the itinerant preachers are so full of life.

Nachman turned to the sixth bar:

To prepare for the real journey. For wherever I travel is only a rehearsal.

Six. He counted the bars from right to left. Yes, indeed six. Then from left to right, and to his astonishment found that they were seven. Again, he counted from right to left: six. Then from left to right. Incredible. Seven! He took a deep breath. Looked out the window to inhale tranquility. No more, he said. No more counting. He understood the hint. The six that are really seven. The seventh that is hidden. The seventh bar was, and was not, on the bed. The seventh reason was not spoken. Not even to himself would Nachman admit that the real reason he fled was to escape from his Lilith-filled dreams.

From Nathan's Diary

> The master always spoke in sevens. Even when he did not speak in sevens, he spoke in sevens. For instance, his story "The Seven Beggars" only speaks of six beggars. But we know very well who the seventh is, may he speedily come to redeem us, Amen! And we all await the twice seventh tale that will follow the thirteenth he has already told us.

What's wrong with me? Nachman thought. First I can't read, now I'm afraid to sleep. He sat on the bed, undressed, ready for sleep. His body told him it was time to lie down and close his eyes, for he was spiralling into exhaustion—but his heart pounded in fear of sleep. Maybe soon the cock would crow. His leg muscles felt weak; he could stand no longer. An odd feeling—hunger or fatigue—plagued his stomach. He stared out at the black night and assumed that the silence and immobility were sleep. Stared until the black turned grey, and the grey rose and blue, and his wish that the cock would crow came true.

In the morning he was dizzy, weak, overtired, as if his night was work and his day repose. At six, a night post-coach made an unscheduled stop at the inn to let off a passenger. Nachman boarded. As soon as he leaned back he dozed off, sinking at once into a dreamless sleep, rocked in his sleep by the sway of the horse-drawn carriage. When he awoke, his first thought was: I didn't see her. I did not see her. He didn't know whether to be happy or sad.

As soon as he began his travels his dreams ceased. What did it mean? That his sinning and lusting at night was connected to a place. Of course it was, he decided, because in Bratslav, by the water, that's where he opened himself to temptation, prayed for it to come, so that he could be like all men. But what did it mean? The message was clear. It meant that when he was away from home, from Bratslav, he was purer; that, like the Jewish people, he was destined for wandering; that Bratslav was Exile, and Exile was sin; that only when he was on his way to Israel was his purity restored. It was true that every mile brought him closer to Vienna; but did not every road lead to the Land of Israel? Wherever

I travel, I am on my way to Israel; and wherever I am, that place is Jerusalem.

Each day another reason for departure surfaced, changing like the face of the land. The valley he saw in the morning was not the mountain he saw at dusk. Town Jews differed from village Jews. Yet their prayers were the same; their faces turned toward the same God in heaven. Only he, only Nachman lacked the letters, lacked his dreams.

Once, as he entered a synagogue before services began, he saw a five-year-old boy reading a Psalm. The boy moved his finger slowly over each letter as if tracing its shape. With tears in his eyes, Nachman watched the lad read, then bent down to kiss his forehead. The surprised boy smiled up at him, he handed him the Book of Psalms, and said, "Do you want to say Psalms too?"

Nachman prayed by heart. He dared not open a Siddur. He closed his eyes, drew an imaginary circle named Jerusalem around himself, and directed his devotions to God. If in a town, he sought out a synagogue. If on the road, he prayed where he was, embracing the fields. At first he hoped the letters would come back outside of Bratslav, locus of his impurity. If the dreams were gone, wouldn't the letters return? But in the first shul, the Hebrew letters on the curtain of the Holy Ark were foreign to him. Travel had not yet brought a cure.

One Friday night he left his inn to look for a synagogue. Soon he heard verses of the Song of Songs floating like petals in the air. "My beloved is mine, and I am his." In pursuit of the melody, he turned into a lane. A young woman stood in a doorway. Was it really she, Lizabeta, the long lost princess? But under Nachman's intense gaze, the girl stepped into the house and disappeared. He found his way to a small, crowded shul. Many of the men wore gold-striped caftans. A cantor with a soft sweet voice stood by the Holy Ark, but the prayers and melodies were directed by a stocky, bearded man sitting on a bench at the side. To the right of the Holy Ark stood a familiar-looking mahogany chair, its back shaped like a lyre. Despite the crowd, no one sat there. After prayers, Nachman asked a worshipper if the stocky man was their rebbe.

"Not exactly. He's our spiritual leader, but we have no rebbe. Our rebbe died at a young age years ago and no one has taken his place." The Hasid looked toward the empty chair. "That's the sign of his continuing presence. No one sits there."

The next morning Nachman wanted to return for morning services. He described the shul to the innkeeper and asked where it was.

The man shrugged. "You must have dreamt it! There's no such shul in our town."

"Are you sure?"

"I know every shul here."

"The leader is a stocky man with a wide grey beard. An empty chair stands to the right of the Holy Ark. Some of the men wore silken gold-striped caftans . . . Their leader died years ago at a young age."

"Empty chair. Stocky leader. Gold-striped caftans." Again he shrugged and grimaced. "Impossible. Not in our village. There is no such shul here. Wait! We once had a collector from the Holy Land who described a shul like that. It must be the Kabbalists' shul, in Safed or Jerusalem."

Nachman travelled by foot; he travelled by wagon. Sometimes he took a night coach and woke at dawn, watching the May countryside coming back to life. The moist and shining blue green mist of morning floated by like a cloud. Nachman was amazed at the changing faces of the landscape. He had never seen vistas from a moving vehicle for so long a time. A passing village beckoned. Here he might live and begin anew; but by the time he pondered it, he was somewhere else. Then he remembered his dream. The good dream. He lay on a stone pillow and an angel stood on a ladder of moonbeams and told him of a treasure.

Haystacks bespoke the changing regions. Little rectangles; pointed arches; hut-size mounds. In one village, the farmers stuck long sticks diagonally into each haystack, like a pin in a woman's bun.

He passed farm girls working in the fields. They gave him water, directions, advice. Blonde and smiling, they all reminded him of Lizabeta. Had her image been scattered like haystacks, like clouds, all over Europe?

From Bratslav he went to Kamenetz, from Kamenetz to Horodenka, from Horodenka to Lvov. Ever westward. The more shuls he went to, the more pleased he was with his own congregation. One Sabbath, in a village shul, he closed his ears to the noise of worshippers talking, and tried to watch the letters he could not understand rising from the cantor's lips. He could not hear the Torah portion over the buzz of conversation. When the Torah reading was completed, the rabbi rose. He spoke of the legend that the Egyptians had immured Jewish babies into the walls. "The Midrash states," the rabbi continued, "that those children would have grown up to be evil men anyway."

Nachman felt a tug at his soul, his heart, his body, as if an angel had seized his shirt and pulled him forward. His body twitched. And don't you disagree with that crude Midrash, rabbi? He wanted to remain silent, not to interfere, but the urge within him to speak out was too strong.

"Is that consolation for a mother?" he shouted. "Can you tell that to a mourning mother? No Jewish child is pre-doomed. 'Would have grown up to be evil men anyway.' That answer befits the Egyptian murderer. Any Jew who says that is capable of murder himself, for he has a built-in excuse, a rationale for his own wicked behavior."

There was a sudden silence in the shul. The rabbi's face reddened. At once Nachman regretted the interruption. He had shamed the poor man.

For a moment the stunned rabbi looked around for support. A trustee walked up to the pulpit. He stopped at the bottom step and then joined the rabbi.

"It's in the Midrash," the rabbi shouted back.

A lame reply, thought Nachman. "But not in the Torah."

"The Midrash is holy."

"Not every word should be taken literally. Read Nachmanides!"

Now the trustee had gathered up enough courage to shout, "Sit down. How dare you interrupt the sermon?"

"Remember that Chmelnietski's Cossacks who cast our children into the fires in 1648? Would you say that the thousands of babies burned alive by those barbarians would also have grown up to be wicked men anyway?" Nachman bit off the last three words.

No one spoke. No one answered. Nachman heard himself take a deep breath. Looked up at the Ten Commandments above the Holy Ark. Egyptian writing? Indian script? Was he dreaming? Is this shul too non-existent? And where did the other one disappear to? Suppose the congregants here opened a Siddur and said, "Read! Prove that you are one of us!"

"Who are you?" the rabbi's voice trembled.

"It makes no difference who I am. What's the difference if I'm Yankel the tailor, the Baal Shem Tov, or the Messiah?"

"Ha," he heard a sarcastic laugh behind him.

"Pay attention to what I say, not to who is saying it. We can no longer say," Nachman dropped his voice to a hoarse whisper, "that God chose to kill us. And it is a sin against His holy name to say that our enemies acted as God's agents."

"Mysterious are the ways of God and blessed are those who believe in Him. Tragedy befalls us only because we have sinned," the rabbi retorted. "We are His chosen people."

"Would you have us believe," Nachman continued, "that Chmelnietski is God's messenger, doing his bidding? Or that the pogrom in Mizhnov two years ago was God's retribution against the eighty-year-old saintly rabbi of Mizhnov and his one-year-old great-granddaughter, that notorious sinner? Would you say that God chose Chmelnietski as he chose Abraham, Isaac, and Jacob? If so, we can no longer say *ato vechartonu,* that God has chosen us. Because if He has appointed"—here Nachman jerked his thumb backwards—"Chmelnietski to kill us, then we are no longer the chosen people. Chmelnietski and his brutal Cossacks are chosen, and we are rejected. And by saying what you have said, we break our contract, our *bris,* with God. If the Cossacks were doing God's holy deeds, we should thank them and not mourn. Some partnership, God and the murderers!"

Nachman felt all the faces turning toward him. Why had he done this? Why had he interfered? For days he had been travelling quietly, restraining himself. But he had also restrained the fires in him. Where he stood had suddenly become the center of the room.

"Who are you?" demanded the trustee.

"Ben Israel," Nachman said, walking to the doorway, amidst the stunned silence. "A repentant sinner in search of music and light."

"Not Ben Israel," someone shouted, "but a traitor of Israel. Heretic! You're probably a Bratslaver. Only they have such crazy ideas."

Nachman walked out of the synagogue. The bright sunshine hurt his eyes.

After fourteen days on the road, Nachman was in a village in Slovakia. He walked into a little bes medresh, unusually crowded for a mid-week afternoon, just as a man, somewhat hoarse, was finishing a story:

". . . and finally the King found the lost princess and they lived happily ever after."

Everyone gathered around the teller. One man walked among the listeners collecting coins for him. Nachman added his. The storyteller's voice was familiar, but Nachman could not place it. He had come in from a rear entrance and saw only the preacher's back. By the time

Nachman made his way through the crowd, the man was out the front door, where a horse and wagon awaited him. He climbed up on the wagon and at once the horse was trotting down the dusty road.

Nachman stood riveted—by the scene, by the familiar motif, by the end of the tale. Who else in Jewish preaching used tales of kings and lost princesses? Why had he come in just at: "And finally the king found the lost princess and they lived happily ever after"? He should have screamed and made the man turn to him. Who was the king and who was the princess? And what, indeed, if Vlodek's daughter were Jewish? If stories reflect the real world, why can't the real world reflect stories? And what difference did it make? No amount of thoughts, dreams, and dream-wishing would bring her back.

Nachman was afraid to learn who the man was, lest he hear an answer that might break his heart or send dybbuk chills down his spine. But finally, after the Evening Service, Nachman asked a congregant.

"You mean you don't know?" the man said. "You don't live here?"

"No. I come from far away."

"That's the famous story-telling rebbe. He's a fourth generation descendant of the Baal Shem Tov."

"Reb Nachman of Bratslav?"

"Then you *do* know him," the man said, chin out, hands on his hips. "Why'd you say you don't?"

"Of course I know of him, but I didn't know that this man was Reb Nachman. Has he been here before?"

"No. But he sent word he was coming and that's why everyone came to hear him."

"That means he's been travelling around these parts."

"Evidently."

"And he accepts gifts?"

"A man has to eat, doesn't he?"

"A descendant of the Baal Shem Tov? Begging?"

"Not begging. Collecting *tzedoka*. Charity for others. Or perhaps to feed his family. Do you work? Do you eat?"

True, a man has to eat. But how? And by what means? By taking on the soul-cloak of another human being? Arrogating his name and personality for personal gain or fame? Nachman stood and mused. Who could that man be? One of the Hasidim who had left Bratslav? No. No one had recently left the congregation. That preacher was an opportunist. To betray one's own spirit by assuming the mantle of another was the height of deceit. For a moment a thought flashed. Could it be the man who was his mirror image, doing what only Nachman could do? If so, then Nachman would have to become a Rebbe's assistant and the assistant would have to travel and tell tales.

At the inn Nachman packed his bags, ready to go in pursuit of the charlatan. To face, rebuke, and shame him. To protect his territory, as a bird protects its young and a lion its hunting ground. All creatures protect their homes. Nachman faced Bratslav, imagined heading back. Immediately, a gloom, a sour feeling of loss came over him. The call of music tempted him even more. Too late now to give chase. Sooner or later the false Reb Nachman will be found out.

But, on the other hand, Nachman thought as he headed westward, perhaps this is a message to me. For no event in this world is without meaning. Perhaps I am *not* Nachman. Perhaps *I* am the false Reb Nachman, who sinned in water and was punished with thirst. Before I can strip the false Nachman-ness from anyone else, *I* must become the real Reb Nachman.

In the towns he passed through his imitator had not appeared. No one knew the false Reb Nachman; no one knew the real one. He passed himself off as a herring merchant. Once, a sharp-witted wheat salesman from Poland frowned. "Herring merchant, huh? When was the last time you sold a herring?" Nachman did not reply. The man scratched his face and said, "Herring merchants smell a mile away. Nothing helps, neither mikva nor steam baths."

Nachman smiled to himself. Not only am I not a good herring merchant, I'm not even a good liar.

Once, as he was rewinding his tefillin after morning prayers, another worshipper walked off with his tallis bag.

"Wait a minute. That's my bag."

"Really? How do you know it's not mine?"

"My name is sewn on it."

The man held the bag with the gold thread letters.

"What name is that? Tell me."

Nachman looked at the strange letters. He knew they should read Nachman. But his head spun as though a force were pulling away the pronunciation of his name. As he looked at the letters, Nachman forgot his name. He felt disoriented, in a dream world where he was split in two, one part with a name, the other without. Is this death? he wondered. Dead and punished, I don't know my name.

"I don't know," he said, helplessly.

"If you can't even read the name in what you claim is your tallis bag, how could it possibly be yours?"

"But my name is sewn on the bag," Nachman whispered. "Where's your proof?"

The man brushed his fingers over the raised letters. "My name is Nachman. It says Nachman, and Nachman is me. So there's the proof."

And before Nachman could say a word, the other man walked off with the bag.

In one post-coach he was the only rider. At the next stop a girl entered who looked like Lizabeta. Nachman thought it a test, so he turned away. I must forget. I must forget. Maybe she stepped out of Bratslav, resurrected, with magic boots—skip, hop, leap, jump—to this region. Or is there more than one Lizabeta in the world? And if there is, perhaps there is more than one Nachman. And they are doomed, destined, to chase each other, tempt each other, and flee. But she did not greet him. Could she have forgotten him? Then she must be dead. For only the dead forget. But don't the dead have soul memory? True, he was dressed differently. His beard was untrimmed; he wore a peasant cap of the sort he had never worn in Bratslav. Nachman whistled a folk tune sung by the peasants of Bratslav. If she responded, if she whistled or hummed the melody, he would know it was she.

But she did not whistle or hum. Instead, she said: "That's a beautiful tune."

"The farmers sing it in our town."

"Oh, I thought it was yours."

"No, no," he said. "I wish it were, but I can't claim it."

"Are you going far?"

"Vienna."

"I've heard of Vienna, but I've never been there. I'm only going as far as Ulpyi."

"Where's that?"

"West of Budapest. That's where my uncle lives. It's a nice town. A tiny town. The post stops there and you can have a nice room in an inn."

Nice room in an inn. I can sing you songs you'll like and then you can take me for a walk in the fields and I'll teach you the names of the flowers and the trees. I'll show you herbs and plants and medicinal grasses that zayde passed down to me. I shall whistle the songs of all the birds and you'll walk in front of me and I'll see your walk and your blonde hair bouncing and the curve of your neck. He closed his eyes. I can't forget, he thought. I try, but I can't.

"Are you sure you're not going to Vienna?" he asked.

"Oh, sure as sure can be. I have no one in Vienna. Why do you ask?"

"Because I dreamt a dream of Vienna. An angel told me that I'll find a treasure in Vienna."

The girl laughed.

"Shall I come to help you find the treasure in Vienna?"

No, he thought. No, a voice in his ear, deep within his ear, told him. This is not the dream. This is not the story. This is not the weave, the spin, the web of the destined dream fabric. Like Jacob, you follow your dream alone. But still, she was a pretty girl and he liked talking to her.

"But what will your uncle say?"

"True, he's expecting me. But if I bring him some of the treasure, he'll be pleased."

Nachman smiled at her.

"Who says I'll share it with you?" he teased.

She looked crestfallen. "I thought if we looked together and found it, you and I would share it."

"Do you have money for an inn?" he asked.

She pointed to a knot in a bundle. "My mother told me not to tell anyone about these coins."

"I won't tell any of the other passengers," he said.

How old was she? Eighteen, nineteen? She sounded even younger. Why was every girl he met so attractive? Why did every girl he met send out invisible signals, fine little lines, each shaped like a tiny fish hook, at once hurting and pleasing.

No, he was sent to Vienna alone. He was exiled from Bratslav, from alphabet, from holiness, because of Lizabeta. So how could he regain city, letters, holiness, if he duplicated his deeds? She was a test, then, to see if he could withstand temptation. Once he had prayed for temptation, and temptation came, again and again. He would show the supernal forces that he was not the Nachman he was/is, but the Nachman he was supposed to be. He made a cane out of a melody, shaped the top into a handle and held onto it; seized it for balance, protection.

"No," he said slowly. "No," he said, against his will, "I fear it will be too expensive for you in Vienna. Within hours your entire bundle of coins will melt away. You had better go straight to your uncle."

When the sounds of Hungarian faded Nachman began to understand the peasants' language. He could read the signs on the inns and roadposts and knew he was in Austria. Since German was not a holy tongue, God had not deprived him of its ken. God is just, not capricious. As a measure against his impurity, the Almightly had taken from him only the holy Hebrew letters. Still, in his long journey from Russia, he had changed only place, not spiritual plane. Nothing had changed. He began to miss his lustful, satisfying, harmless dreams.

One moment countryside, the next—a tumult heard only at the Tower of Babel. Horses flew down stone-paved streets. People rushed by in pairs, threes, crowds. Tall buildings. Dust and cries and strange smells. In and out of the crowd scurried boys selling papers, rolls, apples, and tarts. Men in tatters, men in high hats, policemen, peddlers. Market women carrying fruits in baskets. Were all cities like this? Or was it only Vienna? He held on to his suitcase lest it be taken from him. Buildings tipped in the wind as the clouds sailed by. His head spun.

A square behind a small fountain. Stone men and lions and wolves sprayed water. A quintet of street musicians performing. They wore flat, broad-brimmed hats tipped up at the sides like wings. Under their blue, tightly waisted coats adorned with brass buttons were frilly white shirts and purple scarves. And all had white knee-length socks and black buckled shoes. Fascinated by the performance, Nachman stood at the edge of the crowd. Around him people munched crackers and sausages. They applauded after each selection and joked with the musicians. Nachman recognized the violin and clarinet from weddings back home, but the other shiny brass instruments he did not know. After the concert he approached the violinist.

"Excuse me, can you tell me who is the most famous musician in Vienna?"

The man bowed and saluted. "Bruno at your service, sir. What instrument does the gentleman play?"

"None. I make melodies."

"In that case, you want a composer. Do you want to study composition?"

"Yes. With the best possible teacher."

"You want the greatest or the most famous?"

"Why not both?"

"Because both qualities cannot be rolled into one musician. But if you want the most famous, his name is Haydn," said Bruno.

"What kind of man is he?"

"An angel of a man. In the service of dukes and kings."

"An employee? Subservient to them?"

"Yes, of course. That's the way it is here in Vienna. We all serve someone. Even the Archbishop. And he serves God."

Was Bruno's reply apologetic? Nachman wondered. The violinist cocked his head and eyed Nachman curiously. "Say, are you from the Alps?"

"No," Nachman said slowly. He didn't know where the Alps were. "Why?"

"Because your accent is different. It's like that of the country people from Tyrol. You use different words. You sound as if you were brought up in the mountains."

"I come from an area surrounded by hills."

Nachman looked at the fountain and the stone figures of men spraying water. By now the square had emptied of people. Bruno's colleagues gathered around him. Only the occasional clomp-clomp of horses' hooves on the cobblestones was heard. Nachman turned back to the violinist.

"But you also mentioned the greatest musician."

"In that case you want Beethoven, right Fritzl?"

"By my trumpet," Fritzl said, rubbing his instrument on his sleeve to enhance its sheen, "Beethoven is the treasure of Vienna."

All the musicians nodded. The dream, Nachman thought, the dream.

"And is there a musician who is independent? Who serves no master but himself?"

"So you're looking for a rebel?"

Nachman hesitated for a minute. He looked at the musicians' uniforms, then looked down at his clothing, so different from theirs. But wasn't his outfit a costume too, designed to hide who he was? Perhaps in this country the king imprisoned rebels.

"Well, a spiritual rebel."

"Then it's still Beethoven," said Bruno.

"Where can I find him?"

The violinist exchanged glances with his friends.

"What?" he laughed. "Do you think you can just go and drop in on him?"

"Why not?"

"Well, it just isn't done. Beethoven is like royalty."

All Jews are sons of kings, Nachman thought. I am royalty too. Do you know what God whispered to me one Tuesday morning?

"If you want lessons—and he's not too keen on giving them—you ought to write to him and then wait for a reply."

"He'll wait. And wait. And wait." Fritzl laughed.

"I don't have time to write. Where does he live?"

Bruno shrugged. "Oh well, it's your skin." He raised his violin. "But I warn you, Beethoven is a difficult man."

"Unpredictable," the clarinetist added. "You know how geniuses are."

"See this French horn?" said another musician. "It and God are my witness. He's a man given to fits of joy and rage. He can be charming one minute and sarcastic the next. He may not open the door if you knock. And if by miracle he does—like he did for me when I wanted to show him a piece I'd written for the French horn—he may slam it in your face. I know."

"I'll take the chance. What's his address?"

The French horn player sighed. "On the other side of the Danube, next to the park, there's a tavern. Look for the Sign of the Cockatoo. Two doors over, second floor. You'll probably hear him pounding the piano."

Nachman stood on the other side of the street and looked up at Beethoven's window. Someone, perhaps Beethoven, was playing. So this is my destination. Here my dream becomes real. He crossed the street, walked up the stairs. In the dark hallway, he took off his traveling jacket and donned his clean knee-length waistcoat. Knocked on the door. The music continued. Nachman knocked louder. He concentrated on the wood, sent his knocking into the heart of the wood. Finally, the playing stopped. Nachman heard footsteps.

"Who is it?" a man asked.

Nachman leaned close, spoke into the door.

"You don't know me. I'm from Bratslav."

The door opened.

"Beethoven?"

"Yes?" The composer inspected his visitor from hat to boots.

Nachman had expected a tall, good-looking gentile, like the ones he had seen in the mountains. He thought that a famous musician would be slim, of noble appearance and dress. Instead he saw a short, broad-shouldered, rather plain-looking man. Smallpox scars dotted his large, reddish face. But his eyes, the link to the soul, his eyes sparkled, strange and luminescent.

For a moment the two men stared at each other. An odd thought flashed in Nachman's mind. I'm Nathan begging admittance—and he's Nachman, sizing up a competitor who would replace him. This too is one of the Almighty's wishes in my Exile: that I learn the taste of being the other.

"And who are you?"

"I'm Nachman from Bratslav."

Beethoven placed his hand over his heart and gave a little bow.

"Please excuse me for opening the door myself. I usually have a manservant, but I can't always pay him on time, so—" Beethoven shrugged—"he has gone and left me . . . Can you please repeat where you're from? As you can no doubt tell, my German is provincial, northern, and yours sounds as if it comes from the Swiss valleys . . . . Are you coming now from . . . ?" and Nachman thought that Beethoven said Radumsk.

"I have a cousin in Radumsk."

"Razumovsky," said Beethoven, still standing in the doorway.

Nachman shrugged. Jews say Lipsia; gentiles, Leipzig. Jews, Varshe; gentiles, Warsaw. In Viennese, Radumsk must be Razumovsky.

"Razumovsky," said Nachman.

"Ah yes. The music. From the prince."

"The prince?"

"You have the music? In manuscript?"

"It's in my head."

"Not written?"

"No."

"Can you sing it?"

"Of course. Listen." And Nachman sang a niggun for Beethoven.

The composer stepped back from the shadow. The sunlight from the huge window lit up his broad, powerful face. His eyes glowed. Beethoven waved Nachman into the room. In Bratslav Nachman had seen a picture of a piano but never the instrument itself. Beethoven sat down on the stool. The seat moved from side to side like a wheel on a toppled cart.

"Again. Sing it again and I'll pick up the melody."

As Nachman sang, Beethoven followed on the piano. His eyes warmed as he played; his face became radiant.

"A most unusual melody." Beethoven sang it. Nachman liked his voice, full-bodied and honest. A man's voice, like his eyes, revealed his essence. "I have never heard anything like it. Is this what the prince is sending me?" Beethoven chuckled and gave a rill of chords up the piano. "He has never written in this mode before."

"Excuse me, Beethoven, what prince?"

"The composition that Prince Razumovsky is sending me."

"What do you mean, Prince Razumovsky? This is not Razumovsky's melody."

"Then whose is it?" Beethoven asked.

"Mine. This is my own melody."

"Yours?" Beethoven jumped up. His fingers slipped on the keys and made a harsh, discordant sound. A flush passed over his cheeks. He stood close to Nachman, breathed into his face. "Are you sure you are not passing off Prince Razumovsky's music as your own? The prince would be most displeased"—here Beethoven twisted his mouth and made a slitting motion across his throat—"if he learned of this . . . Think . . . Perhaps in the long trip from Hungary or Russia, or wherever he is now, you, his messenger, forgot that it was the prince's and began to think of it as yours."

"What Russia? What prince? Messenger?" Nachman stepped back. "There is a misunderstanding here. I beg your pardon! I am no one's messenger." Then he turned, picked up his suitcase. "No prince sent me here. I thought you invited me in because I was Nachman of Bratslav, not a prince's messenger. I have no desire to be anyone but who I am." Nachman smiled wanly. "I beg your pardon, Beethoven. . . . Goodbye."

Many thoughts crossed his mind during the three or four steps he took toward the door. If he left, where would he go? Back home? No. The dream must be true. Or perhaps visit Haydn? But Haydn was a servant. Free men seek out free men. Then, just as his fingers touched the door handle, he felt Beethoven's right hand close on his. The composer took Nachman's suitcase.

"Then you are not an emissary of the prince."

"I am an emissary of the angel who directed me here."

Beethoven frowned.

"And the melody is really yours?"

"Of course. Why should I say it's mine if it isn't . . . ?"

"Do you have more?"

"Dozens. I'm constantly creating new ones. In Bratslav where I come from melodies are so abundant, one has to be careful not to step on them."

Nachman saw the smile suffusing Beethoven's face.

"But," Nachman continued, "the problem is . . ."

"Yes?" Beethoven placed the suitcase near the piano. "What is the problem?"

For a moment Nachman was silent. Purposely. He knew that now the composer would be interested. But evidently Nachman was silent too long.

"Why did you come here?" Beethoven thundered. "Who sent you to me?"

Nachman—the little Nachman in his mind swerved, picked up the suitcase, and stalked out—spoke softly. The Talmud taught that a soft voice calms rage.

"I came because I want to learn. I have melodies in my head and don't know how to write them down. They come to me, then flit away. That's the problem. Luckily, I remembered the one I sang to you."

"What's this got to do with an angel?"

"Ah. The one who sent me here. I had a dream in which an angel told me three times that a treasure awaited me in Vienna. So I left my home on the other side of the Carpathian mountains and have been travelling three weeks. Then, this afternoon, when I set foot in the city, I saw street musicians by the fountain on the square. I asked them, 'Who is the greatest composer and most independent man in Vienna?' They told me 'Beethoven.' Then the trumpeter added, 'the treasure of Vienna.' Only then did I know that my dream had been realized."

Beethoven looked down at the wooden floor. He shuffled his feet. Perhaps he was moved, embarrassed, by the compliment.

"What is your name?" Beethoven asked softly.

"Nachman from Bratslav."

"Yes, yes, you told me before, but Nachman what? Your family name."

"In our region we do not have family names. We go by the names of our fathers. My name is Nachman ben Simcha, Nachman the son of Simcha, which in Hebrew means joy."

"You are a Hebrew?"

"Yes, a Jew."

Beethoven beamed. "There are Jews here, but not many in music. I have a good friend who occasionally comes to Vienna, Ignatz Moscheles, an excellent composer . . ." Beethoven put a finger to his lip, as if thinking of something else. "Then the melody you sang for me is a Jewish one?"

"Yes, of course. To one of our prayers. But when I sing a new melody, we call it a niggun, I forget the previous ones and I have no way of remembering."

"I'll teach you to write notes for your melodies."

"Really?"

"Yes. Really. Look." He showed Nachman a sheet of music. "See these marks? It's a kind of mysterious alphabet that anyone can understand." Then Beethoven moved his big head back and laughed. "So it was indeed a dream that sent you to me." He wagged his finger at Nachman. "But don't think you're the only one who dreams. Once, I dreamt I was Michelangelo . . ."

"Excuse me. Who is that?"

"A famous Italian painter. He even made a statue of Moses. I dreamt I was atop a ladder in the Sistine Chapel in Rome and they told me to start painting. They'd given me the finest brushes and paints of the subtlest colors. I held the palate. I tried and tried but couldn't start. Melodies went through my head—nothing else. Finally, I told them: 'I can't do it. If in real life I'm not Michelangelo and cannot paint, what makes you think that in my *dream* I can paint the Sistine Chapel?' "

Beethoven laughed again and Nachman joined him. He had not understood every word. Why couldn't Beethoven paint the walls? Even he, Nachman, back home had dipped a brush into whitewash and painted the inside of his house. But, Nachman supposed, a musician masters only his craft and no other. Beethoven now sat at the piano.

"See if you can recognize this melody."

He played Nachman's niggun once, twice, just as Nachman had sung it. Amazing how the man could recreate what had been in Nachman's mind. A moment later, in the flow of Beethoven's playing, Nachman could no longer recognize his melody. Beethoven added notes and chords and interwove phrases of the melody, as if weaving a basket

. . . . Now he recognized bits of his niggun. Beethoven played the tune quicker, slower. Changed the rhythm. Made the niggun dance. Nachman imagined that the melody turned around corners, climbed up a ladder, jumped from a wall, penetrated mirrors, curled into a magnifying lens.

"Variations on a Theme by Nachman," said Beethoven.

"You put life into my niggun," Nachman said. Now he knew why he had come to Vienna: to discover the soul of melody. He watched Beethoven's quickly moving fingers, but out of the corner of his eye Nachman also noticed changes of colors in the room. "Excuse me, I see the sun is setting. Can you . . . ?"

Beethoven jumped up, looked out the window. "Good God! I have a concert tonight. Come. . . . You'll hear magnificent music. Bach, Mozart, and . . . Beethoven."

"But I have no place to sleep," Nachman blurted. "Can you tell me if there is an inn nearby?"

"Nonsense. Tonight you're my guest. There is plenty of room here." His broad gesture took in the large room with its booklined walls. He gave a little embarrassed cough. "We'll have to dress for the concert. Your jacket is fine but, forgive me for saying so, your trousers look badly worn."

"I have a clean change in my suitcase."

"Good. But first to supper. A bottle of wine and a meal at the Cockatoo next door. That's where I usually dine and the food is quite good and inexpensive."

"Many thanks, Beethoven, but regarding supper . . . You see, as a Jew I have strict dietary requirements. I'd like to have just some bread and fresh fruit and vegetables . . . perhaps some milk. In any case, I've gotten into the habit of eating minimally."

"The Jewish kosher laws, right?"

"You know about them?" For a moment the pleasing suspicion tickled: Beethoven is a Jew.

"Oh, yes. My friend, Moscheles, he keeps the kosher laws too . . . Come, I'm hungry."

The Cockatoo was a dark, wood-lined tavern with carved beams and wood-lace adornments. It reminded Nachman of the country inns he had passed in his travels. As he looked at the menu, Beethoven frowned, one eyebrow higher than the other. Perhaps out of deference to

Nachman he ordered fish. Nachman watched the composer eating. Back home Nachman taught: you can tell the essence of a man by the way he eats. Some eat in a mannerly fashion, others gorge. He thought that the broad-faced, thickly built Beethoven would eat grossly, would take a carnal delight in his ingestion. But no. He ate with refinement. Slowly. He cut the fish into small portions, did not suck the bones. He gazed off into an imaginary forest in the dark-wood distance beyond Nachman's shoulders. Was he composing now too? Nachman wondered. Beethoven patted his lips with a napkin, never spoke with his mouth full, sipped wine delicately. He poured a glass for Nachman, but Nachman declined. To explain the laws for wine was too complicated. He told the composer he did not drink wine.

The waiter presented the bill, but Beethoven flicked it away and muttered, "Add it to my account."

The waiter flushed. He glanced for a moment at Nachman, raised his hand as if to say, "Absolutely not!"

Nachman wished he were far away, deaf, blind, able to wipe out the scene now recrudescing in his mind.

Beethoven's eyes blazed. "You are in the presence of nobility."

The waiter turned to Nachman and bowed.

Nachman stretched his hand to take the bill.

Beethoven jumped forward like a tiger and covered the bill with his hands. "Under no circumstances."

A shock that began as a wave of chills at the base of Nachman's neck quickly pulsed into physical discomfort. He was sure his face was red. My God, he thought, Beethoven has no money. The greatest composer in Vienna cannot pay for his meal.

The waiter clenched his teeth; his cheeks swelled. But he pulled out a notebook and entered Beethoven's sum.

On the way back, Nachman said, "I don't want to impose. Please. Can you find me an inn?"

"No, you are my guest. I told you once already."

"Then let us share expenses. It is a custom of mine to do that."

Beethoven, walking alongside him, stopped. This made Nachman stop. He turned and faced the composer. Beethoven's nostrils were pinched and white, his cheeks red. Like an East European Jew he stood close. Their faces were inches apart.

"I'm the host," he hissed. His teeth chattered between phrases. "And it's *my* custom to treat a guest like a guest and not like a patron at a country inn. Beethoven is not a tavern keeper."

"But I took so much money with me. What am I going to do with it?"

Beethoven put his finger to his cheek.

"Ah, I have it. A capital idea! Do you know what you can do with your money?"

"No."

"Pickle it."

Beethoven had said, "Dress for the concert." But Nachman noted that the composer's flowing bow tie lay carelessly over his shirt and his black jacket did not match his dark blue trousers. Compared to him, Nachman looked elegant in his Sabbath waistcoat and white shirt that old Natalya had lovingly washed and starched and pressed with a hot coal iron. Music tucked under his arm, Beethoven walked quickly.

"Come, we're late. You don't know what a concert is, ha?" he said over his shoulder. "I'll show you. And thanks for that wonderful gift, even if it's not from Razumovsky. Mozart also worked in the minor mode but not quite with such a sustained singing line. Wait till the encore. Ah, of course, you don't know what an encore is, either. I'll teach you," Beethoven said good-naturedly. "I'll teach you everything."

Nachman kept stride with Beethoven's swift pace. The composer had an off-balance walk, as if his legs were in disharmony with his torso. He leaned forward when he walked, with a wide-eyed, slightly wild look. His lower lip jutted out. Parts of his body seemed to strain to move away from, ahead of, quicker than the rest of him.

When Beethoven arrived at the hall, a few minutes late, the concert had begun. But fortunately, he remarked, he was not scheduled to perform until the latter half.

"You go in through this door and sit down," Beethoven winked to an attendant, "and I'll meet you by the side door after the performance, Nachman. Nachman von Bratslav, right?"

Nachman sat in back of the hall. He looked at the program. Earlier that day, a time that seemed like years ago, he had heard five uniformed musicians playing together. That was nothing new, for back home—back home! My God! If morning was years ago, home was centuries past!—he had heard groups of five, even seven, musicians at weddings. But on stage now were twenty or twenty-five musicians playing Bach's Fifth Brandenburg Concerto. Nachman closed his eyes. He was moved. Touched. He had never heard absolute music before. It was like a dream. Like pure prayer, without words. Before he had a chance to absorb Bach, the orchestra began a Mozart symphony. Melodies different from Bach's. Nachman felt he was smelling flowers, hay; heard robins, nightingales; felt he was praying in a meadow, floating on the river on his back, looking up at white clouds against a blue blue sky. He felt light, dizzy, excited. As if dreaming a delicious dream.

During the brief intermission, Nachman looked at the instruments on the stage. At the back stood a harp, King David's instrument. He remembered wandering gypsies, who sometimes came to Bratslav, playing a hand-held harp. He wondered why no one had played that harp during the concert. Was it reserved for a king?

Finally, Beethoven appeared. The audience applauded. Nachman felt happy. He knew the man being applauded. After a quick bow, Beethoven sat at the piano and led the orchestra in his First Piano Concerto. Here again was something new. Not robins, not hay. A mighty tree being felled by powerful axe strokes. A house rising. Hearing Beethoven's piece, Nachman thought of carpenters hammering and yet—of feathers floating in air. While conducting, Beethoven bent low, face red with strain, urging the orchestra, pointing with his finger. He sang with the musicians, jumped up, the edges of his jacket flying. His jowls shook, tufts of hair flapped like wings. Then he ran to the piano, played, and jumped up again.

At the end of the concerto, the audience stood and cheered. Beethoven bowed quickly once more but did not smile. The applause continued. The composer sat, lifted his hands. The applause faded. He began to play, without orchestral accompaniment. This time the piece sounded familiar. How was that possible? Everything was so new, how could Beethoven's music sound familiar? Then, as shivers of shock, surprise, ran down his back, he realized.

Nachman did not want his tales published, he forbade it; they were only for his Hasidim. And now a niggun of his—played before hundreds of people! He felt a tightening around his chest. Portent of doom? Of death? He was going to be recognized. Nachman rose from his back row seat. In the foyer he had second thoughts. Beethoven was being kind. Who knows how many composers yearned to have Beethoven play one of their songs? Nachman peeked through the door, which was slightly ajar. When the composer finished, the applause resounded. Beethoven held his hands up for silence.

"You have just heard a new composition entitled, 'Variations on a

Theme by Nachman von Bratslav.' The composer of this beautiful melody is right here in this hall . . ."

Everyone turned, looked to the side, to the rear. Nachman shut the door. Heart beating quickly. Blood flowing to his face. Why had Beethoven done this? Sit down, Beethoven. Play something else. Turn their attention to another piece. Just then, Beethoven left the stage, followed by the orchestra. The audience stood to leave.

A tap on his shoulder.

"Excuse me. I have the honor of introducing myself. Gerhard Hinter." He gave a short, clipped bow. "I saw you coming in with Beethoven. You are a friend of his?"

"Yes, I know him." Nachman looked at the short, stout, well-dressed man. Hinter wore wire frame glasses and clasped his hands together as he spoke.

"You see, I represent a publisher. We admire Beethoven's music and we want to publish his work. But he's a difficult man to deal with. So self-effacing, so modest. Do you see him often?" Hinter looked at Nachman pleasantly.

"Well, I'm staying at his house now."

"Splendid. Splendid. Then surely you can do him a favor."

"How can I help? Please tell me."

Hinter looked at the outer door and spoke quickly. He unclasped his small hands, then immediately clasped them again.

"Would you be good enough to give, that is, sell me some of his manuscripts—of course we won't tell him anything about it—so that we can make him famous in the world? And for you there will be some payment too."

Nachman looked at the man's eyes, his clasped palms. Beethoven's eyes summed up the man; Hinter's did not. Beethoven might be pleased with the sale. On the other hand, he might be furious at Nachman for taking a manuscript without permission, even though he surely had copies of everything. But on the third hand—with Hasidim there was always the mystical third hand—Beethoven needs money.

"For me, absolutely nothing," Nachman said. "But why don't you meet me in the little park near the Sign of the Cockatoo tomorrow at lunchtime?"

"Excellent. I'll see you then."

* * *

"Thank you for playing my melody."

"Nonsense! Now you know what an encore is. But why did you leave the hall?"

"I don't like people's attention on me."

"But as a composer you'll have to get used to it."

"You're the composer, Beethoven, not I."

"No, no. You created a melody, one of God's greatest gifts. You're a composer."

"Please understand. Use as many of my melodies as you like. I'm honored, but I see things differently. So I beg you, don't call attention to me in public again . . . Can I ask you a favor?"

"Of course."

"Take me to the stage."

Nachman followed Beethoven. He walked between the rows of empty chairs. A few minutes ago there was music. Now there was nothing. Where had the notes gone? Nachman looked up to the ceiling. Had they, like prayers, ascended to heaven? Toward the back of the stage, in the shadow, stood the harp. Nachman approached, touched the gilt frame, held out his hands, embraced it. He plucked the strings, imagined he was David. The sound thrilled him. "Give thanks unto God with the harp," sang my ancestor in one of his Psalms, he thought. He imagined calming King Saul's rage with a melody. Imagined composing Psalms.

Outside, in the light, he felt faint.

Beethoven leaned forward. "What's the matter? You're pale. Don't you feel well? Is this too much for you?"

"I've been on my feet since the morning. I feel I've landed on the moon. The fountain with the spitting lion and wolves is spinning in my head. My first concert. The dream. Beethoven playing . . . my melody . . . Do you know what I mean?"

"Come, let's walk. The air will be good for you. Even emissaries of angels, I suppose, are subject to exhaustion."

On the way home, Beethoven asked Nachman: "Have you heard Bach before?"

"Never." And like water from a spring, the melody surged in Nachman. He began to sing the second movement of the Brandenburg. Beethoven, beaming with surprise and good humor, puffed out his cheeks, imitating the horn, and accompanied Nachman. "Amazing," he said. "Absolutely amazing." He threw his arm around Nachman, ticking his head, oblivious to the stares of passersby. A moment later the composer broke his embrace, turned, faced his friend and tooted the accompaniment as he walked backwards. Nachman, floating, ecstatic, with that heady feeling of vertigo brought on by fatigue, remembered every note. He felt free, tempted to live a life of music, to learn to notate and compose—no not compose, rather ensnare the music bubbling in him—and give concerts like Beethoven.

Suddenly, on Beethoven's forehead, on that broad, distinguished brow, Nachman saw the empty table back home, the Hasidim sitting at the white-decked table, pounding out their—his—sad Jewish melodies, looking at the empty chair he had left behind.

Nachman broke off singing.

"What's the matter, Nachman?"

"Homesick," he replied.

"Nonsense," said Beethoven. "A good night's sleep will cure it. Come to the piano. I have something important to show you."

As Nachman walked up the stairs the entire Bach piece came back to him, compressed and intense, a bright, pleasing, severe light. Beautiful, but not Jewish. Not in the minor mode. Despite Bach's Jewish-sounding name, he has no Jewish elements in his music.

In the apartment, Beethoven went straight to the piano. There, Nachman saw another harp, lying flat inside Beethoven's piano.

"So you have a harp too? Can you teach me how to . . . ?"

Beethoven interrupted with a happy laugh.

"It's not a harp. It's part of the piano. Look. When I touch a key, a hammer bangs at your harp. That's how the sound is made."

Nachman stared in wonder. "Is that the important thing you wanted to show me?"

"No. It's something you can't touch. It's called perfect pitch. Do you know you have perfect pitch? You have the perfect musical gift and don't know it."

"Some people are *lamed vovniks* and don't know it."

"What's a *lamed vovnik*?"

"First tell me about perfect pitch."

Beethoven rilled some chords on the piano. "You sang the second movement in the very same key it was performed, and you remembered every note. Listen, I'll show you."

The composer played three notes.

"This is a C, a D, and an E. Sing the next three notes."

Nachman sang F, G, and A.

"Now, Nachman, close your eyes. What note am I playing?"

"Beethoven, you are fooling me. You didn't play that note before."

Beethoven jumped up. "Bravo! I told you you have perfect pitch. Can you tell me what note it was?"

Nachman hummed and bent his fingers as if counting.

"It's not an F and not G, but in between."

"Exactly. It's an F sharp. Perfect!"

"Is this what you mean by perfect pitch?"

"Partly. Not only recognizing notes is important, but also being able to sing them. For instance, sing me a G."

Nachman complied.

"Now listen." Beethoven played a triad. "Tell me the notes."

"Let me see." It had a Jewish sound, he thought. "The bottom note is C. The top note is G. The middle note is a little higher than D. D sharp?"

The composer clapped his hands.

"Excellent. Actually E flat, but it's the same thing. Look. A minor triad."

A wave of joy went through Nachman. "Test me on single notes again."

Beethoven played one.

"That's an F."

Beethoven played four notes in succession.

"That's H, I, and then you skipped one. Then K and L."

The composer leaned back, opened his mouth, . . . but instead of sounds, a series of choked cries came from his throat. He was shaking with laughter.

"No no no, Nachman. Look here, the keyboard is not an endless alphabet. There are only seven notes, from A to G. Then they keep repeating."

"Only seven? For so many melodies?"

"Only seven. Plus the five half notes makes twelve . . . .Think of how many words and thoughts can be expressed with only twenty-six letters. It's not the seven or the twenty-six, but the skillful combinations you make of them."

"Twelve notes . . . Strange. There are also twelve tribes of Israel, twelve months, twelve constellations. The music of the spheres. There is a mystical connection."

Beethoven frowned. "Well . . . if you wish . . . Come, Nachman, sit here. I'll teach you the musical alphabet."

Starting the *aleph beys* again, Nachman thought, as a wish flew through his mind.

After a few minutes Beethoven said:

"Splendid, Nachman. You learn quickly. Now, the real test." Beethoven played a crashing, dissonant chord with all ten fingers. "Name the notes."

Nachman named them all.

"Excellent. Now you know what perfect pitch is. Only a few individuals on this earth are blessed with it."

"Now I know what it is, Beethoven, but I still don't understand it."

"Don't fret, Nachman. Neither do I."

"But if I have perfect pitch and can remember Bach's piece, why can't I remember mine?"

"Because Bach's piece is not yours. It's always easier to remember someone else's work. Did you notice how quickly I learned yours? . . . Now tell me what a *lamed vovnik* is."

"It's a Yiddish term. Yiddish is such a beautiful language. Oh, if you only knew what joy, what spirituality Yiddish has. If only I could teach you the melody of Yiddish."

"It's like German."

"No, no. Yiddish is to German like your Fiftieth Concerto will be to your First. On a different plane, a different spiritual arena. Believe me, if you put Yiddish into your music, the world will bow before you."

Beethoven grimaced at the word "bow."

"I don't like the idea of people bowing to me . . . You still haven't told me what a *lamed vovnik* is."

"A *lamed vovnik* is a man with perfect moral and ethical pitch. He senses goodness like a musician senses sound. By his goodness he supports the world."

Nachman thought he would fall asleep at once. But he could not sleep. Back home, his worst sins had been committed during sleep. Since his exile from Bratslav, however, his dreams had ceased. The Almighty had spared him that. His days and nights were pure. Perhaps a sign? The onset of blessing? Still, he was afraid to open a Siddur and face the alphabet. Alpha bet. Alpha beta. Lizabeta. *Li za beta*. My God! A Hebrew phrase. Mine is her house. Her house is mine.

He closed his eyes. Knew he was awake. On the other side of the room

Beethoven was sleeping, breathing evenly. Does Beethoven dream? Does he dream of pianos and notes, of music sheets as big as rooms? But Nachman was too exhausted to sleep. In Nachman everything was tired. His legs, his hands, his stomach. In the pit of his chest fatigue pained him. Colors flashed in his mind. Sounds of strings and clarinets. Blare of trumpets and French horns. He heard passing carriages in the street, then fell asleep.

Nachman dreamt. Saw her floating, lifeless, as if he had not saved her. But he had saved her. Had taken her into his arms and brought her back to life, as she too had given him life with her love. She had infused life into him but had taken the letters in return. Then why did he see her floating, lifeless? It meant she was dead, for when people presumed dead appear dead in one's dream it is a sure sign that they are dead. Suddenly she called to him, called for help. But though he swam and swam he got nowhere. He swam in thick sand. Her skin glistened in the faraway water. Did he save her, or she him? Long ago, she had skipped away with his yarmulke. *That.* That was the tragic mistake. Letting her get his skullcap. All the woe stemmed from that. If not for that, his life would be different now. For her father discovered it and beat her and interrupted the service and she ran to the river . . . Nachman shook his head. The shaking of his head woke him. Again a dream. Pure this time. He opened his eyes. Lizabeta. On the dark ceiling he saw flecks of light, as if candles or moonbeams were tracing letters across the ceiling of his imagination. He saw the shape of hieroglyphs. The alphabets of all the world's languages flew by on the ceiling.

Except one.

God's pardon would not come quickly.

Where was he? Just yesterday he was in tiny Bratslav, where Vienna was just a sound shaped by the letters of its name; today he shared a room with Beethoven. The street outside was quiet. In the distance someone hammered on an iron peg. No country sounds. No cows, no dogs, no whinny of horses. Nachman was in the embrace of a city. In the dark he saw the outline of Beethoven's piano. The composer's music still echoed in his ear. Nachman felt his eyes closing.

The next morning Beethoven showed Nachman the music column in the *Staatszeitung*. "How is your German?"

"I suppose I can manage via the Yiddish."

"Then read this. It's by one of the most hard-to-please critics in Europe."

> All orchestras interested in raising the true artistic value and significance of their repertoires should not hesitate to request Herr van Beethoven's "Variations on a Theme by Nachman von Bratslav" and thus offer their audiences a work in which the breath of music of the soul lives. The piece fully guarantees pure and rich enjoyment. Given as an encore, the uniqueness of the melody, a radical departure for the gifted composer, took the audience by storm.

"Well, what do you say to that? You've already received a stunning review." Beethoven looked closely at Nachman. "Do you know what a review is?"

Nachman shook his head.

Beethoven thought awhile. "Think of the synagogue, when the cantor prays beautifully, and later everyone remarks—or reviews—how well he sang."

"I see," said Nachman. "And in Vienna a writer comments about concerts."

"Exactly. And thousands read his views. If the critic likes the music, the composer can become famous. But often the critics do not like a work. It's quite hard to get a good review in Vienna and you've gotten one."

"I'm glad . . . for you . . . It's really your review because you're the composer." Suddenly, Nachman felt a pinch at his heart. An empty feeling, as if he were removed from himself. Although he gazed at Beethoven's bookcase, Nachman saw his Hasidim. He tried to tell himself that he was here so that he would remember for them the Jewish melodies he created. But he knew that that was only partly true. He was here for himself. He stared out the window into the Vienna streets but still saw the Hasidim. In the back of his mind he heard a faint niggun. One he used to sing with them on Sabbath afternoons as the sun was setting and they all tried to stretch the tranquility and magic of the Sabbath beyond the darkness that ushered in the mundane week.

"What's the matter?" Beethoven asked. "You're pale again."

"I have to get some fresh air." Nachman paused a moment, then looked Beethoven in the eye. "You've been very kind. . . . When I come back—I've imposed enough—please take me to an inn."

"Splendid. First rate. Now you've made me an agent for inns. But haven't you come to learn music? First we'll have to get busy learning music, right? With you in an inn and me in and out, an inn seems out to me. That angel of yours, how come *he* didn't recommend an inn?"

Back from his walk, Nachman found the door open. Perhaps the composer had stepped out for lunch. A sheet of music was tilted on a stand. Nachman picked it up. Would he ever learn to read *this* mysterious language? Perhaps if he mastered this recondite script that compressed sounds onto paper, he would re-learn the Hebrew alphabet that compressed thoughts. This alphabet too was beautiful. He turned the sheet sideways, right side up, upside down. Could not tell the difference between one position and another. Hearing footsteps on the stairs, Nachman quickly replaced the paper, then took one of Beethoven's compositions and hid it in his jacket. Even if Beethoven hasn't copied it, Nachman thought, he surely knows it by heart. If I can't remember my songs that's understandable, he thought. But for a composer like Beethoven . . . ?

At that moment, a tall, thin man carrying a violin entered without knocking. He said, "Good afternoon," and, spotting the music on the stand, cried, "Aha!" He pulled up a chair, squinted at the music as if nearsighted, and began to play. Nachman watched him. The violinist grimaced as his hands and body moved. He repeated the same phrase several times, then put the violin down and threw up his hands. "The master's compositions are getting stranger and stranger."

"Wilhelm," came Beethoven's voice from outside. "Are you up there?"

"Yes, I am."

Beethoven entered, stood at the doorway.

"It's very difficult, master . . . For the violin, it is—"

"Do you suppose I think of your wretched fiddle when the muses speak to me? Play on."

The violinist quickly resumed playing. The music was odd, but pleasing, Nachman thought, an off rhythm he had not heard in Beethoven's music.

Beethoven listened; his face turned red.

"Wrong! Wrong!" He stamped his foot. "What are you doing, you fool? Why don't you get glasses? Not one note is right!"

Wilhelm pointed with his bow at the music. "I'm only playing what you've written."

Beethoven slammed the door furiously behind him and charged into the room. "I told you a thousand times, play what you see, not what you expect. What kind of tenth-rate playing is that?"

Beethoven stood over him, arrows shooting out of his eyes.

"But, master, it's what you've written."

"Out, Willy, out! Idiot! Fool! Go home! It's not *my* music . . ."

Wilhelm rose. His hands trembled as he put his violin into the case. His face burned with shame. Nachman, a page of the Talmud floated before his eyes. He could not read it, but he knew what it contained. He who stands by in silence when his fellow man is humiliated is guilty of shedding blood. True, he was a guest, but he could not look the other way.

"Don't shame him!" Nachman cried. "Why are you carrying on like that for a few bad notes?"

Beethoven seemed to be paralyzed. His mouth hung open; his hands were frozen in mid-air.

"Mind your own business! This is a private affair between Willy and me."

"But it isn't private if I'm here. Since there is a witness to the shame, it's public now."

Encouraged by Nachman's intervention, the violinist showed Beethoven the music.

"Look, master, see! Look at the notes!"

Beethoven turned his head and folded his hands on his chest. "It's not my music!"

"But please look, Herr Beethoven. It's your hand."

Nachman felt the violinist's shame. His face too now burned. Beethoven, Nachman thought, is upset only because he has money problems. Money worries cause anger, and anger spills over onto the first available victim.

Nachman went to a corner of the room and began packing his things.

"Please look, master. If you look, you'll see," Willy insisted.

Beethoven, about to look at the music, was distracted. He walked over to Nachman.

"What are you doing?"

"Packing. I told you I'd like to go to an inn."

"I shout at *him* and *you're* insulted. So now *you're* leaving. You stay where you are."

"Master, please look!"

Beethoven clapped his hands over his ears. "What's going on here?

This place is a circus, a madhouse." Finally, he peered at the music and shouted:

"You ox!"

"I'm not an ox," said Wilhelm. "I play what I see. It's true that your music often takes unexpected turns."

"Bravo!" said Nachman.

Beethoven wheeled. "I told you to stay where you are."

Nachman came up to Beethoven.

"It's upside down," Beethoven told Wilhelm. "You've been playing my music upside down. Which means," with a glance at Nachman, "you're playing it like Hebrew."

Nachman placed his hand on his heart.

"If anyone is the ox, it's me. I confess. I picked up the music and inspected it from all sides. I was so taken by the beauty of the notes strung together, like a magical alphabet that only blessed sorcerers can comprehend, I must have replaced it upside down."

For a moment the astonished Beethoven said nothing, then:

"My profound apologies, Nachman." He threw his arms around Nachman. "I'm sorry. I got angry too quickly."

"It's not me you have to apologize to. It's Willy. It's him you called names."

Beethoven muttered, approached the violinist, and stretched out his hand. "Willy, forgive me."

Touched, the other man took Beethoven's hand.

"Please play it again, Willy."

"Which way, master? Rightside up, or upside down?"

"Upside down, of course. . . . But you still should get glasses."

Wilhelm played. Beethoven, eyes closed, concentrated on the sounds.

"My God, Nachman! In one stroke you've doubled my output. Now I can take some of my pieces and play them in Hebrew. You've just given me a host of ideas." Beethoven slapped his thigh in pleasure. "Upside down, backwards, right to left. Maybe even inside out. What do you say, Willy, do you think Bach discovered this secret? Perhaps that's why he has hundreds of compositions."

As Willy left, Nachman followed.

"Where are you going?" Beethoven asked. "You're not leaving, are you?"

"No, I'm just going out to the park."

Beethoven nodded, lower lip thrust out, and sat down at the piano.

* * *

In the park, Hinter's eyes glistened. Nachman held the score. "How much are you offering?"

"One gold coin."

Nachman remembered the haggling at the Bratslav market.

"No, thank you."

"All right," Hinter said. "Two."

Nachman turned.

"Wait," the man shouted.

"I'm sorry. This is an original manuscript by the great Beethoven." He waved the score. But the man wasn't interested in the music.

"All right, how much do you want for it?"

"Ten gold pieces for Beethoven."

Hinter clapped his hands over his ears, rolled his eyes heavenward. "Five is my last offer."

"I'm sorry, then, Herr Hinter. Goodbye." Nachman turned and walked away. Would Hinter, like Beethoven, come and seize his arm? At least, he thought, now Beethoven will not be angry with me for taking a score without permission.

Nachman felt an arm on his. "Here, you drive a hard bargain. Five and three equals eight. No more."

"All right," Nachman sighed. For even in bargaining one must let the other person sense that he too has won a victory. "I said ten for Beethoven but am willing to take eight. But what about something for me?"

"You said you want nothing for yourself."

"I changed my mind."

"Here then, one more gold piece and that's it. I won't pay ten, I absolutely will not."

Nachman nodded, lower lip thrust out.

"Now let's have the manuscript."

But as soon as the manuscript was out of Nachman's hands the tenuous, ill-at-ease feeling in him burst like an abscess. Hinter slowly backed off, as if reading the hesitation in Nachman's mind.

"Wait!" Nachman shouted, approaching. "The composer will be furious . . . Let's do it with his permission. In the meantime, here's your money and please give me the . . ."

But before Nachman could say the word "manuscript" Hinter turned and fled. Over his back he shouted, "A deal is a deal!"

* * *

Back home, Nachman spread the coins on Beethoven's piano. When he had begun speaking to Hinter, Nachman imagined how he would come up to Beethoven with a broad smile. But he wasn't smiling now.

Beethoven, playing, looked up.

"What's that?"

"I took your advice, remember? I pickled my money and it bore fruit."

Beethoven frowned.

"Surprise! I made a sale for you."

"What did you sell? I hope that old-fashioned waistcoat of yours."

"That would hardly bring in nine gold pieces."

"Then what was it?"

Now the trouble will begin, Nachman thought. "One of your compositions."

"What?"

Nachman had not known that a human being could growl like a lion. Beethoven leaped up, face on fire. He pulled at Nachman's hair. "You beard, you Easterner, you mountain hick, you—"

"Go ahead. Say it. Jew! It's all right. It's not a curse. I am a Jew."

Beethoven stamped his foot as if he wanted to make a hole in the floor. Spittle dribbled out of the corners of his twitching mouth. He looked around wildly. An apple Nachman had bought at the market lay on the piano. Beethoven spotted it and hurled it at the wall with all his might. Pieces splattered in all directions.

Beethoven rummaged through the manuscripts on his piano. "My God, it's the Lichnowsky piano and violin sonata. It's been commissioned by the prince. Didn't you see his name on it?"

"No."

"It's clearly marked on the last page."

"I didn't look."

"I have no other copy, you idiot! I did not make a fair copy," Beethoven howled.

"Oh, my God. I didn't . . . I thought . . . When rabbis write rabbinic decisions, they always make a copy."

"I'm not a rabbi." He punched his fist on the piano. The dissonant vibrations sent a shiver of fear through Nachman. Perhaps Beethoven would hit him too.

"It's not quite finished. I don't make copies until a piece is absolutely finished. I had no intention of letting that sonata out of the house. It was commissioned by Prince Lichnowsky."

"Don't you remember it?"

"Not note for note. It's hard to recreate something you've already created . . . You fool, who did you sell it to?"

"Forgive me, Beethoven, I did it to help you."

Nachman looked at the gold coins on the edge of the piano. Now Beethoven seemed to see them for the first time. With a stroke of his hand he swept the coins from the piano, grabbed Nachman by the lapels, and shook him. "Who? Who? Do you know?" A large vein throbbed on his forehead.

"A publisher named Hinter."

"Hinter? Publisher? He's no publisher. He's the biggest wolf in Europe. That thief pays no royalties. He'll see the dedication and will surely sell it to another prince. A neat game of power and extortion."

They heard a knock at the door.

"I'll get that. Does that thief have the gall to come back for more?"

Nachman held Beethoven's arm.

"Don't upset yourself. I'll get the manuscript back."

Beethoven's face clouded.

"No. I'll take care of him." He opened the door and barked, "Give it to me."

A liveried footman, hat in hand, dressed in red with a white breast braid, stepped back in astonishment. He gave Beethoven a card, bowed low, and said:

"His Highness Prince Razumovsky begs to have the honor of your company this evening. His Highness wonders if you will agree to perform one of your sonatas for his distinguished guests."

Without a further glance, Beethoven tossed the card onto a little table in the anteroom.

"No!" he shouted. "Tell His Highness I'm not well."

Beethoven closed the door. A sullen look burned in his dark eyes. His left eyelid twitched.

"The nerve! Summoning me to play for his guests this evening. What does he think I am, a uniformed street fiddler? There's court manners for you. They never consider another man's feelings. No wonder I can't get any work done. Everybody wants something from me." Beethoven paused and slapped his forehead with four fingers. "That was a stupid move."

"Forgive me. I'm sorry."

"I mean me, for refusing to go. I should have gone. Hinter will go straight to the Prince with my score. Yes, without doubt. Now I'll have to hire a carriage at my own expense."

"I'll pay," Nachman said, thinking: How can I reverse time? Joshua stopped the sun, the moon. What shall I do? Beethoven will throw me out and I'll have to return home empty-handed, without the Hebrew alphabet.

The composer ran to the window. "Imagine! He's still standing there, that oaf."

"Then I'll run down"—Nachman scooped up the gold coins from the floor—"and get the manuscript back. After I handed it to him I changed my mind, but he ran off."

"No, no, no. It's not Hinter. It's the footman. Evidently Razumovsky told his servant not to take no for an answer and the idiot is gathering up courage to come up again. I didn't *want* to go to his damned concert and now I'll *have* to go. See what one stupid move causes? Hinter knows that Razumovsky collects my scores. Now I'll have to ask the Prince to buy it from him and then sell it back to me."

Nachman shyly gave the coins to Beethoven.

The composer went to the window and gestured to the footman. At the doorway Beethoven told the retainer: "Tell the Prince that I accept his invitation but Beethoven declines to perform. Beethoven does not perform at three hours' notice. Please have the carriage waiting for me at seven. And tell the Prince that a composer friend of mine will also attend. Can you remember all that?"

Then he turned to Nachman, lifted his hands as if about to place them on his shoulders, then dropped them.

"Before you get any wrong notions, listen. We have to understand something. *You* said 'Jew.' Remember that. Not I."

"Wasn't that what you were going to say after 'beard,' 'Easterner,' and 'mountain hick'?"

"No. Never. I don't harbor such sentiments, so how could I possibly say such a thing?"

"Then what *were* you going to say?"

"I was about to call you provincial and naive."

Nachman drew a deep breath.

"Tell me," Beethoven said. "Who did you do this for? Me, or yourself?"

Nachman stared at him, too overwhelmed to answer at once. He couldn't believe that Beethoven could be so insensitive. Would Nachman do a mitsva like this for himself? To give *himself* the pleasure of a good deed? Wasn't it obvious that he wanted to help his friend who had done so much for him?

Nachman decided to respond in a different way.

"What do you think?"

But this Jewish way of answering a question with another question absolutely astonished Beethoven. He couldn't reply. He looked out the window for a moment and then—as though speaking in a different key—said:

"Come. Let's go to Razumovsky's palace. Maybe with luck we can reverse what you've done."

The horse-drawn carriage passed the gatehouse and entered a long, curved driveway bordered by formal gardens.

Beethoven looked down at the floor. His face sagged, his pockmarks seemed deeper. Nachman didn't know how he could undo what he had done. Even a conciliatory remark might reawaken the anger.

"My only hope is that he's greedy enough to go to the richest source . . . Otherwise . . ." Beethoven bit his lip. "Look! Here we are . . ."

Nachman saw ivory columns, marble staircases, paintings and tapestries and gilt chandeliers, a princely residence depicted only in fairy tales.

Inside, Beethoven was welcomed like royalty. Women crowded around him. For a while he held court like a duke. Then, a trumpet flourish and a personal crier announced the entrance of the Prince. Everyone rose. Razumovsky approached Beethoven before greeting anyone else.

"Please pardon me, Beethoven, for the abrupt invitation. I just returned last night from Hungary on pressing state affairs. We're trying to see if we can stop Napoleon's eastward thrust . . . But I'm pleased you could *attend* . . ." he stressed the word with light irony ". . . the concert anyway."

"Your Highness, I'd like to present Nachman von Bratslav, an astonishingly talented composer whom I've been hosting."

The Prince shook Nachman's hand. It was a cold hand. Nachman could not penetrate Razumovsky's eyes.

"The composer of the theme that you recently played?" Razumovsky asked Beethoven, while gazing at Nachman.

"Yes. But how do you know? You were abroad."

"Good music travels quickly," Razumovsky quipped. "That concert is the talk of Budapest. And anyway, I read the Vienna *Staatszeitung* even when abroad." Then he took Beethoven's arm and with authority directed him toward the grand salon.

The concert hall was lit by dozens of sparkling chandeliers. Hundreds of red velvet-backed chairs were set out in scores of rows. At each arched doorway stood a servant in uniform.

"I can't stay for the entire concert, Your Highness. I have a lesson scheduled for later."

"I'll give instructions to have my carriage waiting. Come sit with me in the first row."

"Thank you, but I'd rather stay in the back by the open windows. I have an awful headache."

"I hope the fresh air helps," said Razumovsky with an aggrieved air.

Nachman watched the orchestra through half-closed eyes. He saw only a silver-headed jewel and many lights, reflecting the countless lit candles. The instruments and the musicians' spectacles gleamed like hundreds of tiny suns. The profile of brass and cellos, harps and basses reminded him of the Vienna skyline at dusk—the harp was Stephen's Cathedral, and the conductor the Opera House.

What would his Hasidim say if they saw him here? Nachman had become a city man. The musicians played and everyone was absorbed in his own thoughts. There was something self-centered in this beautiful experience called concert. Back home in Bratslav, when music was made, it came from the soul, but it also joined people like flames into fire. Hands and shoulders joined. Bratslav niggunim united disparate souls and bound them as one; Vienna music made people feel alone. Now he understood why people went to concerts. To be alone with their thoughts. As soon as the music began, sighs and thoughts turned inward, problems surfaced. Nachman too was alone. He shut out the audience and heard only music. Everything seemed to be in order. But nothing was in order. He had music but missed the twenty-two sparks that fired his soul. And suddenly a longing for the Hebrew alphabet surged through Nachman, a longing so powerful it tore at his heart.

The melodies chased one another. The violins began a motif; a moment later the violas picked it up. A struggle. The chase, hunt, pursuit. Each seeking mastery. Like the struggle between the good forces and the demonic urges in the world. The test of strength between Nachman and the universe. Both on the see-saw. Who would overbalance whom? Nachman sensed a vibration, a cord of thin flame. He felt he could pick up the earth and hurl it to the sun.

For the first time he felt a curl of envy. Talent all around him and he stood there with his dormant holiness pressed into him like seed in a flower. A sudden terror seized him. What if someone tapped his shoulder and asked, "What can *you* do?" Around him the smell of perfume and women's hair. Near the wall stood a beautiful woman wearing an off-the-shoulder ivory gown. But he saw another. Her hair wet, long to her shoulders, dew drops falling from her hair. Little beads of water on her brown arms glistened like gems. Slowly, Nachman began to rise in the air. The woman in the ivory gown saw Nachman. Her mouth dropped. She tapped a friend's hand and pointed to him. Suddenly, her face became drawn, as if hidden wrinkles were now revealed, and Nachman saw old Natalya who cleaned his house and pressed his shirts. He saw the cross glistening on the woman's chest, and quickly he descended.

The music made Nachman forget Beethoven's woe. Through no fault of his own, the composer too had lost something precious. Everyone loses that which is most precious to him.

Beethoven, sitting on a window casement, looked down uneasily at the driveway. Just then he leaned closer, as if to confirm what his eyes had seen. He gave a silent cry and ran toward the stairs. Nachman, afraid to be alone, knowing no one, unable, unwilling to engage these strangers in conversation, ran after him. Beethoven, not a slim man, moved as quickly as an animal on the attack. "It's him," he cried, looking back at Nachman, "it's him."

Outside, the composer charged at Hinter. Dazed, the man was paralyzed for a moment. Then he turned abruptly, skirted around Beethoven, and ran full speed toward the palace.

Beethoven waved his fist and gave chase, hunter after prey. The gap narrowed until Beethoven caught Hinter, shook him, and threw him against a prickly rose hedge. A jumble of arms and legs, then Beethoven rose, holding his music. He folded the manuscript into his pocket.

The composer trembled. "You thief!"

"I'm not a thief. I wanted to publish your sonata—after letting the Prince perform it first. Now you'll get nothing. Nothing." Hinter stood, brushed his coat. "I bought it fair and square. Your agent overcharged me. You're the thief. Help!" he cried. "Robbers! Help!"

Beethoven looked around wildly and shouted, "Guards! Arrest this man."

Seeing guards approaching, Hinter now dashed to the gate with Beethoven in pursuit. "Here, you fool, take back your coins."

"What is it, maestro?" asked a guard, blocking Hinter's path.

"It's all right. Let him go. I've settled it. Show him out the gate."

Beethoven held his chest, took a deep breath. Then he shook himself, looked down, and cleaned the dust from his rumpled jacket and trousers.

"Well, in luck after all. You don't want a carriage back home, do you?"

"No, a walk is fine," said Nachman.

"Guard, tell His Highness that Beethoven walked back home. Do you hear? A carriage will not be necessary."

Nachman clasped Beethoven's hand in a contrite handshake. He bowed his head. Beethoven slapped him on the shoulder.

"You provincial," he laughed. "You're not going to sell Beethoven's manuscripts again, are you?"

Nachman laughed too.

The warmth returned to Beethoven's eyes.

Nachman sighed. A faint trace of letters, each with its own melody, tickled the back of his mind. A good sign.

In the middle of the night, Nachman opened his eyes, fully awake and rested. He propped himself up on his elbows. The room glowed with moonlight. At turns it became lighter and darker. Nachman got out of bed and walked softly to the window. The moon ran through the clouds. Vienna's silhouette was topped by the spire of the cathedral. In the distance, beyond the low houses, the Danube sparkled as waves rose and fell. A fresh breeze came in. The city was still. Not a note of music in the night. Moonlight clothed Beethoven's room in dark blue light. His round piano stool was pushed aside. His upholstered chair with the knobbly curved legs now stood by the piano. Soon the master would sit down and with a crash of three chords awaken the entire city. Where had he seen such a chair before? Yes, yes, the empty chair in the vanished shul. A solitary brass candlestick stood at the edge of Beethoven's piano. The candle had burned down half way—at that point the composer had no doubt decided to go to sleep. And Nachman had dozed off to Beethoven's soft music as though the master had written a personal lullabye for him. Beethoven slept soundly on his side. His hand was near his ear, as if even in sleep he were straining to hear a nocturnal music beyond his ken. Under the piano were stacks of music, neatly wrapped with string. Other compositions were rolled like traditional megillas, scrolls, on the long piano.

In Vienna, no one knew Nachman. He was merely one of the masses. Back home, whether vilified or praised, whether because of his own deeds and tales or his zeyde's fame, Nachman was as well known as the Emperor. Here, in Vienna, he had achieved the quality of *bitul ha-yesh*, the undoing of self, the denial of his name and fame, that trait that medieval mystics and ascetics toiled for years to achieve. Here Nachman was only a husk of himself, stripped of his glory. He was in exile. From home, alphabet, self. He tried to recall the faces of his Hasidim but saw them through a mist. The deeper the fall, the higher the ascent. One of the reasons he had gone into exile was Jewish melody: for the sake of saving the holy sparks of niggunim that floated unredeemed in the world, like dybbuks doomed to eternal wandering.

Maybe now, he thought, it was time for the letters to return. His punishment had endured long enough. But what if he could not tear himself away from Vienna? Would he too become a spark in eternal exile? Still, there was hope. If a stubborn yetzer ho-reh could be driven from a man's soul, then surely Nachman could leave Vienna, a much simpler task. God had directed his feet to the capital, to give Jewish music to Beethoven and to learn the alphabet of music. And God would direct his feet back home. If he could redeem melodies, why couldn't he redeem . . . ?And he repeated God's whisper and broke into a silent little Hasidic dance. Happy with his thoughts, Nachman took out his Siddur, was about to open it and plunge into the sea of letters, awaiting disappointment or exaltation. But something—angel or moonbeam?—held him back. He did not open the prayerbook.

I'm afraid, he told himself. Yes. I admit. I'm afraid. The entire world is a very narrow bridge. The main thing, as one crosses, is not to fear. Still, I'm afraid. But depressed? No. Not depressed. Never that. A man who defies gravity and floats in air can surely relearn the alphabet.

Then, by the light of the moon, Nachman took a clean sheet of music paper from the top of Beethoven's piano and jotted down the melodies for the disembodied letters humming in his mind.

From Nathan's Diary

Our Master taught that every day has its own melody. Every *part* of the day has its own melody. "When I rise in the morning," he said, "the absolute silence I hear has its own melody. Dusk and sunset, each has its own melody. After sunset, the purple sky has its own melody. Every blade of grass has its own melody. Each person has his own melody. God creates harmony in the universe, and that is melody too."

"When we create melody," Reb Nachman said, "we imitate God."

Nachman had been with Beethoven more than a month. He wanted to share expenses, but didn't know how without insulting his host. He thought of paying Beethoven's debt at the Cockatoo but knew what fury that would prompt. Once, the composer overslept. Nachman went to the market and returned with bread, tomatoes, apples, and eggs. When Beethoven awoke, Nachman asked him to share his simple meal. He told him that he enjoyed walking in the market. He loved the aroma of fresh fruits and vegetables; it reminded him of home. Soon, Nachman went shopping almost daily, happy that he could reciprocate Beethoven's hospitality.

Weekdays were the same. Lessons, walks, an occasional concert; increasing familiarity with music and its recondite alphabet. But the Sabbath was special. Beethoven learned that Nachman would not play piano from Friday sunset to Saturday night, so out of consideration for his guest he too would not practice; instead, he sat and composed or revised his scores. The absence of music hallowed the day for Nachman. Even Beethoven commented on the special joy of silence. While Beethoven wrote, Nachman would review in his mind the weekly portion of the Torah. Sometimes he took Beethoven's well-used German Bible and translated the words into Hebrew as he read. And in the park, out for a Sabbath stroll, Nachman wrapped Bratslav around himself, hummed familiar niggunim, and recounted Hasidic stories about Jews away from home.

Did he really miss prayers with his Hasidim? Nachman wondered. There were Jews in Vienna, Beethoven had told him. A small community, in a different section of town. Surely they had a synagogue. But Nachman had not come to Vienna to meet Jews. He had come to study music. Music had become his ladder. Music would purify his soul. Restore his alphabet. He would climb the rungs again. Was, in fact, climbing. But first he had to restore himself. How could he bring salvation—God's whisper, God's whisper—to the world, if he couldn't bring salvation to himself? How could he proclaim himself leader of leaders, scion of the Davidic line, if he couldn't lead a congregation in prayer?

Suddenly, he was back in his bes medresh with his Hasidim. When he led the prayers on a Sabbath and sang his songs, songs that came to him and songs that came down through the ages, the congregation too levitated, but they didn't know it because Nachman brought them down to earth again before they noticed.

Nachman had not forgotten he was a Jew. The only thing he *had* forgotten was how to read. But God takes with one hand and gives with the other. Now Nachman could read music and write down the Jewish melodies he created. He had learned one secret alphabet. Soon, he hoped, he would begin to re-learn the other.

During their weeks together, Nachman and Beethoven spoke mostly of music. With a Jew Nachman would have exchanged personal history and family background within minutes. That was the magic of Jewish contact. But with Beethoven it was different.

One day, however, Beethoven made an innocent request. Once, after lunch, as Nachman was reading in the *Wiener Tageblatt* about Napoleon's army approaching Austria, the composer remarked:

"Nachman, I think it's time *you* became a teacher. I would like to learn the Bible. I'd like to read 'In the beginning God created the heaven and the earth' in the original. Would you teach me Hebrew?"

At once, with a hammer blow, Nachman's spiritual malaise returned. Again, "holy holy holy" upside down. Once more he stumbled over the rock-strewn path of the Hebrew alphabet. He saw the large, hand-drawn letters on the walls of his room in Bratslav. Now, with the composer's request, a carefully closed door burst open and out tumbled all distress. And behind the letters, behind the sun-drenched reeds, Nachman saw the young woman he had tried to escape. Lizabeta.

"You're silent, Nachman." Beethoven's voice shattered the image. It flew in a hundred different directions, like splintered glass. "You're staring into space. Have I said something wrong? It's not against the religion, is it?"

Nachman, pale, shook his head.

"Well, can you teach me Hebrew?"

I'm not Nachman, he thought. Nachman can read, but I'm not Nachman. The other Nachman, back in the Slovakia shul telling stories and collecting coins, he's the real Nachman.

"No," Nachman groaned. He put the newspaper down.

Beethoven licked, then bit his lips. Perhaps biting back a retort. After all my teaching, you can't teach me Hebrew?

Nachman's fingers tapped the armrest as though he were playing scales. He wanted to stand and embrace Beethoven like a brother. Nachman was an only child, like Isaac to Sarah, like Samson to his mother, like Samuel to Hannah. He had not known sibling love. He never knew he could like another man as much as he liked Beethoven. Was there anyone in Bratslav for whom he had as much affection as for this man before him? He loved him like David loved Jonathan. He wanted to embrace his teacher and weep on his shoulder. He wanted to say: You! You are the true Hasid.

Nachman stood, approached Beethoven, and put his hand on the composer's arm.

"Please, Beethoven, please don't be angry. I haven't told you. It's not that I don't want to. I want to very much. I wish I could. I'd teach you Hebrew from dawn to sunset and into candlelight. But I can't . . . Have you seen me open a Hebrew book since you've known me?"

"No. I've wondered about that but didn't want to pry."

"Dear Beethoven. I . . ." Nachman looked down. "I . . . can't read." He regarded his fingers, his nails, as if perchance he might see some letters there. "My ability to read Hebrew was snuffed out."

"But you have no trouble reading Latin letters . . . German."

"No trouble at all. For *me,* they're backwards . . ."

But Beethoven missed Nachman's oblique reference to the reversed score.

"Tell me. Is this why you left your home for Vienna?"

Nachman looked at Beethoven's bookcases, his piano, the fine oak floor. Perhaps his question too would vanish, like the Hebrew letters and the little shul. Beethoven, however, stared at him, demanding answer.

"I killed someone."

Beethoven jumped up. "What? What?" he shouted. "You? You? I don't believe it." He crouched forward, like a cat about to spring.

"I didn't actually kill her." Nachman smiled sadly. "But it's almost as if I did. She drowned in the river because of me."

Beethoven, incredulous, shook his head.

"Why, were you swimming together? Did you see her drown?"

Nachman felt himself pulled into a whirlpool. The more he answered, the deeper he would sink, entangled in the reeds.

"No. I didn't see. Her father told me."

Beethoven licked his lips. He stared at Nachman.

"You don't sound convinced."

"I'm not," Nachman said. "He showed me her bundle of clothes. With her shoes! No one who drowns herself takes off her shoes. Yet all the peasants talk about her death."

"A love affair?" Beethoven's mouth twitched as if restraining a smile.

Nachman shook his head somberly. "No, no . . . Imagine! A healthy, beautiful girl just doesn't go and drown herself. But dead or not, I was punished anyway. It's not a coincidence. My Hebrew letters were taken from me."

Beethoven's eyes sharpened with anger. "Taken? Punished? Just for a little love affair? If God punished me every time I was with a woman I'd be a dead man."

Nachman stared straight ahead. He wanted to look right through Beethoven but he restrained himself.

"Perhaps it's just a coincidence," Beethoven suggested gently.

"No!" Then Nachman lowered his voice. "It's not a coincidence. God metes out punishment measure for measure. When I saw her I compared her to the beautiful letters of the Hebrew alphabet. I even thought that she was lovelier than an *aleph* . . . Then the warning came. First, I saw the words holy holy holy . . ."

". . . is the Lord of Hosts."

"You know it?"

"Of course. I read Isaiah. In fact, once, after a walk in the woods, I wrote in my notebook: The trees cry holy holy holy."

"My very thoughts," Nachman said. "So you know that famous phrase."

Beethoven furrowed his broad brow and gave a half laugh. "You think Christians don't read the Bible?"

"No, it's not that." Nachman smiled shyly. "I see those words in the prayerbook every day. I forgot that it's a verse in the Bible." He pressed his fingers to his lips. For a moment he had slipped into the past. For a moment he was back in the world of before. Before he had lost his alphabet. "And then the words holy holy holy," Nachman continued, "and *only* those words, turned upside down. The message was clear. A few days later, all the letters disappeared . . . I, who wanted to be holy for many reasons, I became defiled."

"A woman's love is not defiling," Beethoven said. "It can be more beautiful than music . . . It *is* music. There is no music more beautiful than love. And my music tries to translate love into melody."

Nachman did not want to talk any more. He did not want to tell Beethoven about modesty, purity, the rungs he had to climb in preparation, the same rungs of the ladder in Jacob's dream. He could not tell him about God's whisper or the Davidic line. Nachman looked up, saw the puzzled expression on Beethoven's face. He realized that his stubborn silence had made the composer uncomfortable. Nachman took a deep breath and sent Beethoven a silent signal to speak.

Beethoven began slowly. "Have you tried to see if . . . perhaps your ability to read has returned?"

"I'm afraid to try . . . Jewish mysticism teaches that worlds are created through combinations of letters, and if I don't have the letters, how can I master my, or any other, world? Do you know I can't even read my own name? All his life a Jew practices reading his name so that when he dies and the angel in heaven asks him his name, he won't forget."

"It's a kind of spiritual depression, Nachman. Don't worry. It will pass."

"Depression? God forbid!" Nachman shouted, as if trying to snap himself awake. "My great-grandfather, the holy Baal Shem Tov, explicitly forbade us to be depressed. Our watchword is, Don't despair! I can't imagine I'm depressed. I'm very happy."

"A person can assume he is happy and even feel happy and yet that is just a patina over his basic spiritual malaise. I know. I know it from my music . . . I also get depressed and angry at times."

"What reasons do *you* have to be depressed? You are successful, your music is recognized. You are applauded at concerts . . ."

Beethoven put up his hands. "You don't know everything. In music, an occasional concert is not enough. Nor is applause sufficient. Publication is important. But I want my music to be published throughout the Continent. And the publishers are afraid to take chances because my music is so new. And don't bring up Hinter. He's no publisher. He's a charlatan."

Nachman looked away to the piano.

"Tell me, Nachman, did you really come to Vienna to study music?"

"Yes."

"And not to run away?"

Nachman sighed.

"I thought if I changed place I would change my luck. But the essence of a man goes with him no matter where he goes."

"Did you try talking to a rabbi, to your spiritual leader?"

Now Beethoven had him cornered. Now the truth would have to come out.

"Tell me, Beethoven, people come to you to study composition. Who is *your* composition teacher?"

"Why, I have none . . . I . . ."

"Of course, *you're* the one they come to. You see, it's the same with me. *I'm* the spiritual leader. *I'm* the rebbe. *I'm* the one to whom scores of people flock for advice, counsel, spiritual uplift. When I saw you conducting, I thought to myself, I wish I could conduct my Hasidim the way you conducted the musicians. So when I fell ill, and lost my letters, there was no one, except the Almighty himself, who could help me."

Beethoven jumped up from his chair, paced around the room. He clapped his hands once as if in anger. "Does God intervene so directly? How do you know you're not cured? Try! Perhaps you're cured now and don't know it."

"I told you. I'm afraid to look."

"Then how will you find out if your malaise vanishes? Perhaps if you look now—Nachman, open the prayerbook!—you'll see that your ability to read has been restored."

Nachman regarded Beethoven. Was he urging him on craftily? But the composer's face seemed perfectly ingenuous. Maybe Beethoven was right. Perhaps now that Nachman could play simple tunes on the piano, he was indeed in a higher spiritual state. Perhaps his exile had gone on long enough.

But Nachman was still afraid.

"No. I'll wait till I get back home. I'll talk to my Hasidim."

"Do you preach to them?"

"Not really. I tell stories. So far I've told them thirteen tales."

"Like?"

Nachman held his chin and thought a while. "Once upon a time there was a king who was in love but could not sing the songs that raged within him. One night he dreamt that he sang. As he sang, silk strands came out of his tongue. The king heard his beloved outside the window. He ran to the window, tripped on the silk strands, and cut his tongue."

"Is that it?"

"Yes."

"But he loses either way. I don't understand it."

"Then you can become one of my Hasidim. Sometimes they don't understand my parables either."

"Do you?" Beethoven asked slyly.

"No," said Nachman with a laugh. "Not this one. I'm also puzzled by the injustice of the story."

Two days later Beethoven sat down at the piano and played the Lichnowsky sonata for Nachman. "First, the violin part, then the piano, and then I'll blend them."

At the piano, Beethoven built a palace out of notes and chords. A palace full of light and air. Nachman entered and was caught up in the waves of melody.

"It's beautiful," Nachman said. "Like the alphabet. Like the spaces between the letters."

"The journey to Graz is lovely too, and it will give you—"

"Me? What journey?"

"Yes, you. Both of us. Oh, I didn't tell you, did I? We've been invited to Graz, to Lichnowsky's palace, for a few days . . . We really ought to see it before Napoleon arrives. His troops are moving quickly."

"But you're the one who's been invited."

Beethoven raised his hand as though about to conduct.

"And I even may play for him your new Meditations on the Hebrew Alphabet."

Nachman smiled. Beethoven had not mentioned Nachman's melodies before. "When are we leaving?"

"Tomorrow." Then Beethoven raised a finger and pressed it to his lips. "Would you mind if I asked you a personal question? Are you married, Nachman?"

"No," Nachman said shyly. "At twenty-eight I should be. It's bad enough I left my congregation for so long. I certainly wouldn't leave a wife for such a long time . . . And, of course, you're not married either."

"The princes are continually offering me their sisters or daughters, but I'm afraid I'll be enslaved, become part of the idiocy of court life, lose my independence . . . You know, I've been called a misanthrope. Of course, I'm not that at all. I like women and need love"—here Beethoven laughed—"but I guess I'm difficult to get along with."

"Nonsense. You are a wonderful friend."

Beethoven shrugged. "And you? Do you also want to devote yourself to art?"

"I still see music as a mystery. As elusive as a woman. But I also see the alphabet that way. Especially now that the letters are gone."

"But you haven't answered my question."

Nachman smiled sadly. "I know. Creating stories from the mysterious letters, and music from *your* mysterious alphabet—things that didn't exist before—is our way of showing we can be like God. No, I don't want to devote myself to art. I want to make God's world better. To bring salvation to the earth."

"God . . . Art . . . Perhaps it's the same thing."

"Can music make the world better?" Nachman asked.

"I don't know. Perhaps in my naiveté I assume that aesthetic beauty can help a person achieve ethical purity. Every good person in his own way attempts to make the world better . . . And music may help. For music is man's way of imitating God." Beethoven stopped for a moment, nodded his head as if speaking to himself. "And even if it doesn't help the world, it certainly helps the soul. In his immortal opera, *The Magic Flute,* Mozart tells us: 'We wander by the power of music through death's dark night.'"

"If the music is linked to prayer," Nachman said.

"And religion," Beethoven said slyly, "has *that* made the world any better? It seems to me that more people have been murdered in the name of religion than in wars."

Nachman watched Beethoven arrange his suitcase. He has the soul of a Jew, he thought. Look at the way he makes variations on my Jewish theme. He doesn't go to church. He has a kindly nature. He's not a drunkard. He devotes himself to the spiritual. His views on God and nature coincide with mine. "The trees cry holy holy holy" is *my* thought. We both feel that music has ethical power and that with music man imitates God. . . . Wait. He comes from a Dutch family . . . and Holland is where many Spanish Jews went after the Inquisition. Beeth-oven . . . *Bet* means "house" in Hebrew, and in Yiddish *offen* means "open." Open house. Hospitality. Traditional Jewish hospitality, which he gave to me. Maybe Beethoven is a double, a spiritual twin, a horizontal *gilgul,* or reincarnation; a *gilgul* in space, not time. Maybe that's why we get along so well.

The carriage wheels turned in the Austrian countryside, and the melody of the first movement of Haydn's 100th Symphony turned in Nachman's mind. Green fields and hills danced to Haydn's tunes. As he saw little villages the key switched from major to minor. The beat of the horses' hooves kept the tympany rhythm; Nachman did not hum but tapped the rhythm on his knee with his fingers.

"Haydn's 100th?" Beethoven's eyes twinkled.

"I don't believe it. How did you know? I wasn't singing it."

"By the rhythm. Just as each composition has its own melody, it also has its own rhythm."

"It's a captivating work."

"Yes, it sings with a life of its own. But Papa Haydn didn't let loose enough—that's what you get when you're a lifetime subordinate to a prince . . . Haydn is retired now, of course, but he used to eat with the help . . . Imagine, with the footmen and cleaning girls. Once he even got a princely boot in the seat of his pants . . . Had Haydn been free like me, he would have soared higher. In that last movement he almost makes a leap, climbing climbing up up up to heaven, but at the last moment—I'll show you when we get back home—he just drops it. He didn't let go, he couldn't flutter his wings for that extra inch to touch the clouds. He brings us up, but doesn't let us go over the wall to Paradise . . . That's the difference between a free man and a servant."

"The same thing once happened to me," Nachman said. "I once heard a cantor. At the end of a prayer he added more and more heartfelt trills, ecstatic trills. Then, suddenly, inexplicably, he stopped. One more note, I told him, and he would have brought down the Messiah."

Lichnowsky's castle, set on a hilltop, was visible from the post station in the valley. In the distance, beyond the rounded turrets, thick clouds were moving toward the town, blocking some of the mountains from view. Beethoven looked up and pointed to something moving down the hill. "There it is. You see that toy on wheels? They're on their way to meet us."

Every few minutes, as the gilded bands decorating the carriage doors met the flat rays of the setting sun, a flash of light announced the approach of the two-horse carriage. Two footmen opened the doors for

Beethoven and Nachman. The ride was slow and jerky. Soon the driver stopped and apologized. One of the axles was loose. There would be a half-hour delay.

Later, when they resumed their uphill journey, Beethoven pointed down to the valley.

"You see the vineyards and all those fields? He owns it all," the composer said. "Everything you see is his. Except the clouds. Lichnowsky is probably one of the richest men in the world."

"So why doesn't *he* publish, or help you publish, your music?"

Beethoven chuckled. "That's how the rich stay rich. They don't part with their money too readily. In fact, he still owes me money for an earlier sonata he commissioned. He's too busy running around Europe serving as a diplomat to remember to pay his debt."

On the top of the hill, the land lay flat. Around a bend a lake appeared. Bordering the water, framed by a huge oak, was the castle. It reminded Nachman of pictures of castles in the illustrated Haggadahs. In the foreground, fruit groves and, set slightly higher, a tiered, walled castle with two turrets. One was rounded with a conical top, the other was square; each contrasted gracefully with the other.

Inside, a footman showed Nachman and Beethoven to their rooms. He said the Prince would see them in twenty minutes.

"Twenty minutes," Beethoven muttered after the man had gone. "What about supper? I'm starved."

"Don't worry," Nachman said. "I brought bread and tomatoes."

Beethoven flicked his hand. "Here I'll get royal fare." He unpacked his bags and carefully set his music on a little polished cherry wood table. Rubbing his hands, he glanced at the door, as if momentarily expecting the invitation to dine.

Later, the Prince, a tall, mustached, elegantly dressed man, met them in the salon. He too had heard of Nachman and his music.

"Your melodies are the talk of Vienna," Lichnowsky addressed Nachman.

"I hope to play a new piece by Nachman this evening."

"Excellent, Beethoven. Excellent. But first, basics. You must be famished. You came a little later than expected—"

"The carriage broke down, Prince . . ."

"The driver and his men are now eating down below. Why don't you join them?"

Suddenly, a flash of lightning and a rumble of thunder like a passage in Haydn's Drum Roll Symphony. The Prince and Nachman turned to the window. A downpour began. Beethoven said something, but the resounding thunderclap drowned out his words. By the time Lichnowsky and Nachman turned they just managed to catch sight of Beethoven going through the door, which he slammed in a fury.

"What a temper! I wonder what got into him. Did I say something to anger him, or do thunderbolts always bring this on?"

Without waiting for Nachman's reply, Lichnowsky strode across a huge Persian carpet to a little table. "Look. He left his music here."

The Prince took the score and stepped into the hall. A footman came up.

"Your Highness. Your orchestra is ready to begin."

"Tell them to hold off awhile. Our guests haven't eaten. . . . Von Bratslav, will you help me look for our naughty genius?"

Nachman followed the Prince from room to room. Lichnowsky opened a door, looked in, then shut it. Nachman wondered what the Prince did with so many richly furnished but unoccupied chambers. Like a dream castle, one room was more elegant than the next: art works in gilded frames, sculptures, brocaded furniture, chandeliers, carpets, silk drapery. The Prince and Nachman turned right into another wing. Room after room, but no sign of the composer. They descended a flight of marble stairs and started the search again. Lichnowsky's patience was ebbing. He too began slamming doors.

"Go start with artists. Feed them, pamper them, patronize them." Lichnowsky shook Beethoven's music as if it were a faulty umbrella.

But you don't feed him, Nachman thought.

Finally, at the end of a corridor, in a warm library, they found Beethoven, calmly reading *Plutarch's Lives*. He looked up in surprise at the Prince and Nachman.

"Oh, so here you are," Lichnowsky said. "It's fortunate there are only one hundred rooms in this wing. Had there been two hundred, who knows how long I would have to search for you. Isn't it beastly hot here with the roaring fireplace? You could have opened a window . . ." Now his voice was gentle, almost friendly. "Come, go eat and play your sonata . . . the guests are ready."

"I'm not going to play tonight."

"And why aren't you? How did Prince Lichnowsky offend His Highness?"

"Did you expect Haydn?"

"Why Haydn? I expected you. Haydn is too old to travel."

"Haydn ate with servants. Beethoven doesn't eat with the help. When Beethoven is invited by royalty he dines with royalty."

"Royalty waited for you, but you arrived late."

"It was your royal carriage that broke down."

"A thousand and three pardons, Herr Maestro. Perhaps you are angry that the payment for tonight's sonata has not yet been tendered. It will soon be forthcoming."

"Not at all, Prince," Beethoven bit off the words. "In fact, it was you who recalled his, not I . . ."

"Come then, it's time."

"I'm not playing for you tonight."

"Please, Beethoven. No time for temperament. I've invited many distinguished guests who are anxiously awaiting you."

Beethoven shook his head.

"Three hundred people are waiting in the Grand Salon," Lichnowsky hissed.

"I am not changing my mind. Let your footmen's chorus sing for your distinguished company."

The Prince walked over to the fireplace and, with his elbows pressed tightly to his chest, rubbed his hands. Then he took Beethoven's music, stretched his hand over the large metal grating, and held the sheets over the flames. Nachman restrained a cry. The Prince smiled coldly. Beethoven did not budge. He closed *Plutarch's Lives*.

"Are you going to play, or must I make a burnt offering of your music?"

Beethoven stood; he clenched his teeth, bit down hard.

"How dare you tamper with the fruit of my mind? How dare you coerce Beethoven? Return my music!"

"Don't give me orders. Mind your station. The music is mine. It is dedicated to me." Lichnowsky brought his hand over the flames, held the sheets with two fingers. "Well, maestro? Are you going to play?"

"What?" Beethoven roared, sprang up toward the prince. "My mind is not a round of cheese or a hunk of meat that can be bought at the marketplace." He drew closer. "Give me my music. I'm leaving."

"Leave," the Prince said calmly, and opened his fingers. The manuscript dropped into the flames behind a metal grating. "Perhaps the cold rain will cool your hot head."

Oh, my God, thought Nachman. A second time. You *did* make a copy, didn't you? Nachman was about to shout. As the flames devoured, curled, blackened the paper, Beethoven stood stunned. Nachman's heart beat quickly. He did not know what to do. Then Beethoven emitted a cry of pain that sounded more feral than human. A moment later he leaped forward and with the full strength of his muscular arms and contained rage slapped the Prince's face with his open palm. The force of the blow thrust Lichnowsky to the side. "Twice," Beethoven shouted. "Nothing is doomed to die twice!" He was about to lunge again, but Nachman restrained him. Instinctively, Lichnowsky's hand reached for his belt. But he wore no sword. His hand touched his face, as if covering his shame.

"In the East, where I have served as Ambassador, I learned a remarkable tradition. You are my guest now, so I won't harm you. But I am going to hunt you down."

"Try it," Beethoven said. "Napoleon's French are approaching Graz. They believe in liberty."

He ran to the door and pulled Nachman with him. They raced down the stairs to their rooms. Beethoven threw his things into his suitcase; Nachman packed quickly too.

Did you make a copy? Did you make a copy? Nachman dared not ask.

"Come, let's get out of here before he sends his servants to kill me. We have some time, since he won't dare show his face with my finger marks."

Outside, the icy mountain rain slashed their faces.

Beethoven pointed his nose skyward. "Let's hope there's a post coach in town. Hurry!"

They trotted down the hill in the dark, using white stones as their markers. Despite his arhythmic walk, Beethoven moved quickly. First Nachman's hat and trousers became wet. Then the unceasing rain penetrated his jacket, shirt, shoes. The cold water sloshed in Nachman's boots. He wished he could fly to a warm shelter, that the sun would shine, that the rain would stop. He thought of floating on his back in the river, the sun shining. But he could not shake the cold. He shivered, then sneezed once, twice. The sneeze triggered a fit of coughing. Beethoven stopped.

"Is it the rain?"

Nachman shook his head. "No, the cold hurts my lungs. It's an old cough. Since childhood."

"Forgive me, Nachman."

Nachman, silent, quickened his pace. An occasional bolt of lightning lit their path.

"Austrian princes!" Beethoven said. "They're just like the rabble they prey upon. Cruelty masked with elegance. They deserve to be destroyed by Napoleon. God! God! God! Why didn't I stop him?" Beethoven shook his fist. "He destroyed my composition. I should have killed him. Why did you get in the way?"

"You wouldn't want to kill a man, despite his unforgivable act. They would hang you. Anyway, it is hardly fitting for Beethoven to stoop to a prince's level."

Beethoven grunted.

"It's the first time I felt the spirit of hatred and meanness in this country," Nachman observed.

"You haven't been here long enough. There is hatred in the air. The Austrians possess it in plenitude. Anything the Germans do, the Austrians try to do better."

The question burst out of Nachman before he had a chance to stop himself.

"Did you make another copy of that sonata?"

"No," the composer bellowed. "Please leave me alone."

"Why? Why? Why? I told you to . . ."

They trudged in silence, too tired to run.

"There's a light down there," Beethoven said. "It must be the post house."

In the carriage waiting room a stove was lit. The old attendant invited the two men to dry their clothes. As their soaked garments were stretched out, another spell of chills came over Nachman and he coughed until his chest ached. Beethoven looked guilty, said nothing.

"You know," Beethoven said finally. "Although Napoleon may not be good for the Austrians, he is good for your people. He has given permission for Jews to resettle Palestine."

A thrill ran through Nachman. "Then indeed we do stand at the threshold of Messianic times."

The attendant approached. "The gentlemen are in luck. The night post coach for Vienna has arrived."

An hour later, the rain stopped. The light of a half moon came in through the window. Beethoven leaned back, absorbed in thoughts. Then Nachman began to sing Beethoven's sonata note for note.

At first Beethoven looked up in surprise. But as Nachman continued through the first movement into the second, Beethoven gripped Nachman's arm. He was about to speak, but only his lips moved. Finally, he managed, "How . . . ?"

"It's Beethoven's, not Nachman's. You played it for me. Both parts, remember? Perfect pitch . . . See, I know . . . I've learned."

Beethoven clapped Nachman's shoulder with affection.

"Not only that. Perfect ethical pitch. A *lamed vovnik*. See, I know too. I've also learned."

They slept in an inn midway between Graz and Vienna. At noon, the sun was in full blaze. It was a perfect day, one that reminded Nachman of his morning walks to the river in Bratslav. Soon, as if in answer to an unspoken wish, the driver stopped by a lake to rest his horses. Nachman looked at the water. Lizabeta, he whispered. Alpha beta. The water radiated out toward him in waves, and urged him, come come come. Nachman made a swimming motion to Beethoven, but the latter said:

"No, I've had enough water for a month. My ears still hurt from last night's downpour."

"Then let me get you some herbs. They should help. It's an art passed down from my zayde." Nachman picked weeds, flowers, herbs, roots. "This weed you can chew now . . . The others we'll boil and you'll drink the water when you get home."

The noonday heat was dizzying. Nachman saw blue, white, and black spots. He walked to the water, as if in a dream where nothing was under his control. Yet he was the dreamer, master of the dream. And Napoleon will let Jews settle in the Land of Israel. Then perhaps—God's whisper—there is hope for me. A bird trilled. He could not tell what sort. Here, far from home, there were different birds. Home. Home. I still think of Bratslav as home. Good sign. Blessed sign. Near a patch of water lilies, a bull frog croaked. In the distance, misty grey clouds. Probably raining again in the mountains. He undressed and plunged in. He went under. The water covered him. It went into his ears, his nostrils. Under his nails. A stream of cold water from an underground spring sprayed him. He felt refreshed inside and out. Purified. He surfaced. Thanked God he was alive. Who by water, who by fire? Who by hunger, who by sword? There were so many ways to die. Runaway horses. Toppled carriages. Lightning and rain. A cruel prince. It's a miracle a man lives to be twenty-eight. There were so many ways to die.

Only one way to live. Daily I will bless God, says the Psalmist. And I, David's descendant, echo him.

Nachman saw Beethoven sitting on the side of the embankment. The composer waved and pointed to the sky. Nachman shaded his eyes.

"No, not there. There!" Beethoven said. "Can't you see it?"

"A rainbow," Nachman cried. Recited the blessing. A rainbow. Promise of peace. The end of war between God and man. A thin band of clouds cut one part of the delicately hued arch. It reminded him of the letter *beys*.

"Look, Beethoven, *beys*," Nachman shouted before he realized what he said. "*Beys*," he said joyfully. "*Beys*. That's the first letter of the Torah. Beginning. And the first letter of your name, Beethoven." He ran up to the composer. *Aleph beys*. Alpha beta. Beta. Beeth-oven. "I see one of the letters," Nachman said. "I see one of the letters. Look up there. One of the letters. The rainbow, cut by a long cloud, looks like the letter *beys*."

Beethoven looked up at the rainbow. "You're cured, Nachman."

A Siddur flashed before Nachman. But its pages were still blank.

One afternoon, as Nachman toyed with the piano keys, he suddenly —as if the letters were never gone—called each note by its Hebrew name. With music—the invisible alphabet—the visible alphabet was slowly returning. An aleph, filled with music, flew by like a bird. The precious gift back from oblivion. The seven notes: *Aleph, beys, gimel, daled, hey, vov, zayin* . . .

The next morning, Nachman prayed from the Siddur. He sensed he had the letters—yet something was still missing. He recited a line of prayer by heart, then read it from the Siddur. But something was wrong. One letter blank, and he could not tell which one it was. This too is a sign, like the six/seven bars of the bed. Perfection, Nachman thought, cannot come in Vienna. It must be realized elsewhere, in the locus of peace, the perfect city of peace, in the land Napoleon was freeing. Nachman took a pen and some sheets of paper, and for the first time in months saw letters of his script running across the pages.

Nachman knew that the time had come to say goodbye to Beethoven. He had been away long enough. If he stayed any longer in Vienna, it would be impossible to return home. But he didn't know how to break the news.

As he thought of ways to begin, the composer approached hesitantly.

"Remember I once asked you to teach me the Hebrew alphabet so that I could learn the Bible?"

"Yes?" said Nachman. He hoped he wouldn't have to start teaching now.

Beethoven scratched his cheek.

"I don't know how to say this . . . But I can't now. I've been invited to tour the Low Countries and England . . . and it comes at a perfect time. To get away from Lichnowsky. And it's a wonderful opportunity to meet fellow composers and publishers."

"I understand. Of course. And I must go back too. You've given me so much. You are a true *lamed vovnik*. My letters have returned, because of you. I grew spiritually, because of you. You gave me the invisible letters. That's why the visible ones returned. I didn't know how to tell you I must return home. So, you see, God has ordained that the separation be easy and natural on both sides."

The two men gazed at each other in understanding. They hugged and, in their warm embrace, exchanged melodies.

"Thank you, Beethoven, thank you very much."

"I thank you, Nachman. I know that music for you is a means to a richer spiritual life. Had you devoted yourself to composition you would be Haydn's equal."

"Not enough for me." Nachman laughed. "Beethoven or nothing."

"You don't want to be Beethoven. You want to be Nachman."

"I do indeed want to be Nachman!"

"I'd like to be Nachman too. I envy your instant facility for melody. And your ability to bounce back when your spirit is low."

"No, Beethoven. You once said that everyone must be the person he's destined to be. So you be Beethoven and I'll be Nachman, even though it's a struggle. But to tell the truth, being Beethoven isn't so bad either."

In the evening, by the light of the moon, Nachman looked around Beethoven's room, painting a picture in his mind. Goodbye piano, goodbye music stand, goodbye books, goodbye window, goodbye Vienna from the window, goodbye wooden floor. Here I found the treasure.

The next morning, Nachman packed. Beethoven approached with a little velvet bag.

"Razumovsky asked me to give this to you when you leave."

Nachman put his hands behind his back.

"I don't accept gifts."

"Oho! Someone prouder than Beethoven? It is not a gift; it is a stipend, a scholarship, an honorarium. Razumovsky knew you would refuse; that is why he gave it to me to give to you. He forbade me to give it back to him. It is not a gift; it is a performance fee. It is earned. It will help pay for your travelling expenses. Guard it well."

Beethoven tucked the little bag with the prince's seal into Nachman's pocket.

"Goodbye, Beethoven. Thank you. If I don't see you in Vienna, I'll see you in Jerusalem when the Messiah comes."

He turned quickly and went down the stairs.

On his way out of Vienna, Nachman passed the fountain of lions and saw the same uniformed street musicians again. They played the same melodies—but Nachman was not the same. Nachman had music and almost all the letters. He knew he was not perfect; still, his pitch was perfect. The musicians were performing a Mozart Cassation. Nachman shook his head. Third-rate players. Today the group did not sound as impressive as it had weeks ago.

At the end of the performance, the violinist came up to Nachman.

"Say, aren't you the gentleman who wanted to study music with Beethoven?"

"Hello, Bruno. Yes, I am."

"Say, you remembered my name! Well, I hope he didn't slam the door in your face."

"No, not at all. The good Beethoven opened the door wide and took me into his house. And I want to thank you for your help."

He opened the prince's velvet bag and gave Bruno a silver coin.

"Why, thank you, sir, and you're welcome, sir . . . Fritzl, the gentleman studied with Beethoven and remembered my name!"

"And would you mind if I made a comment?" Nachman asked.

"No, not at all."

"In the last movement, that high note of the French horn. I think it should have been a B natural, not a B flat."

Book Three

As he walked into Bratslav, the mist of morning still hung in the air. A fresh smell as though after a sunshower. On such mornings he would swim in the river. He passed the familiar path. Knew his heart was knocking. At the house, he kissed the mezuza and came in unannounced. He seized his home like an amulet, hoping to drive away invidious spirits. Murmured, "I'm home." Everything was in its place. If everything was in its place, where had time gone? Farewells reversed; mirror images of goodbyes. Now he greeted doors and pictures, tables, books, and stove. In the yard, he saw the cleaning woman. Natalya sat on the ground and peeled potatoes. An open book with a magnifying lens lay on a stool. She still wore that loose-fitting red checkered kerchief that draped over forehead and eyes. First she bowed her head, then rose and bowed from the waist like a peasant before an icon. Her face reddened with excitement.

She would know. She would know about the drowned Lizabeta.

Carefully, Nachman began questioning the old woman.

"Are you well?"

"Well, praise God. And you, sir?"

"Well too."

Nachman coughed—out of shyness or pain, he didn't know.

"Shall I make you warm milk?"

"Not yet, not yet." He touched a cauliflower leaf. "How is our produce?"

"Excellent. I go to market everyday. To sell and barter."

"You remember there was talk in the village of an accident two months ago?"

"The farmer who was here? That rowdy man?"

"Yes, yes." Nachman breathed easier. It was going better than he thought. "They said a girl was drowned."

"Oh, yes, they found her. But she lost her soul."

"Dead? Dead?"

"Now the soul must seek salvation. No rest until salvation."

Nachman looked down at the ground. So that was it. Finished, finished. Done for. He did not want to get into a discussion of belief with a superstitious old peasant.

He looked at the open book, a Hebrew and Russian primer. An odd feeling coursed through him: surprise, dismay, even shock.

"You're studying Hebrew?" You too will master the letters that are still not mine? "You know how to read?"

"Yes." She glowed. "I want to learn your language. I want to . . ." She dropped her voice.

"Why? Do you know what it means?" He exhaled, breath drained from him. "Do you know the burdens? Our history?"

"I work among Jews. I learned the Jewish kosher laws. I live with Jews. I live in your house, Rabbi. Ruth was not a Jew before she became a Jew."

"So you know that too. So you know everything, old woman."

"No," she said softly. "Not everything. But that's not a fault. There isn't a man on earth who knows everything."

Nachman did not say a word. Anger—was it anger?—moved in two directions through his arms and legs. He would not get drawn into an argument with an old woman.

"According to Jewish law I must say to you: Come back in three months, four months. . . ."

From a pocket Natalya pulled out a little book.

"One of the old women in town has helped me. Look. Listen how I read."

She slowly read the *Shema,* the "Hear O Israel" prayer.

"Very good. You read better than me."

She laughed at his joke, covering her mouth as peasant women are wont to do.

Nachman stepped into his room. His veins hummed. He was disconcerted. The balance he had achieved for weeks and weeks was suddenly shattered. Another problem, another decision. Suddenly, the fatigue of the journey overwhelmed him. He lay down to catch his breath. Created the shapes of the letters on the wall; smiled with joy. Home again.

Now to the—he took a deep breath—bes medresh. A stranger with dust on his shoes; that's what they saw. He measured their slow recognition by the changing look on their faces, as subtle as sky colors at sunset. From cordial welcome of a newcomer to celebration of their returned master. First a dance around him, a circle, of black coats and white skullcaps. And then the embrace.

Nathan entered. His face too changed from disbelief to a hesitant, bashful smile, like a young wife whose husband returns from a trip. At first, he said nothing, but his eyes glittered. Then, softly, "Rebbe, rebbe, *sholom aleichem,* rebbe. Welcome back." For a moment Nathan was on the verge of tears. They clasped hands, embraced. Nathan's hands were cold. Nachman felt that his assistant was hundreds of miles away.

Nachman raised a finger for silence, but one of the Hasidim asked, "How was Eretz Yisroel? Tell us, tell us about our Holy Land. Nathan said your last words were: I'm going to Israel."

Nachman wanted to say: I'm happy to see you and happy that you want me back. Instead, he swallowed, his throat dry. He shaped his mouth into an "O" but said nothing. As if he bubbled out a zero. Nachman's silence intensified the stillness in the room. The white cloth on the long table seemed to flutter in an unseen breeze. The wind of Nachman's discomfort. He looked down at the floorboards. Saw Beethoven's oak floor. Nachman's gaze seemed to say: I was there, but now I am here. Now I am home with you.

"Well, actually, those were *not* my last words. I said: A man's feet take him where he's destined to go. Although every place where I set foot is Israel and everywhere I direct my heart is Jerusalem, I have come back not from the Land of Israel . . . but from Vienna."

Nachman considered the gasp that hung in the air. He began softly, knowing they would come closer to listen.

"Yes, Vienna. I could not . . . I was not prepared to go to Israel." I am defending myself, he thought. I am defending myself. Why should I have to defend myself? "The holy Besht made the attempt and was forced to retreat . . . I was afraid. Yes, I admit, afraid. Not ready. Before one sets foot in the Land of Israel, one must prepare oneself spiritually." He raised his voice; it echoed as if in a deep dark cavern. He held his head as if in pain. "I was afraid." The Hasidim heard his booming, cavernous, fearsome voice and trembled. Again, as on the day Lizabeta's father had come in to the bes medresh, the Hasidim backed off, leaving space between themselves and their rebbe.

"If one is not prepared spiritually, the trip to the land of the living can become a journey," he whispered hoarsely, "to land of the," and quickly placed an index finger over his lips.

With his finger on his lips, Nachman suddenly felt a thrill of remembrance: A conductor calls for pianissimo. Nachman waved them closer. The Hasidim formed a semicircle around him, dressed in black, like musicians. He began a niggun. One Hasid was the clarinet, another the violin. He looked for the harp, the Messianic harp. What wonders memory was capable of. What had taken him weeks of travel, with memory took no time at all. Back to Vienna. The concert hall. Nachman raised his hands and conducted.

From Nathan's Diary

Ay ay ay. Finally, our Rebbe is back. Exhausted from his travels but back. We thought that, like the Jews awaiting Moses at Sinai for forty days and forty nights, he would never return. Now I can be myself again. God be praised, he can read again, but still misses one letter. He sounds like a niggun with a hole in it. He cannot pronounce the *nun*. A sign of humility? That the letter that begins and ends his name, Nachman, is hidden from him? That he is not yet fully present? Withdrawn? Like—dare we make the comparison?—like the Shechinah, God's Holy Presence, in Exile? And will he tell us the fourteenth tale we have all been waiting for?

I told a Hasid to ask Reb Nachman: "Why Vienna, where there is no piety?" For I dared not ask it of the Master myself.

"If you ask why," Reb Nachman snapped, "none of you have understood one iota of what I've tried to teach you . . . that man can rise only after he descends . . ."

Nachman summoned Nathan, who entered with a gloomy, guilt-ridden face.

"Once upon a time there was an old peasant woman who wanted to become a Jew," Nachman began. Then he stopped and looked at Nathan. Not only did he not react, but Nathan's face actually brightened, as if a reprimand he had expected was not forthcoming.

"Who?"

"Our cleaning woman, what's-her-name."

"Natalya."

"Was it you who got her the Russian-Hebrew primer?" Nachman asked quickly.

"Rebbe, I don't know what you're talking about."

"Can you imagine? I thought she was illiterate and here she is studying Hebrew! Met one of our older women who has helped her. Knows about Ruth. Wants to become a Jew. What's happening here?"

Nathan did not answer.

"Our first obligation is to make Jews of our Jews," said Nachman.

From Nathan's Diary

Shortly after our last conversation, the Rebbe began speaking about salvation. "We need the Messiah. . . . He could be here in our midst. He can come from any of us."

"A plain man can't be a Messiah," I said.

"Who said so?" said Reb Nachman. "We are all sons of David. If we magnify our hearts, our wills, any one of us can become the one. It depends upon the preparation. . . . Are you prepared?" Reb Nachman asked me.

"No," I said.

I put my hands behind my back. I looked the Rebbe straight in the eye.

"Are you?"

"All my life," Reb Nachman said, "I have been in a state of preparation. Once you hear that whisper, you can never forget that whisper again."

Nachman felt removed from the Hasidim. Have I gained one thing and lost another? he mused. Have I grown used to the beardless gentile faces?

A map of Vienna spread like a transparent cloth over Nachman's image of Bratslav. Even if a nail had not been moved, a shingle replaced, or a board hammered over, Bratslav was different now. Vienna was a glass pane through which he now saw the world.

Could he recreate the past? Could he walk in the field unperturbed as he had done months, miles, ago? Walk the path to the river in the same way? The Talmud teaches that for complete repentance one has to be tempted exactly the same way a second time and then withstand that temptation. But that was no longer possible. Now her soul hovered somewhere. Still, she seemed so near and he felt an emptiness akin to hunger. The trees, the bushes, smelled the same, in full bloom, the leaves greener than ever. But in each flower he saw the park near Beethoven's house. Vienna was everywhere. Now when he sang a melody, he saw the notes.

From a cupboard in his room Nachman took three of the Hebrew letters that the Hasidim had made. He turned them to their blank white side and cut strips, which he stitched until he had a length of white paper four feet long and six inches wide. Then, with a quill he drew the white and black notes and made a keyboard. Silently, he began to play.

One Friday evening before sunset Nachman prayed in the fields. What kind of melody can express that green? he wondered. Like people, colors had different melodies. Green alone contained a rainbow of colors. A frog croaked at the edge of a pond. Years ago his grandfather had taught him the names of trees and flowers and birds. He heard grackles and jays, a mockingbird in the distance. At sunset, blue turned mauve, green crimson. The Sabbath enveloped him like an ethereal tallis. Nachman welcomed the Sabbath alone.

Night came quickly. The hills were silhouetted. No moonlight. A tiny star, a firefly, lit up in a tree and vanished. In the silence, crickets chirped, shadows moved. God wraps himself with light as with a garment, but at night he wore a different cloak. One could pray at night as well as day. The Master of the Universe had created darkness too, and He was God of night as well as God of light.

Once more, Nachman sat at the head of the table with the Hasidim. Sabbath afternoon between twilight and dusk. He sang with eyes closed, head back, pounding the rhythm on the white-decked table. Everyone floated in air with the ecstasy of Sabbath song. The Hasidim waited for Nachman to speak.

Nachman's words, "I shall tell you a story," broke the silence. He hoped their anticipation would spark a tale. But the silence built upon itself; it climbed lugubriously through the empty space of the room. Nachman looked from face to face, saw the emptiness growing wider. Then, sensing the punishment from on high, he rose and returned to his room.

From Nathan's Diary

"Tonight, the Rebbe told us a story which probably has never been told before," I said to the Hasidim. "A story of the highest order, like motionless dance, which the Rebbe says is the highest rung of dance. Could it have been the perfect story? He looked at each of us and, without saying a word, told us the story deep in our hearts."

But I did not tell them what I truly sense: The Master's strength is ebbing.

A few days later, after the Afternoon Service, Nachman responded to a question about the Besht:

"It is said of the holy Baal Shem Tov that his soul was on the same level as King David's. Every night he heard Torah from the mouth of the Holy One Blessed Be He. Zayde's friends asked him if he could hasten the Redemption. So, accompanied by his daughter, Eydl, my grandmother of blessed memory, he began his journey to the Land of Israel. By Passover he was in Istanbul, where he took a ship. A heavenly voice warned him not to travel farther. But he paid no heed. On board, he suddenly could not pray; he could not read. Hours later, a violent storm came and Eydl was swept overboard. The Baal Shem Tov recited the *Shema Yisroel* and jumped into the raging sea to save his child. 'Save her,' he told God, 'and I'll go back home.' At that instant the storm ceased and they returned home. Who knows? Perhaps if that holy man had set foot on the Holy Land the Messiah would have come."

Nachman hadn't realized his eyes were closed until he opened them, came back from Istanbul and the sea, the tumultuous green blue sea, and saw his Hasidim before him.

"And you, Reb Nachman, are you planning to go?" Nathan asked.

This was the tremulous question he heard in the thick twilight. The question raged in his mind like a skiff in a storm. Did Nathan want him to leave so that he could play Rebbe again?

"Yes," Nachman said flatly. He said "yes" without ecstasy. He said "yes" without joy. But as he replayed that "yes" in his mind a flood of confidence surged. Nachman did not budge, but once more felt elevated, as he did in Razumovsky's crowded salon. "What can *you* do?" the beautiful woman in the ivory dress had challenged him and he, responding, had risen in ecstasy.

"Yes," he shouted. But as soon as he said it he felt the Hasidim pulling back. "You've heard of Napoleon. Some Jews side with him, some oppose him. He is a conqueror, but he has restored the rights of Jews. He has proclaimed that Jews can settle Eretz Yisroel. So, indeed, perhaps the time has come. If the powers of the world support us, perhaps the hour is ripe. I shall go and see. If it is possible, then all of us will go up to our Holy Land." Nachman lowered his voice. "We are close, brothers, close to Redemption. The light of the Messiah is all around us. One has to be blind not to see it!"

One Friday night after prayers, the Hasidim spontaneously rose and gathered in a tight circle around Nachman at the reader's lectern. They drew him into a dance, embraced him with their love. As if they didn't want to let him go away again. Another time, as though he were a groom or a bride, four Hasidim lifted his chair while the others danced and clapped around him. Still, his lips were clamped.

Now that he had said yes to the journey, Nachman asked himself if he should leave again. In Hasidic life, Hasidim made pilgrimages; rebbes stayed home. But in Bratslav, the rebbe was the wanderer. What was missing in his life? The trip to Vienna had perhaps restored the letters, given him music. But what good were letters if the words and sentences were gone. Perhaps, he thought, it is preordained that I tell only thirteen and not fourteen tales, twice the perfect sum of seven?

And then another woe returned.

The dreams.

Why am I being tormented? Nachman wondered. Is it because in Vienna I longed for these dreams? He knew the old tradition of reciting the entire Book of Psalms in one day as a sword against the yetzer ho-reh. One morning he chanted all 150 Psalms.

In vain.

At night, Nachman fell into a sopor, a deep sleep as if he were drunk or drugged. A sleep so thick that had the Holy One Blessed Be He come to remove a rib and fashion a helpmeet for him, Nachman would not have been aware. His dreams seared with desire—and satisfaction. Again Lizabeta, night after night. Again and again.

One night, after the Evening Service, Nathan came in with two letters.

"The old caretaker handed them to me. Natalya said a passing wagoner brought them."

Nachman smiled, recognized the handwriting on the top envelope. Was transported at once miles, cities, away.

"So the master is writing to me," Nachman said softly.

"Master?" said Nathan. "*You* have a master?"

"My music master. Beethoven . . . From Vienna. And the other, the other is from someone whose hand is unfamiliar . . ."

At once, Nachman saw Beethoven at the piano, conducting, strolling in the woods, hands behind his back, chin out, walking disjointedly as if torso and legs did not belong to the same man. Nachman saw the familiar room with the view of Vienna's skyline, a room he knew as well as his own. The piano, the oaken floor. When he opened his eyes, Nathan had gone.

At his table, he happily, eagerly, tore open the envelope.

> Dear Nachman,
>
> I hope you reached your destination safely. My trip, thank God, was a total success. Your friend Beethoven made a high impression on the Low Countries and England as well. The only bad news is that my hearing is worse. The doctor traces it back to the Lichnowsky debacle when we walked in that merciless downpour. How is your music? Are you composing? I've managed to publish my Third Symphony which, for a while at least, until he became a conqueror like all other conquerors, was dedicated to Napoleon. Now Napoleon has a new enemy: Lichnowsky. As I predicted, his land, including his castle, were taken by Napoleon's forces, and Lichnowsky is furious. Now he is on an ambassadorial mission trying to round up support against Napoleon. And Napoleon, as you probably know, is in Palestine, which he has promised the Jews; and you, dear Nachman, are, I presume, in Bratslav, where I hope this letter reaches you and finds you happy and reading words and music well. I think of you often and

Razumovsky sends you his kindest regards. If you come to Vienna again, he wants you to spend some time in his palace as guest composer.

Yours with affection & esteem,
L. Beethoven

Nachman jumped up. Napoleon in the Land of Israel and I here? Soon I too shall join the better part of me that is already there. For me there will be no obstacles. He picked up a pen and wrote:

Dear Beethoven,

I hope this letter finds you well. Yes, your letter reached me in Bratslav, but I had already been thinking of the Land of Israel, to which I soon hope to go. Your letter prodded my spirit, like a good rebbe prods a Hasid's spirit. Yes, I think of music, of Vienna, of you, and I now remember the melodies I compose. But here there are no concerts, no symphonies, no string quartets. In short, no music, except what we create from our souls. I play a cardboard piano with my imagination. I pray that you are well and that your hearing will improve.

Your friend,
Nachman of Bratslav

He looked at the second envelope. It was smudged and wrinkled, as though it had passed a long journey. Nachman tore open the top. The letter was in Russian, dated one month ago. Another folded sheet within, labelled: 'For my father and mother.' He quickly skimmed the short sentences, saw the name at the bottom. Something rose, fluttered in him, as if another soul within him had been given life. A sky blue joy rose in all his limbs. So you were right, Beethoven. You were right, master. Like a child with a candy saved for last, he delayed reading the second letter. He ran to the bes medresh, the image of Beethoven's study and the Viennese streets precise as a painting in his mind.

"Listen," Nachman cried. "Listen carefully," he told his Hasidim. He caught his breath. A pain in his chest, a huge fist closing in on his lungs. "Remember this." He stopped. All eyes were on him. The men were seated now around the table. "In our world. Beneath the canopy of heaven. There is nothing, nothing as perfect as music . . ." And as he said this, Beethoven's variations on his own niggunim echoed in his mind. He heard the violin sonata that Lichnowsky had burned. "This is what I have learned. There is nothing as perfect as music. Music can make one rise." And he remembered rising as the beautiful woman in the ivory dress—Beethoven told him later it was Razumovsky's lascivious sister—gaped at him in amazement. Nachman looked at the long, white-decked table in the bes medresh. He felt the palpable darkness descending. Darkness settled like crows in the crevices of the walls. No one spoke. The weight of an untold story hung like a leaden mantle on his back. The Hasidim waited.

"I . . . I . . ."

The Hasidim leaned forward, expecting, hoping for a story.

Nachman too was hoping for a story, a hope as mute as his tongue. Earlier that afternoon, Nachman had studied an old mystical text he had not seen before. Despite his lack of one letter, he could still make out the meaning. One sentence was directed at him. "In order to attain holiness, one must first pass through defilement." He had known it; now found proof in a text. Yes. One must descend to Vienna before rising to Jerusalem. One must descend to lustful night visions before climbing the angel's ladder of sun-filled dreams.

"Do you see me?" Nachman asked suddenly. "You think I'm here."

"Yes," the Hasidim answered. "We see you."

"No. You don't see me. The I of Nachman is not here. The essence of my I-am is *there*. I am not here anymore. I am more there than here, and I must go where most of me is. One must descend to Vienna before rising to Jerusalem. I have been to Vienna, now I must ascend to Jerusalem."

A beam, a small bright beam, a hundred candles in one, lit in his mind. If I go to Israel when I am on my way to Vienna, how much the more am I on the way to Israel when I go to Israel. But the light he saw was not reflected on the sullen faces of the Hasidim.

He returned to his room. Again a sweet elixir suffused all his limbs with joy. Now I know what happiness is. In his room, heart thumping, fingers shaking as he held the letter, Nachman read slowly, but his mind inserted "she's alive" between each word.

> Dear Nachman,
>
> I am far away from you. In the village where I live now. What can I say? I miss you. I miss seeing you by the water. I remember the water. I wish you well. I remember you. I think of you. I cannot write all the things I feel. I have beautiful

> thoughts of you. But as I pick up the pen, my thoughts flee. Please give the enclosed letter to my father.
>
> Lizabeta

He held her letter to his nose, disgusted with himself, but he hoped for her smell, perhaps a lingering scent from far away. None. Dry paper. He couldn't write to her even if he wanted to. So this is the woman who haunts my nights. He remembered a verse from the Song of Songs: "Strong as death is love." It is good she is far away. To reduce my temptation.

Nachman slapped his forehead. If she's alive, perhaps I'm not punished after all. "Alive!" he shouted. The year is 1800, he thought. A hundred times *chai*. The year of life. He jumped up and down like a Jew saying "holy holy holy" in the repetition of the Silent Devotion. Again he jumped and stayed in the air for a moment, feeling light as a Mozart melody. Then another verse from the Song of Songs came to him: "Floods cannot quench love, nor can rivers drown it."

He ran back to the bes medresh. Some men were at the door. Others stood talking. The mood in the room said departure. Nachman sat and closed his eyes. Silence. No one moved. He tapped a rhythm on the table, hummed a tune as if it were an overture.

"Once upon a time there was a king . . ." he said.

The Hasidim sat and listened as though it were a Friday night or a Sabbath dusk meal.

Then he opened his eyes. Saw the joy on their faces. Their rebbe was telling a story again.

"He lived in peace, this king I speak of, but sensed that God was distant from him. One day the king told his ministers, 'God is removed from us, like a lover parted from his beloved. But this increases our longing for Him.' That is what the king said. And true, we do long for Him. How we long for Him! We long for the land where His presence dwells. And with God's help I shall go, like Abraham, and explore the land for all of us, unless the Messiah precedes us, may he come speedily and in our own day and let us say, Amen."

Nachman expected, as indeed he always heard, the chorus of Amens. When he did not hear Amen; or rather, when he heard the loud space of silence, his heartbeat was suspended. Instead of that resounding Amen, he heard a vacuum so loud he sensed the blankness, a clear warning. It stung his heart. Why are they silent? Is it because I went to Vienna and not to Israel, as I had announced? Or is it because they can hear that one missing letter and consider me imperfect? Or is it because I'm going to leave them again? Or is it because they realize that what I told was not really a story at all, but a confession of my sins?

That night Nachman was afraid. He locked the outside door. But the dreams were unrelenting, the lustful dreams he fled. At night, Lilith and demons took over. On silent hinges doors swung open, and in slid dreams. He remembered the Yiddish folk saying: In dreams, it is not the dreamer who sins but his dreams. He sought consolation in folk wisdom. For his cough, and as a spiritual amulet, every night the old woman brought him warm milk and honey, visible symbol of Israel. But he knew, he knew that milk and honey could not counteract potent dreams. Dreams were stronger than amulets because they came from man's secret wishes. Only one place would help. Not the symbol, but the place itself. The Land of Israel, God's perfect place, would cure him. There, there completion would come.

His eye wandered to Beethoven's letter. Happy, he picked it up and read it again. When he came to the end, he was disappointed there was no more. He turned it around, hoping there would be another message, between the lines perhaps? Once more he was in the composer's room, listening to concerts, strolling with Beethoven in the Vienna woods. A happy time, a happy time.

Then Nachman took Lizabeta's letter to her parents out to the old woman.

Natalya sat cross-legged, a candle lit on an overturned pot. She put her book down.

"The rabbi looks happy. Why is the rabbi so happy?"

"Well, you know that Jews believe in resurrection of the dead."

"Yes, like Jesus."

Nachman bristled. And this, this wants to be a Jew. You're going to be a Jew like I'm going to be a dog. "If you want to be a Jew, you cannot say that," he said gently. "It goes against the grain of our belief."

Abashed, the old woman lowered her head.

One cannot make a yarmulke out of a sow's ear, Nachman thought.

Natalya looked up. "But Rabbi, you didn't tell me why you're so happy."

"I'm not happy anymore."

"Please," she said.

"Do you remember that girl who I told you had drowned? She *didn't* drown. She sent a letter to her father."

Nachman watched to see if she would cross herself. If she made the slightest motion with her hand he would tear the book away from her.

"It's good she's alive, but I wonder about her soul." Natalya's eyes glowed fervently.

He waved the letter at her.

"Could you deliver this for me tomorrow? It's for a farmer named Vlodek who lives about two miles from here."

The old caretaker began shaking her head as soon as she looked up at the letter. Her face showed agitation. The heightened color made it almost youthful. Could she too have been a pretty woman years ago, desired by the village youths? Nachman grew dizzy watching her head and kerchief moving.

"No no no. Bad luck. Bad luck. Where I come from it's bad luck, bad bad luck, to deliver a letter that's already been delivered. Many hands, tsk tsk tsk. Pp, pp, pp." She spit three times to ward off the evil eye. "I don't want these hands to wither." Natalya held her hands behind her back.

Irritated by her thickness, Nachman turned abruptly and walked out. He doubted that this superstitious woman would become a Jew.

The next morning he saw two boys playing with a prayer stand in the bes medresh; one pushed, the other caught.

"Don't do that," Nachman said gently. "You may think it's only wood, but objects have an inner life too. If you throw prayer stands, you may next begin to throw books. And my mother Feige of blessed memory always said, 'The way you treat books, you treat people.'"

The pale, shaken boys were silent. They had not moved while Nachman spoke to them. One lad still held the prayer stand at a tilt.

"Here. You can do a mitzva. Run and bring this letter to the farmer Vlodek. Follow the path almost to the river, and then, instead of bearing right to the river, go left and you will soon see his farm. It's a white house with a broken fence and a huge birch tree. You can leave the letter by his door. If he's there and asks, say a passing wagoner gave it to you."

During the day Nachman thought about his trip. By evening he decided. He would delay no longer. Later that night he stepped out into the fresh night air. Crickets trilled. Insects, cats, a cow lowing: all of God's creatures were making music in the night. God's symphony. Suddenly he found himself before the open windows of the bes medresh. How had he come there? Had he blanked out for a minute or two? The curtains were drawn. The Hasidim evidently assumed that Nachman had retired for the night, for as Nachman passed, he heard someone saying:

"What's wrong with him? He can't sit still! No sooner is he back after a long stay in a *goyishe* city than he plans to leave us again. He's away far too much. It's not right."

"Yes, I agree. What kind of rebbe is it who *travels?* Hasidim travel. A rebbe stays home."

Nachman's heart, someone plucked it like a bass viol string. It vibrated. He said my words; those are my words he said. Who spoke my thoughts?

"Shh, what kind of talk is that?" said a third man.

"You know I'm right." It was the louder of the two critical voices. "You know it but won't admit it."

"Yes," someone else ventured. "He still misses a letter. The rebbe has always taught us to see signs. Maybe it's a sign to us that he's not perfect. Maybe what other Hasidic courts say of him is true. He's a sinner."

"Yes, he sins with his ideas!" someone whispered loudly.

"Not fit for leadership."

A smack. Someone's face had been slapped.

"That's for the rebbe. If he were here, he would have slapped your face himself, you impudent boor."

"Have you ever seen the rebbe lift his hand?" the slapped one said.

There was a scuffle of chairs and people moving, as if a fight were about to begin. And then, silence.

"No!"

"Then don't lift your hand, either."

Who could it be? Nachman wondered. It's starting, he thought. The rebellion. First no Amen, then no rebbe. Now coming to blows like in a gentile tavern. He tested the voice he heard. Set it up against faces he knew. But the curtain muffled the sounds. He had wanted to go into the bes medresh to see his Hasidim once more, but now was ashamed to enter. He did not want to embarrass the man, or shame himself. Arguments, rebellion, blows. Again the history of the world compressed into a short dialogue. And that Amen not uttered—it was as if God were telling Nachman that there were waves in his sea, disharmony in the music he created. And then he heard another voice.

"No," someone replied. "If the rebbe is going to Israel, there must be some great significance to it. Don't take such a hazardous journey lightly. Who knows? Perhaps salvation may come of it."

Who said that? Was it Nachman's heart speaking aloud, or had someone else said this? On the other hand, if he were a Hasid, he too would want his rebbe to be accessible. What kind of rebbe was not present to help, console, offer succor? But I, Nachman defended himself, devoted myself to the salvation of a people. Any rebbe can advise his Hasidim, but how many rebbes seek to penetrate the harmony of the spheres? Or stand, like common eavesdroppers, listening to words not intended for their ears? Nachman withdrew from the window. A sour feeling rose from his stomach to his mouth. He returned to his room.

Then, a timid knocking on his door. Perhaps the old woman bringing milk.

"Yes, who is it?"

"It is I, Rebbe, Nathan."

Nathan's eyes were tear-filled as he stepped into the room. So he's about to confess, Nachman thought. I should have recognized his voice. Why didn't I recognize it? Again the resemblance between himself and Nathan struck him. So this is how I look when I weep. Nachman knew he was afraid to confront him with the question: Are you the storyteller who impersonated me when I travelled to Vienna? Suspicion was bad enough, but an admission would be worse.

"What is it, Nathan?"

He wants me to stay. But I will go, Nachman thought. I must go. Prayers, incantations, were not efficacious. Milk and honey, the essence of Israel, were of no avail. My dreams of lust wrack my body and soul almost every night. Even if they stop for a few days, it is just a torment to make me believe they've gone. Then they begin again. I must go. To restore the missing letter. To hear God's whisper again.

Nathan gazed into Nachman's eyes and then down at his clasped hands. He looked ill at ease, and this discomfort sent waves to Nachman.

"Rebbe, I wanted to talk to you . . . I feel . . ."

"I know," Nachman said. "I feel it too. A strangeness. Instead of melodies, there is dissonance between us."

"Maybe I've been here too long," Nathan said quickly.

There. There was that chill again, as on the day he returned and saw Nathan after a long absence. How long can a man be expected to be subservient to another? He has to shape his own essence. A tiny rowboat, a miniature rowboat of fear and anguish, coursed through Nachman's body. It seemed to him that his name and essence were suddenly melting. *Not fit for leadership. He sins with his ideas.*

Nachman took his assistant's hand. As soon as he said, "I know what you did during my absence . . ." Nathan's hand began to tremble. Now he's told me what I wanted to know, thought Nachman. But why did he choose the region where I was travelling? Because, he realized, Nathan had assumed that I was going south to the Land of Israel, not west to Paris or Vienna.

". . . and I appreciate it. I left knowing that everything would run smoothly. As if you were another I, my alter ego."

Nathan looked down at the floor; he licked his lips. Then he directed his glance into Nachman's eyes, as if he were Nachman and Nachman were Nathan, the mirror reversed.

"You're not leaving because I'm leaving, are you?" Nachman asked.

Nathan laughed. "Why should I do that?"

"Then go. You have my blessings. Go for as long as you like." Every man must be himself and not another. He must be the person, as my friend Beethoven said, he's destined to be. "But I ask only one favor. Can you stay until I return? Then, when I come back, you can go for as long as you please, to as many places as you like. Is that agreed?"

Nathan was silent.

He's afraid of being my substitute. He fears temptation more than responsibility.

"I'm afraid," Nathan said. "Afraid of telling stories."

"I know. But don't be. I need your help while I'm gone. Can I count on you once more, Nathan—to be Nathan and not Nachman?"

"Yes," he whispered.

"Promise," Nachman shouted in an unearthly voice. "Promise to stay!"

Nathan paled, bowed his head.

Nachman lifted his chin gently.

"Some of the Hasidim are against my going. Have you heard?"

"No. I haven't heard a thing."

Nachman looked Nathan in the eye. He inspected his cheeks, looked for a vein swelling on his forehead. Looked for a betraying finger motion. Saw nothing.

"Maybe they're right in complaining. What have I done for them? I couldn't even fill a thimble with my deeds. Breathing, eating, sleeping here? Is that enough? Is merely being a descendant of the Baal Shem Tov enough? So, then, do I have your blessing to leave?" Nachman said with a slightly ironic tone, which he tried—too late—to withdraw.

Nathan either had not noticed, or was too kind to react.

"Even rebbes need blessings," Nachman whispered.

Nathan took a step closer. Nachman thought he would kiss him.

"Rebbe, go in peace and return in peace. May you have a good journey on land and sea, and if angels or magical birds come to transport you on their wings, then a pleasant journey too by air."

"Thank you. Now tell me: 'May God whisper to you again.'"

Nathan looked puzzled.

"Don't ask. Just tell me: 'May God whisper to you again.'"

"May God whisper to you again."

"Amen," said Nachman.

From Nathan's Diary

I looked at the dried inkwell on Nachman's table and thought of the Rebbe's imagination. The imagination he sought to revive by having God whisper to him.

"Rebbe, on your journey," I said, "think of tales. Come back to us with stories."

"They're sleepy as it is."

"Who? The stories?"

Nachman shook his head. "No, the people. Mothers tell stories to children to make them fall asleep. I tell stories to wake people up. But they fall asleep anyway."

"But that doesn't mean you'll stop telling stories." My voice hung in the balance between question and statement. I was hoping he would not say: "I won't tell any more tales." Because then *I* would have to start. And if I started I would not be able to stop.

She knocked on the door, brought warm milk, and said shyly: "I heard you're going. Alone. Take me with you. I too want to see the land that is holy."

"You're too old for the journey. When the Messiah comes, we'll all go together."

"I've travelled, even though I'm old. Look how far I've come to get here. But I'll go anyway. I'll see the land. No one can stop me. Please take me."

He didn't want to argue with her, but signalled the conversation was at end by closing his eyes.

After she left, he opened the door to the bes medresh. Nathan was sitting there, studying a text by candlelight.

"When I leave tomorrow morning, keep that superstitious old woman away. Imagine! She wants to come with me. Distract her. Think of something. I don't want an old woman's hysterics on the eve of my journey."

As he did on his first journey, he bade a subdued goodbye to walls and books, bed and chairs, then set foot outside. But he did not feel the surge of joy in going up to Israel. He was leaving a congregation behind, stripping them of soul, of music. Of mantle and light. But I shall return with an even finer light, he thought. I shall return with salvation; it is long overdue. The time has come.

He stood in the absolute silence of the dawn and suddenly heard again the first movement of Haydn's 100th Symphony. Just as he had when he travelled with Beethoven to visit Prince Lichnowsky. He stopped at the phrase Beethoven had singled out: at this point Haydn could rise no higher because he was a servant. Nachman closed his eyes. Vienna floated into view. Removed from Vienna, he saw the city more clearly than when he was there: the Danube Canal, which he had crossed countless times, amazed at the proximity of water and buildings; the magnificent opera house down the street from the Cathedral. He retrod the cobblestones of Vienna as he stood in the fields of Bratslav. He saw the children playing in the Prater. He realized with a pang that he knew Vienna better than Bratslav. Could he draw a map of Bratslav? No. It existed without him. But Vienna existed within him. In Vienna everyone spoke of the beginning of the 19th century. The year 1800. For him 1800 was 100 times *chai*. Life. And if he were to return to Vienna? He'd return to a fulfilling life. He would compose. His works would be heard. Perhaps he would take up residence with Prince Razumovsky and compose music that all of Europe would hear, melodies the world had never heard before. Could anyone in Bratslav understand this?

If wherever he set foot was Israel, then what difference did it make if he went west instead of east? Vienna too could be Jerusalem. Pass through defilement. That is what the Zohar said. Perhaps more of that was needed before he raised himself to heights. And the Prince's sister. Now she looked alluring, to the tune of Haydn's Symphony still moving in his mind. To see Beethoven again. To hear his compositions played by soloists and orchestras. Had it all been real? If an artist paints a picture, it remains forever—but music flees with the wind. Only memory remains. And yet there was a third choice. To go neither east nor west, but to stay right here and relinquish grandiose hopes. At the crossroads he looked north and east. From both directions carts were approaching. Mystical sign. Tested again.

He remembered last night's dream. Another journey, another dream. It was a relief of a kind, that dream, a respite from the dreams that pursued his body, lured his soul. He dreamt that King David spoke to him and blessed him with a safe journey. "God will give his angels charge over you and no evil shall befall you. You will tread upon lion and adder and rise above the serpents. You will call and God will answer. He shall be with you in trouble and deliver you. Every *aleph* is made of music. Soar on its wings. Take my book of Psalms and read it." Then the vision vanished.

Nachman looked eastward for a moment at the approaching cart. In the distance he saw the silhouette of Vienna. Memories increased, almost to the point of pain. Then a mist, a cloud, obscured the city. Nachman faced the brightening sun. The light blanked his memories. He turned slowly to the north and waited for a south-bound cart that would lead him to the land of every Jew's dreams.

Book Four

Days later, out under the open summer skies, clouds accented the arching blue. As he walked, the green of pines and clover was like velvet before his eyes. In front of him a large, yellow, spotted butterfly tasted a sunflower, then flew to a mignonette. Nachman too moved from place to place. Running away. The dreams, he thought, again the dreams. They destroy by night everything I achieve by day. Perhaps the lesson is: God made us as we are. We can only add dimension, not change nature.

But as soon as he left Bratslav, the dreams of forbidden love disappeared again. So that, *that* is the place of my defilement, the town I wanted to make a holy community. As he travelled south, toward Turkey, he tried to suppress memory with prayer. But could not erase the white curtains, the misty faces in the bes medresh, the complaining voices. If two people uttered such heresy aloud, who knows how many thought the same in their hearts? They said I sinned with my ideas. Ha! Nachman was startled by his outburst. He looked around. Walked on. The sun shone. The fields, squares of green and beige, showed careful farming. Haystacks shaped like mushrooms. In the grey distance, hills spun slowly in the heat. If the Hasidim only knew the true nature of my spiritual state, they would exile me.

And perhaps they have. But I am not in exile from myself.

Nachman closed his eyes for a moment. The summer scene of pines and clover was shut away. He contemplated himself. He could see his hat, his shoes, his hands. But he could not imagine his face. His face was a blank, an unfinished portrait. He shivered; in a fright, touched eyes, nose, cheeks. Another broken rung. Could others see that broken rung, that unimagined face?

One day he was near the city of his birth, Mezhibezh. He was tempted to go into the town he hadn't seen for years. Surely no one would recognize him in his workman's clothing. But he was afraid to hear zayde's admonition: Return. Do not undertake this journey. The time has not yet come. Afraid he would hear his grand-uncle Naftoli's warning voice: Fear Istanbul. But Nachman felt the time for salvation *had* come; he did not want to hear the word "Return." He avoided Mezhibezh; did not tempt visions.

In towns on the trade route to Istanbul, Nachman gathered information. From travellers, from merchants, from innkeepers, from a Jerusalem fund collector familiar with Istanbul. Before Nachman arrived in Turkey, he knew where to stay and where to pray. He learned how to book passage for a ship, how often ships sailed, which ticket agents to avoid. He was told that Istanbul, with 750,000 people, was one of the biggest cities in the world. He learned that Jews lived in the Galata quarter and, like the Turks, wore turbans and blue slippers. Above all, he was cautioned: the Turkish Jews were suspicious folk—it was best to keep one's distance from them. "They are business brokers," the fund collector said, waving a scrawny finger in Nachman's face, "and agents . . . of intrigue."

As he walked near the river, he expected to hear the city noises miles away. Yet two miles from the walls of Istanbul a desert-like silence reigned. The plain was quiet as a country village. Across the eastern horizon a team of oxen dragged a plow. In the water, on long narrow boats, Turks reclined on cushions and smoked long pipes. A Sabbath stillness pervaded the region.

And then, tranquility became whirlpool. He entered the capital of Byzantium. At the city gates, he looked up and saw what he saw, but could not believe his eyes. Did not want to look again, but against his will he raised his head. In silver dishes on ledges near the top of the gates, human heads were on display. Nachman shook his head. Sodom and Gomorrah. Yet people calmly come and go. And no one cries out, for shame, for shame? And he remembered Lichnowsky's threat, after Beethoven had slapped him.

On the streets beggars, beggars and chanters, the lame, the crippled, the mad. Not music, not Mozart in an elegant square, but from up and down a cacophony of voices greeted Nachman. From the ground, where cripples writhed and moaned with outstretched palms, to the top of minarets, beige in slant sunlight, where muezzins called the faithful to prayer. If one listened with half an ear the Arabic sounded like Hebrew. But Turkish, thick as dough, was full of *ek-mek* bursts. Nachman saw tight crowds on narrow lanes. Not at all like the broad boulevards in Vienna where walkers could dance in the streets. The throngs of Vienna had been pressed into an Istanbul vise. The Turks hawked pottery, pushed carts. On their hands they carried huge rounds of cheese, jugs of oil, baskets of almonds, walnuts and dried figs, and trays of pitta. Passersby jostled him, barrows nudged him. Bony donkeys grazed his arms and shoulders. He smelled spices, roasting rice, boiled honey. His appetite rose; he swallowed.

In the Galata district he almost took a room, but the tight grey leaden houses depressed him. He was tired. A heat, vest-shaped, pressed his ribs when he drew a breath. As he crossed the crowded bridge to the Hassa Kui quarter, he looked down into the murky water. Why should the river remind him of last night's thoughts? He found a small inn on a side street. In bed he floated on a cloud of darkness until he fell asleep. In dreams he wandered through the vast library of the Sultan; saw a vellum manuscript of the Book of Psalms, indited by King David. If you bring this book to the Land of Israel, Nachman heard, the People of Israel will be closer to salvation. Was it God's whisper again?

The next day he went down a steep street to a synagogue whose address he knew. Behind a stone wall lay a quiet courtyard, a world apart. Its well-tended garden had palm trees, yellow roses, a lemon tree, carnations. As Nachman stood by the gate, an old bandy-legged Turk in a soiled white turban and ragged grey robe pasted a poster on the wall. It bore the crimson crescent, the royal seal. Immediately, a crowd gathered. When Nachman turned back, he saw a tall, solidly built man with a blue fez leaning against the lemon tree. He smoked a long pipe and stared with curiosity at the crowd near the gate.

"Yehudi?" Nachman asked him. "Do you speak Hebrew?"

The man smiled; his eyes warmed. "Shalom," he said in his Sephardic accent.

"Sholem," Nachman said in his Ashkenazic one. "Will you have a minyan for the Afternoon Service?"

The man placed his right hand on his heart and bowed his head. A faint scent of anise wafted from him. "Yes, yes. Welcome," he continued in Hebrew. "Where is the visitor from?"

"From the north."

"You come from the north, and my family stems from the farthest ends of the west, like my Spanish ancestor, Yehuda Halevi."

"The famous poet and philosopher? A noble family line," said Nachman. He watched the gathering crowd anxiously. Some men now stood in the interior of the courtyard, but still the Turkish Jew puffed his pipe contentedly.

"Why is that poster attracting such a crowd?"

With a head motion, the man signalled Nachman to follow. He ambled slowly to the gate and looked at the poster. Nachman watched his face. The man pursed his lips, raised his eyebrows, scratched his cheek with the stem of the pipe.

"Hmm," he said in astonishment and moved his head diagonally a few times, as if saying yes and no simultaneously. "Very interesting. And with the royal seal too. The Sultan Selim must be in despair. His child is sick and he is turning to the public." The Turkish Jew took Nachman by the arm and walked back to the lemon tree. "The poster proclaims that anyone who cures her will get a fortune and be free of taxes forever. In other words: 'Up to half the kingdom,' as Ahasuerus told Esther."

Nachman's heart leaped. My pre-Vienna dream! Go to the big city and find a treasure. True, the dream had said Vienna, but do dreams know geography?

"What's the matter with the Sultan's daughter?"

The Turkish Jew put his pipe in his mouth for a few moments and regarded Nachman. "She apparently has a malady no one can cure. Not anything physical. The Sultan's men do not speak of it, but through our connections with the court it has come down to us." He bent close and quickly tapped his head.

"In story books," Nachman said, and remembered with a shiver the city gates, "if someone tries and fails with a Sultan, he may chop off your head."

"*My* head? No, no, first *your* head. This head stays right here. Between my fez and my neck."

Nachman apologized. "I didn't mean *your* head. I meant the head of anyone who undertakes a mission and fails."

The Turkish Jew laughed. "Oho! No, no. This is not a storybook world."

"Tell me. Who orders those heads to be displayed on silver dishes?"

"I see you worry a lot about your head. Are you interested in curing his daughter? Do you want to try? Are you a doctor? A philosopher? A musician?"

"Why musician?"

"Because the poster says knowledge of music is necessary. Do you play an instrument?"

"Isn't it time for the Afternoon Service?" Nachman said.

The Turkish Jew raised a finger. "I see you hesitate to answer my questions. I don't blame you. You've probably been warned about us Turkish Jews, warmhearted, hospitable, noble sons of Sepharad, but inquisitive and suspicious. Our friendship has hooks. True, we are like that, but not I . . . not I." He pulled a candy from his pocket and placed it in his mouth.

"Are Jews well treated here?" Nachman asked. "Is the Sultan a good king?"

"We are all friends. And as a friend let me tell you to be careful . . . By the way, how long are you going to stay here?"

"I don't know."

"Have you come via Greece?"

"No."

"Are you sure? Think! Don't answer right away."

Suddenly, a chant, quavering, rising and falling, split the air. It came from up above. Others joined the dolorous cantor. Now there were three, five, ten voices.

"What is that?" And then realized, just as the Turkish Jew said:

"The muezzins. The Moslem call to prayer. Every evening at this time . . . You say you're not from Greece?"

"No."

"Well, that's fine with me, but let me advise you to be careful. The Jews here are suspicious. Given the power of the Sultan, one should not be surprised. They always suspect visitors of being foreign agents."

"Why?"

"Because most of them are."

First Nachman thought the man was joking—but his expression did not change. So Nachman, inspired, cupped the palm of his hand around his mouth and said softly, "The walls have ears. Who knows but that the Sultan's spies are listening."

The Turkish Jew backed off. "We live at the mercy"—he raised his voice, placating all the secret agents listening—"of our glorious Sultan, long life and all honor to him, from his loyal servant David Hacohen. Now the Sultan Selim is in a bad mood because of his daughter, and so"—here his voice dropped—"we must be careful, ever on the alert."

Nachman turned and walked into the synagogue, followed by Hacohen. At the doorway, Hacohen excused himself and pressed ahead. He said something in Turkish to the others in the synagogue. Soon they all crowded around Nachman.

"Who are you?"

"Where are you from?"

"Jewish or a convert?"

"Where are you going?"

"How long are you staying?"

A man with a blue turban whispered into Nachman's ear. "Did Hacohen tell you he's related to Yehuda Halevi? Don't believe it! He's a descendant of the poet like I'm Queen Isabella's grandson."

"Ferdinand!" Hacohen called to the man with the blue turban, "why don't you lead the prayers tonight?"

Another told Nachman: "If you go to Israel bring me back a sack full of Eretz Yisrael dust so I can lay my head on it when I depart this earth."

"Don't do that," said David Hacohen. "Bendicho has already gotten so many sacks of Eretz Yisrael earth he can open up his own country."

"When did you leave?" asked one.

"Are you going to Israel?" asked another.

"Are you going to bring back dried dates and trade in them? How much is your price?"

"Yes and no," said Nachman. "All is likely." He looked for the charity box. It stood on a window sill. He took out a few coins. They clanked in the empty copper box.

"Guess where he's not from?" David Hacohen asked.

"Greece!" they chorused.

No modulation in Istanbul. The streets were noisy, the people loud, the smells overpowering. Fried fish, baked nuts, spiced, skewered lambs, breads baking over open hearths. Also, no lean men or women. No, the Turks could never be Bratslaver Hasidim. Quivering with fat, they rolled, they waddled as they walked. The women were veiled, the men had sleepy, lidded expressions. In Istanbul, the circle dominated, not the angle. Posters lined the route. I shall cure her, Nachman mused. And then the Sultan too, along with Napoleon, will be favorably disposed to Eretz Yisroel, which is a tiny dot in his empire.

In the inn he changed clothes. Now he held a walking stick and wore an elegant black cape, which he discovered several days after leaving Vienna, in the bottom of his bag, with a note attached: "This is not a gift, but a memento of Beethoven." He was proud to wear the composer's cape. As it flared behind him he floated, across several squares, on his way to the palace. He was a magician now, a wonder worker, a metaphysician. He entered the long formal garden that led to the Sultan's quarters. Here, for the first time, the luxury, the breadth, the openness reminded him of Vienna. All along the path stood groups of people watching who would enter to offer a cure. Nachman strode by; a princely feeling surged in him. He looked about. No long lines of prospective healers. Nor did he see any failed candidates being led to execution. Were they beheaded and disposed of by a rear entrance? A yellow-turbaned guard with a scimitar tucked into his belt stepped out of a booth.

"English, Deutsch, Español, Français, Russki, Polsku?"

Nachman did not want them to think he came from Russia, so he spoke in German.

"Who are you?" the guard asked.

"Benhabesht, the famous musician and metaphysician." Nachman spread the wings of his cape for effect. "I came to cure the Sultan's daughter."

Someone immediately translated this loudly into Turkish, upon which the crowd burst into laughter. Someone drew his finger across his throat in a slitting motion. More laughter. Nachman looked at them with disdain. Evidently it was a sport here to listen to the fools who came without talent or skills to seek reward. This is also a test. I was tested in Vienna and I am being tested here. Decades ago his grand-uncle Naftoli had died in Istanbul before reaching the Holy Land. The Besht got as far as Istanbul, even into the waters beyond, but was permitted to go no farther. They too were tested.

One of the officials standing near the guard booth approached. He inspected Nachman and gave an approving nod. He pulled out a sheet of paper and read in German. "The Sultan Selim is not only looking for an intelligent man, but a clever one. Any fool can be intelligent; only special fools are clever."

Nachman responded:

"His Highness shall find none cleverer than I, nor more modest."

The Turk pointed to the sky-blue palace a hundred yards away. "Follow the garden path to that central doorway. They speak your language there."

The domed roof of the palace was gilded. Blue and green, mauve and lilac tiles decorated with geometric designs, tendrils and leaves lined the walls. In the arched doorways, three large bronze doors were ajar.

Nachman stood at the central doorway. A swarthy man in an orange turban chewed sunflower seeds and casually spit the shells out of the side of his mouth. Two soldiers sat impassively on the floor.

"Hey you! Are you another doctor seeking gold?"

Nachman resented the impertinence. The hair on his forearms bristled. He sniffed, short of breath, and concentrated his anger into the blaze of his eyes. Without a word, Nachman stared at the man in the orange turban. The Turk's face froze. A sunflower shell wagged slowly at the tip of his tongue. He removed the seed with two fingers and held it.

"Are you applying to attempt to cure Her Highness?"

Nachman nodded like a king.

"Do you know music? If you don't, stop right here. Turn around and march back home." Then, catching himself, he added, "Those are my orders."

"Why is music so important to cure the Sultan's daughter?"

"Because she loves music and a way must be found to approach her with it."

"I know music." I once played a harp. Playing the harp, Nachman thought, runs in my family.

"Then listen to this . . ."

The Turk then began to sing a melody with Arabic half-tones.

"Do you know it?"

Nachman repeated it.

"How about this one?"

The second melody was even more intricate, but Nachman sang it with all its subtle trills.

The Turkish official then opened a side door and summoned someone. "If it pleases the kadi to sing."

An old, white-bearded musician entered, holding a zither. He sang a Moslem hymn in the minor mode with many cantorial dips and turns.

Nachman closed his eyes. As his fingers opened and closed expressively, he repeated the melody without the words.

The Turk in the orange turban took a deep breath.

"Ya Allah, there are not many who can sing the three songs! Now you may pass into the Sultan's chambers. These two soldiers of the Royal Guard"—at the snap of his fingers they jumped to their feet—"will lead you."

In the great hall the lights were dim. Torches burned in glasses on the walls. Thick were the green oriental carpets underfoot. Coal-burning braziers, generously spaced, gave off a cozy warmth. At the doors servants stood on guard.

The Sultan was seated on a broad red plush cushion. His dark, round, fleshy face could have been a baby's suddenly grown up. Pox scars, covered perhaps by an unguent, dotted his cheeks, chin, and forehead. Beethoven also had smallpox marks on his face. Wouldn't it be strange if the Sultan were suddenly to pull off a mask and reveal himself as a smiling Beethoven, pleased with his joke? But the eyes were different. Languid and sleepy, as though he spent his nights worrying about his daughter. When he spoke, an intermittent pallor crossed his face; he looked as if an illness passed over him like a quick cloud. His mouth opened as if to yawn; his eyes fluttered; it seemed as if he were about to drop off to sleep. In an arc behind him a dozen courtiers stood at attention. Floated a faint odor of burning incense.

A courtier stepped forward and told Nachman, "I will be your interpreter before His Highness."

The Sultan opened his eyes wide. Clever eyes, Nachman saw. When awake he is alert. An untamed power rolled out of his eyes.

Sultan Selim spoke a few sentences. His voice flowed like oil. Only a fat man, a regent in full control, could have such a harmonious voice.

Then the interpreter said, "The Sultan tells us that he who seeks to cure must also be clever. That will soon be determined. We have already learned that you know music. What experience have you in curing, asks His Highness?"

Nachman could not tell if the translator had rendered an accurate account. He used far fewer words. Perhaps the Sultan was more poetic and the translator spoke plain prose.

Nachman swung his cape. "I am the most famous metaphysician in the Greater Bratslav region, O Sultan of Sultans, O Sultan Selim. From miles away hundreds of people come to me to be cured of maladies physical and spiritual, metaphysical and metaspiritual. I've cured commoners and royalty, most notably the Princess Lizabeta. I know roots and herbs, grasses and flowers, and the medicinal properties of each. I know notes and the infinite spaces between the notes. I know letters and the miles of sounds and petals that curl around the letters. I can make letters fly and disappear. I know, I can see, the interstices of the human soul."

The interpreter began, but Selim waved him aside. "First of all, what is your name?" the Sultan asked in perfect German.

"Benhabesht."

"Where are you from? You're not a Turk. And you don't look like a typical European."

"Originally, way back, from Egypt."

"Do you practice Islam?"

Nachman took a chance with his reply. "No, Sire."

"Christianity?"

"No," Nachman said quickly, "as an ex-Egyptian metaphysician, I have a monocredal tradition."

"Yes. I believe I've heard of it."

"In Alexandria alone we have sixty religions."

"Very interesting, you Egyptians. Where did you learn German?"

"My ancestors, my kinfolk, travelled."

"It isn't pure German, right?"

"That is correct, Sultan. You have a perfect ear."

The Sultan's eyes nearly smiled. "Your German has an Eastern lilt, Benhabesht."

"We come from Eastern Egypt."

The Sultan weighed that; then—"If you're not a Moslem, how did you sing the kadi's hymn so perfectly?"

"I have perfect pitch. I am learned in music."

"What other special skills do you have?"

For a moment Nachman thought of showing the Sultan his special skill. In his mind he already saw himself rising slowly, enjoying the amazement of the Sultan and his court. But he controlled himself. No, I am not a magician, nor sorcerer, nor clown.

"The power of a clever mind," he bit off each word, "that can thwart presumed destiny."

The Sultan's leathery eyes gleamed. They seemed to say: I'll pull you down a notch.

"If you can answer these two questions, I will let you proceed. One: where do you look down to see up? Yes, you heard me. Where do you look down to see up? Two: where do you look out to see in? Answer, and I will believe that you can see beyond seeing."

"Do you want the answer now?"

The Sultan's lively brown eyes lit up.

"Why? Are you prepared to answer?"

"Well, you see," Nachman said, "in story books, when a king asks a wise man a riddle, he is usually given three days."

"That's precisely what you have." The Sultan's eyes gave a hint of a smile, as if pleased with Nachman. "Come back in three days with your answer."

Nachman did not have to levitate. Confident, he turned and walked away.

"Just a moment." The Sultan's lethargic voice pulled him back. "I understand you are afraid . . . in case your cure does not succeed . . . No, no, don't ask who told me. News travels quickly in Istanbul. Just let me assure you that there is no penalty for failure."

Nachman licked his lips. His mouth was dry. "You see, in all the tales I've read, if a doctor fails to cure a princess, he is put to death. . . ."

"But you are not in a story now."

In the tumult of streets again. For a moment he had been somebody; now, once again, he was entirely unknown, unable to speak the local language. If a cart came and knocked him down, no one in Istanbul would know that a Nachman who had heard God's whisper and sought salvation had been there. He watched the streets, stayed close to the walls. Then a sudden fear tapped, like a bird's sharp beak. He had to stop and lean against a building to ease the shaking of his body, to shoo the bird away. I am far from home. Alone. Without language, culture, knowledge of the country. How could zayde have survived here? He breathed deeply, infused calm into himself, ambled through the din of the market.

No one knew where Nachman slept. Even a spy wouldn't have been able to follow him. For he weaved in and out of the countless lanes and alleys of the bazaar. The sounds and smells enticed him. He lingered, absorbing its music. Just as every man was a world unto himself, so was every corner of the bazaar. Here beans and nuts; there dried fruit; further the smell and oven heat of bakeries. A right turn under an archway—the donkey market and the leather stalls. To an outsider the bazaar seemed relaxed, pervaded by a quiet hum of music. But it was a coiled spring. Merchants, even youngsters, sat amid their merchandise, their wary eyes moving like candle flames. Nachman moved on. Copperware and hammer blows sounded in syncopated rhythms; little children banged designs in bowls and trays, their faces reflected in the shining metal. Nachman liked the vessels. He was tempted to pick one up but he had to keep moving. To Israel. The Land of Israel.

Another turn, and spices: mounds, bags, wagonloads of it. The assistants were dusty with the colored powder, beige, red, ochre. Fat, mustached shopkeepers in billowing white aprons stood and watched. Nachman sneezed, quickened his pace. Veiled women with trays of sweet-smelling cakes on their heads passed him. He pressed against a wall to make way for donkeys with baskets on both flanks.

On the third day the heat of the city weighed on him. Nachman walked along a broad boulevard that led to the palace, seeking shade. He thought of the river back home, imagined floating on the raft in the river as unknown eyes watched from behind a tree. He knows whose eyes they are. Lizabeta's. He smells her hair. Lizabeta. Invader of his sinful dreams. He gazes down at the water. Sees rolling clouds break the stillness of the water mirror. Nachman snapped his fingers with delight. Some men on the street turned. So that's it. And the two riddles are obviously connected. Where do you look out to look in? He imagined himself in his room at night. He walks to the window, looks out in the black night, seeking peace and tranquility, seeing his own anxiety instead. Nachman quickened his pace and smiled again.

The Sultan also smiled when Nachman said, "Where do you look down to see up? Down at water to see clouds. Where do you look out to

see in? Out a window of a lit room at night to see your own reflection."
Not only did the Sultan smile, he actually laughed. His cheeks shook; a look of merriment invaded those cautious, oil-gleaming, leather brown eyes. But he did not deign to shake Nachman's hand.

Nachman took a deep breath, loosened his cape.

The Sultan's huge reception hall was dimly lit. The glowing braziers exuded heat and mystery. Servants and guards stood discreetly along the walls. Everyone watched the Sultan of Byzantium.

"Clever. Very clever. That is right. It is as if Allah himself has sent us down his blessings. You have earned the right to see if you can cure my child. Musical and clever. Yes, you may proceed."

"Sultan Selim, may I ask what the Princess suffers from?"

The Sultan beckoned with a finger. Nachman drew close, bent over to hear his soft words. "We do not speak of it publicly, and I shall ask you, on your honor—"

"Yes, of course."

"It is forbidden to reveal it to anyone."

"As you know, I am a stranger here, Your Highness, on a temporary visit. I know no one and talk to no one."

"That is excellent. You will easily diagnose Edirna's malaise as soon as you are brought in to her. The diagnosis is simple; the cure evades us. All possible help will be given to you . . . a full range of potions and medicines and salves . . . Now why don't you ask about the reward? Doesn't that interest you?"

"But I haven't cured her yet. The reward is given not for attempting, but for curing."

"You are clever indeed. The other doctors . . ." he stopped and signalled to Nachman to speak.

"Sire, I understand there is a fortune. But I am not interested in it. Not in money, not in possessions, not land, not power. If I am successful and you feel I have earned the reward, then I shall ask only for a small item—one book from your fabulous royal library."

"Is that all?" the Sultan laughed. "Do you hear that, chamberlains?" And Sultan Selim spoke for a few moments in Turkish. "A book? Only a book? Granted. Granted willingly."

Nachman was led to Princess Edirna's room. The door closed softly behind him. The silk-lined walls contrasted oddly with the sparse furnishings: one table, one small sofa, no chairs. Dishes were strewn on the floor. Nachman did not know how old the princess was, what she looked like, what ailed her. He looked around. Saw no one. The table near the wall was draped with a white cloth that reached the floor. It reminded him of the table back home in the bes medresh where he sat and told the Hasidim tales. Once upon a time there was a sick princess. Doctors were consulted but they could not cure her. One day, from a foreign land, came a prince, a healer, handsome of countenance and sharp of mind . . . But what if the princess were another Lizabeta? Where would the tale go from there?

In a corner of the room hung a curtain. He pushed it aside. It enclosed a small, closet-like space in which stood a chamber pot. At the far end of the closet, near the floor, was a foot-high wooden door, from which servants evidently removed the pot without entering the room.

"Hello!" he said tentatively. Looking up at the ceiling was foolish. But perhaps Edirna thinks she's a pigeon and flew up to a lamp. Coo-coo-coo! Impatient, he turned swiftly. Saw no one. Except table and sofa and a window whose light was muted by brocaded silk curtains.

"Are you here? I am! Hello! Edirna, where are you?"

A dog barked. If the dog is near, can the mistress be far off? The barking mingled complaint and satisfaction. A well-fed dog. Of course. Amid this splendor and wealth, no dog goes hungry. Nachman wondered if the princess might be hiding on a balcony. He walked to the window. No barking there.

The dog noises commenced again, from under the table. Whistling to the pup, Nachman lifted the edge of the tablecloth and—he could not believe his eyes—saw a young woman crouching under the table. She snarled at him, raised her head, and growled. Nachman's heart stopped. Oh, dear God, first human heads on silver platters and now a king's daughter who thinks she's a dog. He looked at her with pity, but did not move or say a word. The snarl soon turned into a pathetic bark. Nachman planned to talk calmly, reasonably, to use logic, persuasion, as he would with a recalcitrant Hasid. What to do now? Everyone who aspires to salvation is tested. Perhaps this is my test. Then suddenly he had an idea.

He sat down on the floor next to Edirna and began barking softly. Into his barking he put all the nuances of human speech. He introduced himself, said where he'd been, where he was going. He had his sorrows, his malaise, but he had hopes too. *Never despair* was his motto. The world was a very narrow bridge. The main thing is not to fear. Barking lightly, plaintively, merrily, he told his story, then asked about her. At first he barked as though it were make-believe, as though he knew they were both playacting. But then he saw the dull, doggish look in her eyes, devoid of human intelligence, and he began to bark again. He whined and yelped, pleased with the musical variations of his yipping sounds.

In response, Edirna moved from under the table and barked back. Even though she had been a dog much longer than Nachman, her range of expression was limited. She had deep blue circles around her eyes. Like her father, she was chubby and thick-lipped; lifeless eyes marred her pleasant face. She barked and extended a paw as if to play. Nachman smiled and barked softly, softly, ever softer, until the barking became a poem, a melody, a lullaby, and the princess stretched her limbs and fell asleep.

Nachman stepped out into the antechamber and told the three guards, "Please take me to His Highness."

"At once, doctor."

A few minutes later Nachman stood before Sultan Selim.

"Now do you understand?" Selim said.

Nachman nodded.

"What is she doing now?"

"Sleeping on the floor."

"Sleeping? During the day? How did you manage that? Did you give her drugs?"

"No, Sire. Nothing at all."

"Edirna never napped during the day and she sleeps fitfully at night. That is another problem."

"I sang to her."

"Sang? Are you telling the truth?"

"Of course, Sultan. Why should I lie?"

"Ever since the onset of her illness, the princess abhors human music. We tried the music she loves, but she reacts violently. She breaks into fits of wild barking."

"Then why did you want someone who could sing?"

"Suppose her condition improves? We must be prepared. We cannot predict anything with this ailment."

"How long has it been?"

"Two months. More. Ten weeks. Doctors have prescribed potions and pills. The royal physicians have been dismissed. Snake charmers from India, magicians from Persia, spiritual healers from Rhodos have come and gone. Nothing has worked."

Nachman did not ask where they went.

"Was she afraid of dogs . . . or was she particularly fond of one?"

The Sultan frowned. His brown eyes darted into life like a furry animal awakened—a furry animal with sharp little teeth. "And she is such an intelligent girl. Private tutors. Speaks English, French, German, Arabic. Could be an ambassador, if she were a man. We tried leeches and herbs . . . Do you think it's hopeless?"

"Hopeless? Why use that word? Not at all hopeless. My guiding principle is: never despair. But I need help and time. I think I—but no, I don't want to anticipate, or raise hopes; but I do need your cooperation."

"Can the ruler of half the world not provide that? What is it you wish?"

"First of all, a piano."

"A piano?"

"You said she loves music. I need a piano. Secondly, I want a week's supply of washed, uncut, raw vegetables and fruits—"

"She has been eating meat daily."

"Meat is dog's food. That's just what she should *not* be eating. It deepens the dogness. I want raw fruits and vegetables served on two trays, along with a flask of water for each day and two new dishes never before used, and a never-before-used paring knife. And I don't want to be disturbed for at least seven days."

The raw power of the Sultan's eyes rose. He gave out a sarcastic laugh.

"Under no circumstances will I permit that. It is against our tradition, Benhabesht. We send someone in to wash her daily."

"So she will go unwashed for a few days. You want your daughter cured. You have been depressed and your mind is not on your empire. You want very much to have your daughter restored to normality. I abhor depression. It is not the natural state of man. So if you want me to help, I must spend the next few days with her. Alone. Otherwise, everything I gain by day will be lost by night. If our treatment is interrupted, it may take years. You want your daughter whole, and quickly."

The Sultan nodded.

"I assure you, no harm will come to her. If you hear her protest, come in and behead me. But I must be alone with her. There must be no interruption."

The Sultan, still sitting crosslegged—Nachman had never seen him erect—tapped his fingers on the red cushion. His eyes were sunk in his head, his hands in his lap.

"Do you trust me, Your Highness?"

The Sultan looked into Nachman's eyes. Nachman looked back. Could not tell what lay behind those leathery oriental eyes. Nachman enveloped the Sultan with his glance.

"I trust you. But beware of false moves."

"When can I expect the piano?"

"Tomorrow morning. And the trays of food and water and clean utensils, just as you wish."

Edirna slept.

He crawled under the table. His hand grazed an uneven surface on the floor. A cut in the wood. Gently, he tapped his fingers as though slowly playing a scale. A square, a trap door. Curious, he lifted it carefully. Put his hand down, felt steps. He lowered himself till his feet touched stone. Counted five deep steps until he came to a door, then quickly, on tip toes, returned. Does someone come up the steps at night to lie with her and then leave in the morning? If a woman could come to him in his dreams, why couldn't it happen to Edirna in waking? He wondered where the passageway led. If I go down and open the door, my journey will start again. I will travel through Russia and Turkey until I arrive at the outskirts of a large city. Its noise will overwhelm me. I will see a poster proclaiming that the local ruler has an ailing daughter whom no one can cure. I will enter her room, crawl under the table, and see a trap door. I will lift it and it will lead back home. Or perhaps these steps lead to Israel. Perhaps this is the entrance to the magic cave, the fabled short cut to the Land of Israel that Jews have dreamed about for centuries. Perhaps *this* is why I'm here. This is why I've come.

Edirna stirred. He lowered the trap door and moved away from under the table. She scampered back to her favorite spot. He lay awake, listening for sounds of an illicit assignation behind the white cloth. In vain. He heard only her breathing. That too, even when she slept, was dog-like, rapid, with an occasional sibilant, nasal whine.

When Edirna fell asleep, Nachman crawled under the table and slowly raised the trap door. Heart beating, he bent down and listened. Silence. He descended step by step. Before him the door; he felt a latch. Aha. This meant that no one could come in, only leave. He unhooked the latch, opened the door, stepped into a long, decorated hallway. The silence hummed. The door had been so cleverly installed as part of arabesque molding on the wall, it was impossible to discern the presence of an opening. Who knows when it had been made? Perhaps generations ago some Sultan had cut this now forgotten secret doorway for access to a chamberlain's wife. Every few feet in the hallway large niches for lamps and lanterns were gracefully indented into the walls, which were painted with green and blue tendrils. At the sound of footsteps, Nachman stepped into a niche, out of sight. Just where the carpet ended, he heard a door open and close. He saw something strange. A man in a fez gave a knife to someone in a doorway. Nachman saw only the hands of the receiver. The man in the fez clasped the other man's fingers around the haft, as if providing him with sight by touch. Perhaps that is the knife that cut the heads. The man with the fez took a few steps in Nachman's direction. Nachman pressed against the wall. The heat of the lamp warmed his face. What would he do if caught? Say he fell down a trap door? Nachman edged his face away from the hot lamp. The footfalls receded. The man with the fez had evidently changed his mind.

Nachman retraced his steps. My God, where was the door? All the panels looked alike. A hot flush of panic swept over him. His heart, he heard its pounding echo in the hallway. Finally he touched and found the panel. Then, a second fright. Perhaps the door is latched shut, he thought. It was a trap—and this was to be his tomb. As soon as he had gone into the hallway, Edirna had run down the steps and locked the door. But he opened it without difficulty, hooked the latch, and climbed up the stone steps. Home. Nachman laughed bitterly. When one is a dog, even under the table is considered home.

Crouching on all fours, he growled at Edirna; she barked back. He lay on his back, kicked his legs, righted himself, chased his tail until the room spun—but still the tail was out of reach. He lapped water from the dish. Rolled on the floor, barked, yipped, whined. He watched her do the same. I am sinking lower and lower, he thought. I am becoming, I have become, a dog. But I know who I am. From the depths of my defilement I shall rise. One must sink low in order to rise higher. This state is just a ship. I am sailing forward in time until I reach the ship. The rowboat on the river when I was a lad; the raft on the river when I looked down to look up took me farther. This room, this palace, this event lead me to the real ship that will carry me to the Land of Israel. Each step is a predestined rung on the ladder of salvation.

He pushed the tray of food under the table and ate there, sloppily, slurping, slobbering over the bites. He gulped the water greedily. Heard a knock on the door. The princess scrambled under the table and whined. Nachman lowered the tablecloth.

From behind the door a man called: "The piano."

Nachman rose, unsteady at first on his feet. Walked with uneven gait to the door, opened it. Two men pushed in a piano. Not wishing to talk, not knowing if he could still make human sounds, he signalled: close the door after you. Since his conversation with the Sultan, Nachman had not said a word. He sat at the piano and hummed as he softly played Hasidic melodies, then switched to Beethoven's country dances and some of the master's variations on his niggunim.

Edirna did not bark, but she breathed heavily. Nachman played a few of his own melodies, which made him long to compose more. He remembered Beethoven's room, Razumovsky's palace, where that woman in the ivory gown hovered. Was Vienna a dream? Is Istanbul a dream? Was Bratslav a dream? Was Nachman, standing on his two feet, climbing a ladder, also a dream?

Wherever he went in this world was a dream. But then there was a problem. If wherever he went was Israel and wherever he went was a dream, then Israel too was a dream.

What is not a dream in this world?

He crawled up to the princess.

"Edirna, do you like music?" he barked tenderly.

She blinked. Nachman thought he saw tears in her eyes. Were those eyes more human now?

Nachman scrambled back to the piano and picked out three melodies he had heard from the Muslim cantor. Edirna listened and fell asleep again.

One day, then another. They both ate vegetables and fruits. Nachman gave her the daily rations. At first she left most of the food untouched; he forced himself to eat hers too. Then, as she grew hungrier, she finished everything on the tray. Once, Nachman tilted his head back and said, "Coocooreecoo!" He crowed like a cock; but the princess frowned a doggish frown, as if to say, whoever heard of a dog crowing like a cock?

A few more times the Sultan's daughter stuck out her paw to him, but he retreated each time. Lately, her dead eyes seemed to be resurrecting.

Otherwise, no change in her. Edirna barked, crouched under the table, bayed plaintively into the air, ate like a dog. On the fifth day she scampered up to the piano, put one hand on the chair and with the other banged a cluster of jarring notes. She yelped happily and crawled away. Nachman too barked with delight, but avoided the piano. He lost count of when last he'd touched it.

Hours, days, melted. Nachman had become a dog. True, a dog does not play piano. A dog does not have foresight. Still, he ate, drank, slept on the floor. How easy it was to be a dog. Why hadn't anyone thought of it before? This princess was a genius. You ate, slept, were fed. The phrase, "A dog's life," expressed disdain. If he could only speak, he'd tell the world what joy it was to be a dog in the palace. No more tefillin; synagogue neglected. Prayers unintelligible, in language neither Hebrew nor doggish—a language like the undecipherable script he once dreamt of. No responsibilities. Yet he remembered David's Psalms in the library. But what need has a dog of Psalms? Do dogs say Tehillim? He heard a note on the piano. For days he had not gone near the piano; but Edirna, with rascally delight, frequently ran up, banged once or twice, more and more often a single note or two, not dissonant clusters, and then ran away. What greater affirmation was there than playing piano? Even if, as back home in Bratslav, it is only a paper keyboard that makes soundless music. And reciting Psalms makes one human too. Psalms draw one up. You know, dear God, that deep in my soul I am a human. But it is less of a headache being a dog.

On the seventh day, Nachman heard a clatter around Edirna's tray. She pushed it away. Her eyes shone from within. Her bark half-hearted, make-believe. Nachman was still bent over his tray, devouring the vegetables and slurping the water.

Suddenly, the girl rose on her haunches and, as though awakening from a trance, stood. She put her hands behind her back, straightened it with difficulty. Edirna lifted her chin and made a series of noises. Nachman assumed she had barked—and barked back. But then realized that her flippant growl was rusty Turkish coming out of vocal cords long unused to human speech. Again he barked and attacked his tray with a hungry yelp.

But she was speaking.

She tried English, French, German. Upon hearing her speak German, Nachman barked joyfully.

"Get up," she commanded. "What's the matter with you? Is that a way for a grown man to act? You ought to be ashamed of yourself." She bent down to him. "Up! Up on your feet!"

From the distance he heard her faint voice. The words were soft, garbled, as though spoken through water.

Nachman continued barking. "I like it here. It's pleasant. No responsibilities. No weight on my shoulders. No community. No Hasidim. No dreams. No God's whisper. No salvation."

"Get up at once, do you hear?"

Nachman whined, entreated; have pity. As a dog he'd have no more concerns. Leave salvation for others. She would care for him, feed him, play piano for him. The mystics believed in transmigration of souls. Perhaps this was the destiny of his soul, its final form.

"Up, up this minute!" As if reading his mind, she went to the piano and picked out a simple melody. "You are a man, in the name of Allah, not an animal."

The music, the music. The music curled into his ears. He imagined Beethoven, the noblest of men, coming on a tour of Turkey and being shown the famous man-dog, who had cured—and assumed the illness of—the princess. Suppose she began to scream at him. Just suppose she screamed and the guard posted at the door with the scimitar rushed to execute judgment before he heard a word of exculpation. A dog's death.

Nachman barked once, half-heartedly, almost mocking a bark, then with an inner shudder he leaped back into manhood with a cry of joy. For a moment he wanted to run to her, embrace her, take her by the hands, swing her around in a dance of celebration. But no, this too was a test. This too was a test—and he had passed the test. He looked at the princess. Edirna seemed awake, alert, alive. The pointy, canine features had softened and her round face was pretty now. He could have been tempted. Alone with the woman for seven days, he never once thought of her, dreamt of her, as a woman. He was beyond that now. Once, with Lizabeta, his body had rebelled against his spirit, but now he took control and put the evil yetzer in its place. Now the way would be clear. He had sunk into defilement, into sin, into dogdom—and had risen. Blessed is He who cures the sick. Now he was rising again, climbing that ladder made of sunbeams and silk, of notes and letters, of petals and songs. He would fly upward with his musical *aleph*.

The world is a narrow bridge, which he had safely crossed.

A spurt of energy coursed through his legs. He wanted to dance. Joy is a mitzva. Dance is joy. How long was it since he had danced? He heard music. Not a Hasidic niggun, but a Haydn symphony with all its rhythmic elegance. Yes, in one leap he had gone from dog to man. He leaped again, now to the music. The princess drew back, frightened. Ay, he cried, ay ay ay, and moved his legs, spun his body, floated legs apart, waved his arms, snapped his fingers, stamped his foot, leaped up up up, again, staying in the air longer than he should have. He looked at the Sultan's daughter. Saw another face there. Closed his eyes, could not undo the image. The blonde hair was there. She smiled at him, and he smiled back at her. Danced for her. In his dance of celebration, he knew there was defeat; into the mitzva of curing the sick was intertwined, with subtle serpent's venom, the tiny curl of sin. His heart sank. He thought he had uprooted Lizabeta as zayde, the Baal Shem Tov, had uprooted despair. But she was there. And now he was not dreaming. He could not blame it on dreams beyond his control. He was awake, seeing her face on the face of the princess. He leaped and danced, could not stop his liberating movements. But, dancing, he knew he was still a dog, had not really risen, still could not read all the letters, still could sink down again and lap water from the bowl, still had not yet reached the Land. One was always far away until one set foot on her soil. Despite the dream there was no divine promise that he would succeed. Again he had fallen, and again would have to rise.

He stopped. Felt the perspiration on his face, inside his shirt. He breathed quickly. Shovels and picks worked in his chest. He coughed. How many times in a moment *can* a man rise and fall? Exhausted, he wanted to sink to the floor, but knew that if he did he might not rise again, but crouch and bark, whine and hide behind the white cloth. Forever, perhaps. He had no strength to rise from the floor again. It was so good to rest. Legs shaking, he girded his will, stood and coughed into his sleeve.

Over his elbow he glanced at Edirna. She watched him, no longer frightened, fully awake now, smiling, as if pleased with Nachman's dance.

Nachman ran to the door, opened it, and cried, "Call the Sultan. His daughter. The Sultan," he roared in a cavernous voice. "Call the Sultan."

The Sultan came. For the first time Nachman saw him on his feet. He had a rolling, waddling gait. A troubled walk, grave mien, eyes on guard. Selim no doubt thought his daughter's end had come. Nachman jumped, trembling, spun about, almost danced again. Where was his cape? He would have loved to swirl his cape; instead, turned an imaginary one.

"Cured! Your Highness, your daughter, Edirna! Cured!"

The princess stepped from her room into the antechamber. At once the Sultan's face changed. He beamed, face flushed. An incredulous look; mouthing a certain phrase in Turkish again and again. With open arms he rushed to his daughter, embraced and kissed her. A servant ran up with an ewer of water and towels. Nachman and Edirna washed their faces and hands.

"Music . . . musicians," the Sultan commanded.

Within minutes, a wedding-like procession made its way through the great hall. Cymbals and cornets, zithers and baglamas, tambourines and ouds played as the Sultan and his daughter proceeded, followed by Nachman and the royal entourage. A servant ran up and draped Nachman's cape over his shoulders.

From an outer door, a chamberlain ran toward the Sultan with a message.

"Sire, the Ambassador is here."

Before the Sultan could speak, a side door opened and the ambassador walked in. Seeing Selim, he bowed low. Nachman looked once at the well-dressed man and did not know whether to keep his cape on to enhance the disguise, or take it off, for fear that the ambassador, if he had forgotten him, would recognize the cape. Nachman folded it and held it in his hand. Suddenly, the symbolic significance of Beethoven's gift struck him. The mantle. Indeed, like Elijah's gift to Elisha. Continue to compose, said the composer's cape. With the musicians playing, the Ambassador paid no attention to Nachman—he did not even look his way—but beamed at the Sultan.

"What a welcome, your Highness! The Kingdom of Austria appreciates this most royal musical welcome. I shall write at once to the Emperor about the warmth of your reception."

The Sultan nodded. "We know how to welcome guests in Turkey, Prince Lichnowsky."

The two men shook hands. Lichnowsky cast a glance at the Sultan's escorts. His eyes rested for a moment on Nachman, hesitated, then passed on. Perhaps he won't remember me after all, Nachman thought.

"Did you wish to see me immediately?" the Sultan asked.

"Yes, your Excellency, on a state matter of utmost urgency. About the grave situation in Palestine. Napoleon, that dog! . . ."

The Sultan waved once. Everyone began moving quickly. Musicians, servants, chamberlains, in a vortex away from the Sultan.

"Escort the princess to her suite," Selim commanded, then turned to Nachman. "You stay."

Nachman quickly grasped Lichnowsky's intent. He was seeking an alliance; he wanted the Sultan to fight back, not desultorily, with the indolent local forces in Palestine, but with a full commitment, so that Lichnowsky could avenge the loss of his ancestral lands in Graz.

"And this," Nachman heard, "is the noted healer, Benhabesht, who has performed a miraculous service for our house . . . Prince Lichnowsky."

Nachman and Lichnowsky shook hands. The Prince stared at Nachman's face.

"I believe we've met," Lichnowsky said with an undertone of sarcasm not evident to the Sultan. "Healer? I thought you were a composer . . . I didn't even get your name then, did I? Or if I did, I've forgotten it." Then, to Selim: "I didn't know, Sire, that he was a healer. But he did save my life in Graz . . ."

"Yours too?" the Sultan interposed, turned to Nachman. "Then your reputation is indeed worldwide."

Nachman looked down modestly.

". . . when a brutish composer friend of his almost killed me. I never did thank you, Benhabesht, for restraining your friend."

"Despite what you did . . ." Nachman said and stopped, but Lichnowsky spoke over his words, saying quickly: "May I speak to your Highness?"

"You can speak in his presence. I consider him a member of our household . . . Just a moment, please. You must be thirsty!"

The Sultan clapped; a servant appeared whom Selim drew aside.

Lichnowsky stepped up to Nachman.

"Are you his advisor?"

"Well, as you heard, I have helped him."

"Please accept my apologies for having to return home in that downpour that night, but our friend Beethoven is really impossible."

"You ought to apologize to him. Exposure to that rain has irreparably harmed his hearing."

"You saved my life."

"But you ruined his. Beethoven is going deaf."

"We're talking about you," the Prince said stiffly.

The Sultan approached.

"Do you have influence over the Sultan?" Lichnowsky whispered.

"Come," said Nachman, "the Sultan is summoning us."

Selim reclined again on his red cushion. An attendant brought a brazier of coals closer. The proximity of light accented the pox marks on the Sultan's face. Another servant carried a tray of drinks.

"What is your wish, Prince?"

"As you know, Sire, the situation in Palestine is worsening. Napoleon's desire for conquest is unlimited. Now he is biding his time in a fortress in Northern Palestine. If he keeps advancing he will block our trade routes to the East. Yours and ours! We must stop Napoleon with all the forces at our disposal before it is too late."

The Sultan looked at Nachman.

Lichnowsky looked at Nachman.

Nachman felt that the sides were drawn; he and the Sultan against the Austrian prince. Now Nachman was on the ladder. But what if in the subtle and surprising course of human relationships the sides shifted? After all, they were both more powerful than he. Who was Nachman? He had only cured the daughter. Suppose Lichnowsky discovered he was a Jew? Wouldn't the two unite against him?

Lichnowsky pleaded silently. He wants his castle and vengeance against Napoleon. Austria does not interest him. Yes, Napoleon is a conqueror; that's why Beethoven withdrew his dedication of the Third Symphony. But, on the other hand, Napoleon has permitted the Jews to settle in Palestine, which neither the Moslem Turks nor the Christians had allowed.

"Austria," the Prince was saying, "is prepared to offer you an alliance, if we send massive joint forces to Palestine to destroy that dog."

Nachman held his cheek with three fingers, sent silent signals to the Sultan. The clever Sultan noticed.

"Think over your kind offer, Prince. Come back in three days." Here the Sultan glanced swiftly at Nachman. Nachman read a private message in his eyes. "You have had a long, arduous journey to reach our land. Perhaps your offer is too rash. Think it over. No, no. No more on that now . . ."

"But time is of the essence. Ships are leaving today, tomorrow. They could be loaded with men and weapons."

"Here in the East, Ambassador, time moves slowly . . . Go home and rest . . . and I will think it over too."

After Lichnowsky's departure, the Sultan asked:

"Well, what do you think?"

"I am neither ruler nor ambassador, Your Highness."

"But you are a clever man. You have done what others could not do. I permit you to speak. No—" the Sultan's sleepy brown eyes danced— "I urge you to speak."

"Do you like music?"

"Very much."

"And your daughter has inherited your taste."

"Yes, of course."

"What would you do if someone tore up the only copy of the music to a hymn like this?" And Nachman repeated the kadi's beautiful song. "And no one else knew the melody."

"I would display his head on the city walls."

Nachman's heart sank; a sour feeling curled through his abdomen.

Selim narrowed one eye. "I understand. So Lichnowsky destroyed music."

Nachman bit his lips.

The Sultan shook his head. "A man like that cannot be trusted. He may act purely for selfish reasons. I'm thinking out loud. If we don't tie up Napoleon in Palestine, he'll get tired and move on to more important prizes: Russia. Perhaps he'll get that big bear's paws off Istanbul and the Bosporos Straits . . . It's settled."

Dear Beethoven, Nachman wrote a letter in his head: I've succeeded in paying Lichnowsky back for his brutality.

"But let's not forget the reward . . . You have done the impossible . . . Come, you can choose anything you like."

The Sultan rose. Guards and servants standing by the walls converged on him. He signalled them to wait.

"Follow me, Benhabesht. I want to show you something."

Selim led Nachman into a narrow underground passageway without daylight or windows. Glass-encased candles and lamps lit their way. Rugs the colors of the rainbow were scattered on the floor. I've been here before, thought Nachman.

"My private passage," the Sultan said.

The rugs stopped just before they reached a door. As the Sultan was about to open it, something tweaked at Nachman's heart. His hand was quicker. He restrained Selim's. A blaze of fury crossed the Sultan's face.

"Please," Nachman said. "The man inside has a knife. Be careful."

"Can you see through doors?"

"Sometimes . . . You haven't been here for six or seven days."

"That's true. How did you know?"

"I told you I was a metaphysician."

"I've been too busy with affairs of state. I've had to neglect other affairs."

The Sultan knocked.

"Yes?" came the reply.

"Fatim. It is I. I have some guests here. Come out."

"Yes, Your Highness." A fat man in a white robe came slowly out of a tiny cubicle. "But you never knock, Sire."

"Hold up your hands, Fatim."

Fatim obeyed. The dull, blank look on his face did not change.

At once, Selim slapped his face with all his might. The crack echoed down the hallway. Off balance, the man put his hand to his face, as Selim swiftly ran his hands over his body and found the knife tucked into the folds of his robe.

Again and again Selim slapped Fatim. He shouted one phrase at him. Fatim turned white. He fell on his knees. He seemed to shriek, "No no no." Again the Sultan spoke. Fatim groped for, found, and kissed the Sultan's feet. Selim drew back in disgust. He asked a question. Fatim spoke softly, quickly, in monosyllables, reciting a litany that sounded like a list of names.

The Sultan turned to Nachman. "You've broken a conspiracy . . . My trusted guard!" Selim said with venom. "I'm more indebted to you than ever . . . Come, this is what I wanted to show you."

Nachman stepped into Fatim's tiny room. The Sultan snapped his fingers at Fatim. Cowering, he made his way in and opened the other door.

Nachman did not remember what struck him first, the sight he saw or the steambath dampness. He thought he had been granted a vision of heaven or hell. The smell of hot water overwhelmed him. He saw a long pool. Scores of young women sat at the edges or played in the water.

Some were naked, others wore skimpy gauze shifts. When the girls came out of the water, they dried themselves with towels and then put on the white, gauze-like robe. The river, the river, the river blazed in Nachman's mind. God, why have You brought me here? I'd almost forgotten and now You let the worm back in. Here too there were no straight lines, but domes and globes and rounds. Hadn't the Sultan told him to choose? A woman instead of a book? He turned swiftly on his heels, like the guards in the palace. No more. No more! I'll lose the ladder, the sunbeams, the silk, the petals, the songs. The *aleph* will fly away again. I'll strip myself of the "I" that I have been looking for. Nachman stepped into the guard's room. Fatim looked at a point beyond the wall. Selim pulled a key from his pocket and locked the door to the pool.

Fatim drew in his breath, as if about to speak. But he said nothing. When the Sultan left the cubicle, he locked the outer door. Fatim gave out a piteous cry.

"That takes care of him," said the Sultan.

As they walked down the hall to the library, Nachman asked:

"What do you mean, Sire?"

"I gave him a choice: either beheading or remaining in the little room." Selim's leathery eyes glistened.

Or perhaps Selim said: "My harem's pool."

The pool was enveloped by a warm, clinging mist. He looked out toward the rear wall, beyond the naked women sporting in the water. Saw a girl with a forlorn look who stood at the edge of the rectangular pool. So that's where Lizabeta went. She wandered from village to village until she was captured and sold as a slave to the Sultan's harem.

"That one. That one," Nachman said. Through the gauze he saw her perfect form. He tried to control his excitement, but it bubbled out, pinpricks of shivers in his voice.

"What do you mean?"

"I choose that one . . ."

As she came closer, Nachman saw that her face was darker, the lips more rounded. Had she swum across the pool and cried for help, would he have saved her? Would he have jumped into the water in the presence of the ruler of Byzantium? Releasing a captive from bondage is a great mitzva. Jews throughout the ages have bought slaves just to release them. Freeing a slave is a greater mitzva than acquiring a book, even if it is King David's Psalms. No book is worth a human life.

Selim burst out with words he could not understand. Then he stuttered:

"What do you mean, you choose? That one is my favorite."

"You said I could choose anything," Nachman said weakly.

"Anything? Are you insane? I meant in the Library. I just wanted you to have the privilege of seeing what no other man can see and live . . ."

"The doorkeeper?"

"The doorkeeper? But he's blind."

In the grand salon, books and manuscripts shone out from all the corners. As if in a dream, just as in a dream, precisely as in his dream, Nachman approached, saw an old leather-bound vellum and chose it. No need to look inside. Just as he could judge soul fever by pressing a man's hand, so he could tell that this was the book by the warmth, the melody it radiated. For wasn't it all foretold in his story about the ailing princess cured by the stranger who scorned half the kingdom and the hand of the maiden for a seemingly modest book?

The Sultan took the volume from his hands. He didn't open it, just inspected the binding.

"You would have to choose one of the oldest manuscripts in our collection . . . Are you sure you want this? Make another request. Anything! Won't you take ten other, newer books, or a pound, no, ten pounds of gold?"

Not for a thousand pounds of gold or ten thousand books, Nachman didn't say.

"Ten pounds?" Nachman said wonderingly.

"I'll give you twelve pounds of gold."

Nachman thought for a while. He stretched his hand out, as if weighing the gold on his palm.

"No," he said slowly. "I set the condition, and it would not be proper for me to change my mind."

"Very well. I made a promise and I shall keep my word. You cured my daughter. I did not ask you how, but you cured her. You saved my life, even more than my life. The book is yours."

Nachman's heart rose. Yes, it was worth descending to dogdom to rise to possess my ancestor's words. A tender look came over the Sultan's face. Nachman had never before seen such an expression. The Sultan's face looked relaxed, unworried.

"Go in peace, in the name of Allah," Selim said kindly, and then, continuing in the same key, as if the words were but an extension of the melody, "but I'd like to send you something else. Where do you live?"

Careful, Nachman thought. Be careful, be clever. He felt like a squirrel that stops and raises his quivering tail at a suspicious noise. That calculated sameness of melody hid something. Nachman remembered a Hotel Crescent.

"Why are you silent? This is not a riddle, Benhabesht. You don't have to request a three-day postponement. And instead of asking for Edirna's hand or a basketful of gold, as was your right, you asked for less, not more. I may wish to send you something extra anyway. Where are you staying?"

"The Hotel Crescent."

"They too know how to welcome guests."

Nachman bowed. Selim did not offer his hand, but Nachman stretched out his. The Sultan now could not refuse. He pressed Nachman's hand in farewell. A warm, dry hand. Small, with pudgy fingers. Low class, poor breeding. Soul fever. Not to be trusted.

On his way out of the palace—the news of his cure had evidently spread—even the guard at the first entry booth bowed low to Nachman. The Sultan is going to take back the Psalms, Nachman thought as he made his way through the market. If I can see through doors, I may know too much. I must depart immediately. He kept looking back to see if he was being followed. But in Istanbul everyone followed everyone else. There was no one *not* being followed. Except that the followers and the followees kept changing. So crowded were the streets that no one ever walked alone. To be on the safe side, Nachman walked into the Hotel Crescent and asked the clerk a few questions, then sat awhile on a stool in the waiting room, imagining what it must be like to be a Greek spy. Later, he walked out and, via a circuitous route, returned to his inn.

In his room, he held on to the Psalms, even as he slept. What if the princess were beautiful? Could I have accomplished the same thing, or would her womanliness have depleted my imagination? Now I know the meaning of the daily blessing: "Blessed are You who frees the imprisoned." You have imprisoned me in the body of a dog in the palace of the Sultan and have unbound me from both incarcerations.

The next day Nachman weighed the blue sky. Bright sunshine erased the drear of the streets. The warm, bright blue day, as blue as Turkish slippers, flooded his heart. He did not look over his shoulders. Was the confidence from David's Psalms? But then his joy evaporated. Has Istanbul eaten into me? He sensed again the Sultan's men were after him.

On his way through the bazaar, Nachman felt shackles on his arms. He opened the door to his room slowly, expecting someone to jump at him. I have to make a quick decision. Then he set swiftly to the task. He went down to the innkeeper and borrowed the implements. Contrary to Jewish practice, contrary to the traditions of his bearded fathers, Nachman shaved off his beard. When one's life is in danger, anything is permitted. In the market he bought a new yellow scarf, which he wrapped turban-like around his head. With new headgear and a smooth face, no one would recognize him.

And so Nachman stepped out into the Byzantine streets filled with spies, informers, the headed, and the beheaded-to-be, amid crowds of people robed in ivory and blue, pressed so tight the colors blended. Face gaunt, smooth shaven, with yellow headdress, he was a new Nachman, Nachman of Istanbul, waiting to board a ship for the Holy Land. The Book of Psalms was pressed under his arm. In the ticket agent's office, he pretended to be mute. He wrote the word "Palestine" on a sheet of paper. But all tickets were sold, said the agent. No ships for another month. From his suitcase Nachman withdrew Prince Razumovsky's velvet bag with the royal seal and waved it in front of the agent's face. The man brightened and looked through his papers. He smiled. A Greek ship would be leaving in a few days. The man promised arrival within two weeks, before the new moon. Before the Jewish New Year, Nachman realized.

He moved to another inn, in a different section of town. In his room he read Psalms and recalled events on paper. He saw no one until his departure. He boarded a four-masted vessel, stood at the railing as the ship began to move. Just then a troop of horsemen clad in the royal red crescent galloped down the street to the dock. But it was too late. A good breeze was blowing. The ship moved like a pursued doe. The Psalms were safe. No. Not in exile from myself, Nachman thought. God knows to whom He has whispered. And that is why He is letting me go to the Holy Land. And Nachman, a surge of wind and spirit—in Hebrew the word was the same for both—billowed in him, like sails in the breeze.

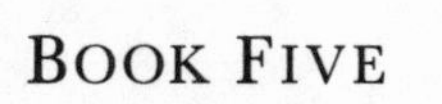

Book Five

The ship hugged the coastline. Soft, cap-shaped hills and stubble-covered fields glided by. A shepherd sitting on a cliff waved. Like its name, the Sea of Marmoris was green blue marble, calm, unmarred by waves, a mammoth painted immobile sea. The ship's motion engaged Nachman. Delighted as a child, he walked west while the ship sailed east. Decks and railings circumscribed his strolls. With David's Psalms pressed to his side, he sat down, his back against the base of a mast. The boat rocked. Deck and mast creaked, swayed to and fro calmly, like a Jew in prayer. Sails puffed like cursive Hebrew letters. Up and down went the horizon, a taut laundry line in the breeze. He saw a little red-haired boy playing on deck with a piece of string. His mother stood nearby. Nachman envied the lad who was going up to Israel as a child. He closed his eyes, floated in a tranquil world on a tranquil sea.

I am Nachman, he told himself. The true Nachman, even without a beard. Nachman von Bratslav, Benhabesht, even the shaven Nachman of Istanbul, taught him to become a truer Reb Nachman. Stripping away layers to get to essence. Falseness peeled away, like skins of an onion. He ran his hand over his face, grasped his chin as though his beard were still there. I, I alone, am the true Nachman. Aboard, only he knew. The few other Jewish passengers who spoke Yiddish did not know the identity of the strange, yellow-turbaned man. He chatted casually with them, did not hold himself aloof, but answered questions with another question or with generalities. People were really more interested in talking about themselves, Nachman knew. Personal questions addressed to him were just ploys to mirror questions back to them.

The perfect weather did not last long. On the third day the vessel dipped and rose from bow to stern and rocked from side to side. Gusts of wind changed the shape of the sails. They snapped like whips. A thick canopy of clouds rolled overhead. Darkness plummeted from the sky. The deck was angled in the storm, like a steep Istanbul street. On the third day, God hurled a howling wind into the water, a mighty tempest in the sea. The frightened mariners scurried back and forth. The masts wavered. It seemed the ship was in danger of breaking. Each spray of mist was followed by a mountainous wave that crashed down on deck. A gust cracked a smaller mast; it groaned like an old tree felled in a storm; mast and sail crashed down aft. The ship whirled around in the raging sea.

Nachman felt nausea rising. A message from God? Perhaps He is telling me: I sent your zayde back with a storm. I'll send you back too. Do not seek the End of Days as yet. The horizon, like his stomach, dipped slowly, and slowly rose. Perhaps the master had lost control of the vessel. Nachman ran down to the cabin section. He passed the red-haired boy and his mother going up. He took the Psalms manuscript from his bag. The room was too dark and cramped; he clambered up again. On deck he clung to a rope. Thunder rumbled; not overhead; to the side, near his ear. Bolts of lightning, vicious and close, crackled through the dark sky. The air smelled of singed linen. The sea hissed. Screams began; the women cried out in Yiddish, Turkish, Arabic; the men shouted in the words of the Hebrew prayer: "Help us, save us." Sailors crisscrossed the deck; some tightened ropes and loosened sails; others did the reverse. One man brought down a torn canvas; another climbed a rope to right a sail. Others poured water in buckets over the side.

Is this the way I end my life? Nachman wondered. Who by fire, who by water? Measure for measure. Those who sin in water die by water. He closed his eyes, dizzied by the pitching of the ship. Both zayde and he had lost the alphabet. Zayde had gone to Istanbul, so had he. Jews always repeat their past. Perhaps a great fish would swallow him and then—instead of Nachman writing a fourteenth tale—a story would be written about him. From under his arm he took David's Psalms, held it up like a talisman. To no avail. He opened the book and began to recite. The wind blew chill, then warm, then chill again. In the scudding clouds, rays of light opened, then closed. Goose pimples formed on his skin. He coughed. Wave after wave lashed the ship. Before one broke, another thundered in its wake. Just then, a wave higher than the tallest mast inundated the ship. The force of the water swept him back. Heard screams around him. But over the screams came a long, unceasing shriek. A cry of terror. The mother of the red-haired boy tore her hair and screamed, "My son! My son!" Her face was pale. She pointed to the railing. She didn't stop for breath but screamed, "My son, my son." Nachman ran, bent over. The boy clung to a rope that ran along the side of the ship. "He's hanging on," Nachman shouted. He called a sailor. "Hold my ankles." The sailor called others. Nachman bent over, his face in the spray. The sea rose. The world tumbled, upside down. "Hold, hold," he cried. "I'm coming." The men gripped his feet. Lower and lower he went, until his hands, free now, so free he didn't realize till later how free they were, descended below the rope, below the boy's hands, to his chest. But the boy, his red hair matted, wild-eyed, clutched the ropes with white fists. He would not let go. Blood pounding in his head, eyes clouded, Nachman said, "I'm taking you back to your mama. Let go, dear child, leave the rope. The men are holding me. Pull," he shouted to the sailors. He grasped the boy's chest firmly. "Up, up." The boy's hands slid on the rope, his fingers opened. Up went Nachman, the boy in his hands. How red was the world, blood in his face. In the water, in a spin of light, a whirlpool of light, something revolved, lifted up, as if counteracting the downsucking motion of the sea. He sensed the empty space under his arm. Nachman's heart tumbled. Hands seized him and the boy. The sobbing mother enveloped both with her embrace. Hands clapped Nachman on the back. The Psalms were gone.

A life is worth more than any book, came the whisper. Any book. If you are worthy, you are David's son.

* * *

Day in, day out, the full moon weakened, halved, quartered. Soon it would wane to a crescent, to resemble a Turkish flag. Nachman asked anxiously if the ship would arrive before the new moon. Again and again he was told, yes, *inshallah,* yes, yes, Allah willing. Before the new moon.

One night, by the light of a silky crescent moon, he stood at the railing watching the sea. The night clouds sent a mute grey light toward the water. A shiver of cold rilled over him. Soon the month would end, the moon would disappear, a new year would begin. Suddenly, lights cut through the fog.

"Land! Land!" came the cry.

The deck filled. Sailors and passengers ran to the railing. Closer and closer came the light. Nachman smelled the damp sand, saw lanterns on rocks. Smaller craft surrounded the ship, which moved slowly forward. He breathed the scents of strange, salty flowers. The noise of the port flooded his ears. Crates were being hammered. A donkey brayed. The cries of porters.

Through the waves, above the din, a familiar sound. At first Nachman thought he was dreaming; he turned to the rocks, the source of light, and heard his name. "Nachman! Nachman!" He became frightened. Who knew he was here? Had someone from Bratslav preceded him to Israel? Who?

On shore, he thanked God for a safe voyage. Like Yehuda Halevi, he bent down to kiss the ground. As he lowered his head, Nachman was empty of feeling. But as soon as his lips, hands, flexed knees touched the earth, thin lines vibrated in him, like a violin string without music. The same feathery feeling he felt when he created a tale. He wanted to dance. "Think of stories," Nathan had told him. But now Nachman's mind was empty. His eyes flooded; the flow of tears singed his eyes; he did not notice he was being helped up by the man who had called his name.

"I would have asked—It is you, isn't it, Reb Nachman of Bratslav? But I need not ask. Only a scion of the holy Besht with sparks of the divine in him could have kissed the land with such ecstasy and longing."

Still on his knees, Nachman saw a tall, full-bearded, heavy-set man, in half-European, half-Turkish garb. A robust man in his sixties, he wore a white tarbush, but like the Hasidim back home he also wore a long grey sashed waistcoat and a white shirt without a tie. His paunch was girded by a thick black silk sash. In his hand, a white cane.

The large man regarded Nachman's beardless face with a puzzled look.

Nachman lowered his voice, touched his stubbly chin. "I was being pursued in Istanbul. I had to shave my beard . . . How did you know I was coming? . . . How did you know me? Has someone . . ."

"No . . . no one . . . I'm Reb Leybele the Hasid, of the Kabbalists' shul in Safed."

"Have we met before, Reb Leybele? Perhaps in Mezhibezh when I was a child?"

"No, we have not met." He tapped his white cane to accent his words.

"Strange, I never forget a face."

"Forget forgetting!" Reb Leybele sang out his responses as if chanting a prayer. He tapped the earth with his cane again. "I was born in Safed and have never left the Land."

Nachman, doubting, looked at the man again. Reb Leybele smiled a secretive smile. His warm brown eyes—one was slightly larger than the other—sparkled. Firm short nose, face exuding health. Where do I know this man from? I have perfect pitch for faces. Could he have been in the Istanbul synagogue? "Synagogue" awoke a little signal in him that said: Yes, you are on the right path. Synagogue. A little shul. On the way to Turkey? No. Vienna.

"The shul. Your shul," Nachman cried delightedly. "I prayed in your shul one Friday night on my way to Vienna. In a small town in Slovakia or Hungary. But when I looked the next morning, I couldn't find it. You sat at the center of a long table and conducted the songs from there. There's an empty chair. The windows are two feet thick and the casements are painted sky blue."

"A Moslem folk tradition. To ward off evil spirits . . ." Reb Leybele laughed. "Yes, that's our little shul. Yes, an empty chair." He looked intently at Nachman and nodded. "The long winters are bitter in Safed. We build good thick walls. Now you understand how I knew you were coming."

"But that was months ago. Then I was on my way to Vienna, not Israel."

"Vienna is but the obverse of the Holy Land," Reb Leybele gently reprimanded. "And, as you see, you are here. One of our Kabbalistic teachings is: No matter where a Jew sets foot, or whither he directs his feet, he is on his way to the Land of Israel . . ."

Nachman, about to say, "But that is my teaching," was stopped before he began by Reb Leybele's firm, upraised hands.

"Nachman, for years we've been reading the signs . . . Don't you know what we know? Surely . . ." His admonishing look said: Come, tell us the truth. "We knew you would come before Rosh Hashana. That's why I waited for you and called your name out in the dark, even before we could learn if you were aboard. Even if a hundred people had shouted: 'There is no Nachman here,' I wouldn't have believed them. I knew you would come. That is why we met that mystical night on your way to Vienna. Our floating shul. You too read the signs. That is why you came."

Nachman tried to swallow. The inside of his mouth felt dry.

"You can admit it," Reb Leybele continued. "Have no fear. Join our common destinies. Let us not lose this holy opportunity. The people of Israel have suffered long enough. Isn't that why you came? To unbind the Messiah: Isn't that the true reason for your journey? Haven't you too interpreted the signs, you descendant of the holy Besht?"

Nachman looked at Reb Leybele's face but didn't see it. He saw only the shapes of Hebrew letters, tumbling and fading.

"I am sworn to secrecy," Nachman said softly. God's whisper filled his head.

"Tell me, Nachman, tell. I am not one of the rabble."

"Of course you're not. God forbid that I should think that . . ."

Nachman hesitated. Why should he tell Reb Leybele what only God knew, what he shared with no other man?

But Reb Leybele pressed him.

"I stand in the Holy Land. So do you. I come from a long generation of mystics who lived and studied in the Land of Israel. My great-grandfather once travelled to Mezhibezh and for a while taught Kabbala to the Baal Shem Tov. We are blood brothers of the same line. To me you can reveal the truth, and that truth, if properly revealed, can be of great significance. For he who understands will truly understand."

Nachman's head felt light, as if air were suddenly swirling in his skull. Dizzy, his strength spent. His mouth was dry. He was exhausted, chilled to the bone. He had to get to an inn.

Still, Reb Leybele silently urged. He twisted the white cane into the ground. From his girth, his size, came the command: Speak.

"Let me explain," Nachman began. "God seeks to elevate man from his spiritual depths, and He chooses various means for this. Sometimes we sink . . ."

"Yes, yes."

". . . and know not why we sink, and only later do we learn the reason . . . to rise in greater purity, out of the defilement. And for me, you see, the Holy One has . . ."

From his chest to his throat rose a spasm. Nachman coughed, choked. He felt a warm flow from the depth of him, hot and wet. Putting his hand to his pocket quickly, he drew out a handkerchief and covered his mouth. A spurt of blood, half the size of his fist, stained the white cloth.

Nachman caught his breath, wiped the tears. "You see. It is ordained from above that I stop speaking."

Reb Leybele put his hand on Nachman's shoulder.

"Come up to Safed with me," he said softly. "There is an excellent doctor there . . . Have you coughed up blood before?"

"No. Never. I've been coughing since I was a child, but never blood."

"Perhaps it's only a strain from the voyage. Seasickness."

"Yes, no end of seasickness."

Nachman felt rooted to the spot where he stood. Then he took four steps. "Enough!" he shouted. Reb Leybele withdrew in fright. "I have achieved my goal. To set foot in the Land. That is all I had to do. That is all the Baal Shem Tov wanted to do. Just to touch the Land—and go." He crumpled the bloodstained handkerchief into his pocket.

"No, Nachman, no. Stay. You have been waiting a long time to come here. We too have been waiting. See the land where Abraham, Isaac, and Jacob walked. See the holy cities: Jerusalem, Safed, Tiberias, and Hebron."

Nachman shivered. How tiny he was. How large was the land. The scouts that Moses had sent to Canaan returned saying the land was occupied by giants. Reb Leybele too was a giant.

"I am small, too small for this land. Its greatness overwhelms me. This blood may be a sign that I should not be here. The holy Besht was forbidden to come. He got as far as the sea by Istanbul when a storm drove him back. To get to Israel one must make oneself small. But to make oneself small one must reach the proper degree of greatness. The Baal Shem Tov had become so great that he could not make himself small. And he, great as he was, could not set foot. And I, I who have not even climbed out of thimble tininess, how can I enlarge myself to small? Since Israel is the highest of the high, one must make oneself very small indeed. For the Besht such descent was impossible. For me, such height is unattainable."

Reb Leybele listened patiently. He put his cane into his sash like a sword and wedged his hands into the silk; his thumbs played with each other.

"He who is authentically great and makes claim to his smallness has already attained the requisite smallness to be in Israel. And that is why you are here, Nachman. I beg you, do not go back. In two days the holy festival will begin. Spend Rosh Hashana with us. Why should you spend the Days of Repentance at sea? Pray with your fellow Jews. Fulfill your mission. Come to Safed."

Nachman turned. Sailors carried crates from gangplank to shore. Porters bent over carrying luggage on their backs. Carts filled with merchandise rolled to and from the ships. Men and women with parcels on their heads boarded. There was a pervasive smell of fish. Not far off stood a Jew, as if waiting for someone. With an agility that belied his massive frame, Reb Leybele pulled out his white cane and pointed it regally at the Jew, and then waved it toward Nachman, as if to say, Move off, don't stare at this man.

"If we leave at once," said Reb Leybele, "we'll arrive in time. I have donkeys waiting."

Nachman shook his head. He looked into Reb Leybele's eyes, but heard the noises of the port, the mishmash of languages, the cries of porters and carters.

"Go in peace, Reb Leybele. Perhaps I shall come up to Safed later. I don't feel well enough for that donkey ride as yet. In any case, I should see Jerusalem first."

Reb Leybele tapped the ground with his cane and sighed.

"If you go to Jerusalem and then to Safed, Tiberias is on your way. Of course you'll see Reb Avremele there. . . ."

"Reb Avremele? I heard of him when I was a child. How is he?"

"Quite well. He too must know. See him. Speak to him."

"Please, Reb Leybele, don't tell anyone I am here."

Reb Leybele pressed Nachman's hand. He understood.

"A healthy, blessed year. As the mystics say in Safed, may this new year bring salvation."

* * *

Nachman held his bag. Donkeys and carriage drivers lined the street beside the port. He asked who could take him to Jerusalem. The drivers refused, for they would not return in time for the holiday. He walked up the street away from the port to search for an inn. Gone was the smell of fish and damp sand. He heard footsteps and turned. Saw a man with a stiff, awkward gait approaching.

"Excuse me, I heard you speaking to the saintly Reb Leybele," the man said, breathless. "And if he gave you such a welcome, you must be a decent man." He stopped, took a deep breath. "I need your help. Please. Let's walk a bit farther." He turned to see if anyone was following. "Reb Leybele pointed his cane at me and then at you. It was a sign to me. You are the man."

Nachman stopped under a tall palm tree to look at the small, stocky man with the wispy grey beard. Like all short men, he held himself erect.

"Please. You must help me." He ran his fingers lightly over his high black hat, stiff and straight as his posture. "I'm in great danger. I've just come back from collecting money in Poland for the yeshivas in Tiberias. When I set foot ashore, one of the drivers who knows me told me that a local Jew has informed to the authorities . . ."

"Informers? Here? Jewish informers?"

"Yes. Don't be surprised. We have all kinds here. If they find it, all the money I collected will be confiscated. The Turks, you see, do not permit us to distribute monies collected abroad to the local Jews. Of course, the informer will get his share. So, please, take the money. I trust you. Deliver it for me. I'm in great danger."

"What?" Memories of Istanbul and intrigue swept over Nachman. "Am I in less danger than you?"

"Yes. You don't live here. The authorities don't know you. They won't search you. Me they know. I live here." The man looked around. "I'm afraid for my life. Please. We must act quickly."

"I know no one in Tiberias. Except the name of Reb Avremele."

"You see? It's destined, a Godsend! No wonder Reb Leybele pointed his cane. Reb Avremele is the one. Bring it to him. He knows who should get it. Thank you. Thank you very much. When will you be in Tiberias?"

"I'll start out the morning after Rosh Hashana."

"May God bless you, your wife and children. May you live to see the coming of the Messiah."

They stepped into a dark alley between a row of houses. Again the man turned. Seeing no one, he lifted his hat, took the bag of money resting on his head, and gave it to Nachman. At once Nachman placed it under his yellow turban.

By ten in the morning it was already hot. Nachman looked at the vaulting blue sky as he rode on the horse-drawn cart to Tiberias. During Rosh Hashana, Nachman had been downcast. His body was in Eretz Yisroel, but his soul—where was that? He would not call this feeling depression because it was against the principles of Bratslav. If the entire world is a narrow bridge, he was hanging from it by a finger. He had thought that Eretz Yisroel would elevate him. But neither the holiday nor the prayers helped. On the contrary, the scroll of sins recited in public confession showed him how depleted was his spirit, what infinite ladders he still had to climb. The blue sky gave him no joy.

The Arab guide rode on a mule before him. Poppies and sunflowers taller than a man blossomed on the sculpted hillsides. Silence all around. He wondered if silence was really tranquility. As he ascended the Carmel to make his way down to the valley, Nachman saw for the first time the broad expanse of the great blue sea.

A faint cry came from the Arab driver. The mule stopped, the cart halted. The horse whinnied even though he had not been whipped. Dust rose. Engrossed in his thoughts, Nachman had not noticed the troop of Arab horsemen who now surrounded the cart. A trap, he thought. The authorities found out. Perhaps *he,* that stocky Jew with the wispy beard, perhaps *he* was the informer. Perhaps, as in Istanbul, everyone was a spy.

But these were bandits, not the Turkish authorities. The horsemen carried no official insignia. The Arab driver handed over the fare he had collected from Nachman; he did not protest or cry out. Evidently he was used to highwaymen. Very likely these highwaymen even knew him and only pretended to rob him too.

One of the bandits gestured for Nachman to step down from the cart. They searched the floor, the seat, looked through his bag, found nothing. The man then felt along Nachman's legs. Nachman began to crow. Standing on tiptoes, he let loose a "Coo-coo-ree-coo" at the top of his voice and flapped his wings. The Arab backed off. Nachman continued crowing. It was morning. God had created the world for the cock; He let him sense night from dawn and provided him with a coop full of hens. "Coo-coo-ree-coo!" His head felt small, but the plumage on his back—that he was proud of. Then the bandit began to search him from the waist up. Now Nachman barked and growled and snapped his teeth. He wished he had Edirna here with him to bark in unison. The Arab bent down, patted his legs again. Nachman crowed. When he swiftly went up to his armpits, Nachman barked.

"He's crazy," the highwayman spat. "From the waist down he's a rooster. From the waist up, a dog. This madman has nothing. Let's leave before *I* start crowing."

The horsemen mounted and galloped off. As Nachman got back on the cart, he gave the robbers a departing series of barks and cock-crows. For the next fifteen minutes he breathed the dust of their hasty retreat. Soon Nachman sighted a small mud-brick village that hugged the sloping terrain. Black-kerchiefed women worked bent over in the fields. In their white aprons, they looked like nesting herons. He passed an Arab on a mule, followed by a woman balancing a huge bundle of twigs on her head. Soon, the cart arrived in the village. Noon silence. Men sat against the walls of the houses smoking water pipes.

Near the well in the small square the driver announced he was going no farther.

"But I paid you to take me to Tiberias. Either take me or refund my fare."

"Those thieves, may the pit open up and swallow them and their fathers' fathers, may Allah give them from the bounty of his curses, they took all my money. So how can I refund your fare?"

"But how shall I now get to Tiberias? I have no money either."

"I don't know. I must return to Haifa. My animals are frightened. Sun and bandits blinded them. Not dependable today. Cocks and dogs. The heat. Perhaps if Allah wills it, a passing wagon will take you. There are always wagons and donkeys going to Tiberias."

Nachman drank and rested for a while in the shade of a house. The villagers stared silently at him. The Arab on his mule clomped by. His wife with the twigs on her head followed. Nachman rose and began to walk. The raging heat in the valley had a life of its own. Mountains in the blue distance of Lebanon shifted in the hot haze. Purple spots danced on his eyelids. Was he getting a sunstroke? He passed his hand over his eyes and forehead. A stream of cricket noises followed him. An orange lizard darted on a rock. On the dusty road grasshoppers leaped, stopped, leaped again. Were they too on their way to Tiberias?

Later he heard hoofbeats once more. Another troop of horsemen—three this time—descended on him with drawn swords, shouting in Arabic.

Nachman pointed to his mouth and ears and shook his head. The Arabs looked away and spoke among themselves. "Yahud, Yahud!" they said. The sunlight glinted on their swords. My God, is *this* the end? Have I been spared from water to die by sword? To be killed like Yehuda Halevi by Arab horsemen on my way to a holy city? Nachman made groaning noises in his throat, and beckoned to them with a crooked finger. Then he began the hymn the kadi had sung for him in the Sultan's palace. Hearing the Muslim prayer chanted so perfectly, the horsemen bowed their heads. Their expressions softened. They put their hands to their foreheads and heart and presented their palms to Nachman. He touched their palms. A stream of apologies, none of which Nachman could understand, now poured out of the Arabs' mouths. Nachman stretched out his two hands, holding imaginary reins—above his fingertips he saw grey green olive trees, gnarled and majestic—flexed his knees, and moved up and down. Then he mouthed, "Tiberias." They understood. Two of the Arabs assisted Nachman as he climbed on a horse. They rode slowly, careful with their holy charge. By evening Nachman was safely in the city. The highwaymen departed, palms up again, looking for other victims, and Nachman, depleted of crows and barks and Moslem hymns, looked for Reb Avremele.

Reb Avremele was born in Tiberias of a Hasidic father and a Sephardic mother. Nachman had heard of him back home as a child. He was the only Hasid who came from Spanish stock, a most unusual combination; in fact, in a community like Eretz Yisroel that divided itself strictly into nationalities, even the Jewish groups—Sephardim and Ashkenazim—were divided, and no marriages between them were contracted. Except Reb Avremele's father and mother. That's why Avremele knew not only Hebrew and Yiddish, but Ladino and Arabic too.

Nachman asked some children to show him where Reb Avremele lived. They brought him to an old, whitewashed, sunbaked, one-story house. Nachman introduced himself in the rabbi's tiny study. Despite his seventy or more years, Reb Avremele was youthful and slender as a young birch.

When Nachman clasped Avremele's hand, the old man trembled. He shook, the table quivered. Reb Avremele held on to his cane to steady himself. His cane too was white.

"I never dreamt . . . or perhaps I did . . ."

Nachman looked over his head. He did not want to see the old man crying. Bindings torn on many books. A musty smell of mildew. Why did he carry a cane? Surely the vigorous Avremele did not need a walking stick.

Reb Avremele looked up at Nachman. He hooked his angular chin in his hand and slowly nodded. Yes, one could see his Sephardic heritage in his swarthy skin, the slightly bulging eyes.

"Is it really you? I never dreamt I would see . . ." and at once he took Nachman by the arm and led him through a door. The little laugh wrinkles around his eyes deepened. Before Nachman could stop him, Reb Avremele banged his white cane on the floor three times and announced to the men in the synagogue: "The great-grandson of the holy Baal Shem Tov."

Where Reb Avremele's private room was modest, the synagogue was ornate. High ceiling, mahogany pillars for the Ark, marble bimah. Hearing Reb Avremele's words, the worshippers stood, withdrew, and left space between them.

"The holy Besht's great-grandson. The holy Baal Shem Tov's great-grandson," they whispered.

"I didn't want anyone to know," Nachman leaned and murmured into Reb Avremele's ear. "I wanted . . . I had to maintain the secret . . . Now . . ." Angry, he turned abruptly and went back to his host's room. The elder man followed and shut the door.

"You've upset me, Reb Avremele," said Nachman. "Forgive me, but I'm displeased."

"I didn't know . . . I didn't know your wish . . ."

When Nachman began to remove the turban from his head, Reb Avremele started in surprise. Nachman gave him the bag of money and told him everything.

Reb Avremele shook his head in wonder.

"And how long do you plan to stay in the Land?"

"I was thinking of . . ." Nachman stopped, piqued.

"Returning home? But you've just come. No, no, don't tell me. Walking four cubits in the Land was enough for you. In those few strides you absorbed its holiness, and took into yourself all the sanctity of the Land."

"How do you know?" Was Reb Avremele's remark a mocking reproof? Or were four cubits indeed enough and that was why he felt he could go home?

"Kabbalists know everything . . . You must stay, Nachman."

"I had already planned to leave. Then by chance I met the fund collector and so I had to come here."

"There is no such thing as chance. You know that. All is determined from above. I suppose you'll see Reb Leybele in Safed now that you are here."

"No," Nachman replied. He wanted to let Avremele know that from now on, *he* would choose where he would go. "Perhaps I will go to Jerusalem. I also want to see Beersheba."

"But that's in the desert. A wild, uninhabited, dangerous place where jackals roam."

Reb Avremele stood and pulled a book from a shelf. He had long arms, long legs. Slim as a Bratslaver. He consulted the volume and hummed to himself.

"According to the holy Ari, Isaac Luria of Safed, there is a cave near the Dead Sea, past the oasis of Eyn Gedi, where the great mystic Rabbi Shimon bar Yohai once lived . . ."

"I didn't know that. But that's where I'm drawn."

"You want to meet him, the one you came to meet?"

A chill went over Nachman. The words reverberated slowly in his ears, as if time had stretched and space had opened up, like the infinite spaces between the letters he had once seen in a waking dream. "What do you mean?"

Reb Avremele read from his text. "No Jew goes near that cave for fear. The Arabs say that at times an old man garbed in white is seen near the cave. But no one has ever spoken to him or knows who he is." Reb Avremele looked up. "We all know the Arabs have great imaginations and like to tell tales."

"Perhaps I've come here because of that cave," Nachman said casually.

Reb Avremele shut his book. Dust rose. He shut and opened his eyes like a great bird. Leaned forward.

"Is that really your reason for coming?"

"Please. I cannot speak. Please don't press me. Reb Leybele questioned me. He insisted and insisted until I could resist no more and when I answered I coughed up blood." Involuntarily, Nachman's hand went to his pocket where his handkerchief lay. "I am forbidden . . ."

"And yet you are drawn to that cave. . . ." Reb Avremele pulled another book down. "There is an old story that the cave is no cave at all, but a passage to a beautiful land where Jews dwell in peace."

Nachman jumped up. "I'm going."

"Where?"

"To Eyn Gedi. To follow David's footsteps."

"Wait! Yom Kippur is coming. Spend the holy day with us."

"No. Please! I must go south. Now."

"Are you determined?"

"Yes."

"Nothing will stop you? Perhaps a visit to Jerusalem?"

"No. That might come later."

"Then your mind is made up."

Even as Nachman wondered why the rebbe was trying to deflect him from his course, Avremele stood and offered him his hand.

"Go, and may God be with you. It is destined that you go. I saw in a dream, the very same night that Reb Leybele in the holy city of Safed dreamt of your arrival, that you will go to Eyn Gedi and Sodom."

"Then why did you ask me about Safed and Jerusalem?"

"To test the truth of my dream. To test your feelings, your determination. Go, lose no time." Reb Avremele gazed at him, taking in Nachman's face with his eyes. "And you are not afraid to go to that cave."

Nachman could not tell if Averemele's remark was a question or a command.

"If one does not fear death, one has no fear of lesser things."

The older man picked up a book of Psalms and said, "Come. In Tiberias we recite seven Psalms before a journey. It is good protection against all dangers."

A wave of fright overcame Nachman. The same lines vibrated in him as they had the moment he kissed the ground of Israel. But now they were not a source of strength; now they drew the energy out of him. He was deeply afraid; he feared he would start to tremble uncontrollably and the shivering would make him cold and the chills would prompt another attack of coughing. He saw the crumpled red handkerchief in his pocket, did not want to cough up blood again.

"Let's say some Psalms by heart," Nachman countered.

"No, no, Nachman. I have it by tradition from the holy Besht to say nothing by heart. Is it not your tradition?"

Cornered, Nachman had to admit; he could not lie. "Yes, but—" and then and there in Reb Avremele's tiny study with its tattered, well-read books, a room smaller than a yawn, he felt that if he did not unburden himself, he would begin to shiver until he trembled his last. Nachman spoke and poured out his heart for the first time. Reb Avremele slowly backed into a high, narrow wooden chair. He listened, then stood and held Nachman's shoulders with great love and awe. He reminded Nachman that the Besht had also forgotten how to read; imperfection was a sign of being human, and Abraham and Isaac and Jacob were human and had flaws, and Moses and Aaron and David were human and they also had flaws. And as for the Book of Psalms, Nachman was destined to rescue it from the Moslem's possession; but it was not destined to be possessed by one man, but by God. For is it not written in that same Book of Psalms that heavens and earth, sea and sky are the Lord's?

Reb Avremele's eyes shone. Like a father he patted Nachman's cheeks. Nachman thrilled to the touch, the love. He had not had such parental affection in years. Avremele's elegant, aristocratic fingers were firm. They looked like tiny trees. He had an unwrinkled ruddy face, a wiry beard. Nachman wished that his entire body had the strength of one of Avremele's slender fingers.

"But what if . . . but what if . . ." Nachman asked, "losing the Book of Psalms is a sign that I may fail here too?"

Reb Avremele thought a moment, then smiled. "God doesn't give straight answers. If he did, we wouldn't open a book tomorrow. We're Jews. So we try . . ." He pressed Nachman's arm. "Let's read slowly."

They began, letter by letter, then gathering strength, letters into words, words into verses. Like a cantor at the prayer stand, like a symphony reaching its crescendo, their voices grew louder, clearer, more impassioned. If he read the missing letter, Nachman did not know it, for they read in unison. They started with *Ashrey,* "Happy are they who dwell in your house," and before Nachman came to the end he realized that Reb Avremele had stopped and Nachman was reading by himself, including the verse that began with the letter *nun.*

Reb Avremele nodded. He was pleased. The air in the little room was thick. Nachman wiped the perspiration from his face. The letters hung in the air like motes of a sunbeam.

Nachman, suffused with joy, seized Reb Avremele's shoulder and began to dance. At first, they went in circles and Avremele kept rhythm by calling, "Hawp, hawp, hawp!" Then, seeing Nachman's inspired dancing, Reb Avremele withdrew. Nachman rose and descended; he spun and rolled and dipped like a ship pitched by waves. Leap, bend, bow, raise his hands, upright masts, the moving oars, point, clap, pound his feet. Storm came, then calm. Nachman waited for Lizabeta to appear in the midst of his voyage, hoping, fearing that she would. When she did not, he knew his dance was pure, of the highest order, akin to a motionless dance.

Nachman stopped. Exhausted. A hot stone in his chest sought exit. If that stone would go, he would feel better. He wanted to cough, could not, dared not. That stone was on fire in his chest. He walked a few paces, felt a sudden weakness. His heart beat quickly.

"What is it, Nachman?"

His legs had turned to stone. Nachman coughed into his handkerchief.

"Go. The dry air is good for your lungs. Go into the wilderness. Elijah went. We know why you are here. Go and bring us what we are waiting for. Suffering is everywhere. The time has come."

Nachman's Bedouin guides followed the caravan routes. They were trustworthy, Reb Avremele had said. He knew them well. They served Nachman, saw to his every need, helped him onto the camel's back. Soon his body fell into the languorous camel rhythm. Dunes and hills turned slowly. The sun rose over a ridge. Down a long hill went the caravan. The stone walls blocked the sun. Then up came the sun again. I saw the sun rise twice in one day, he told himself. He saw shrubs and palms and tamarisks illumined by the glaring desert light. Moses had seen a bramble bush like this one in flames.

He turned and looked at the camel drivers behind him. Their dark faces were like masks. They did not smile. When they spoke, their lips did not move. Nachman used sign language with them and they repeated his wishes in Arabic. When he understood their words for water, *maya,* for bread, *lachma*—so close to the Hebrew *mayim* and *lechem*—sudden smiles broke out on their somber, kafiya-cloaked faces.

The first night, from his tent, Nachman looked up and saw the canopy of night descending. Untold stars sparkled in the sky, black as a scribe's ink. I have no fear, not of the desert, not of evil, he told the stars.

One star brightened. It seemed to direct its light at him. He recalled Reb Avremele's remark: "The time has come." Indeed, he thought, perhaps the time *has* come. True, God had whispered to him. But was he the one? His forbears were unique. And he? He was nothing. The Baal Shem Tov and the others would be remembered. No one would remember him. What *could* he be remembered by? The thought came slowly at first. It seeped in, then left before he had a chance to capture it. It swooped down at him, a bird in swift flight. If he could save a single human being and a community, why couldn't he save all of Israel? The holy Baal Shem Tov had hinted as much to Nachman's mother, long before Nachman was born: "Who knows? Salvation may come from your son."

So, then, he could become the Messiah. For could the Besht be wrong? Nevertheless, Nachman shuddered. Others before him—Shabbetai Zevi and Jacob Frank—had also claimed to be the Messiah, only to bring disaster upon themselves and upon all Jewry. Even one hundred years later, the Jews had not yet fully recovered from these shocks.

The word "Messiah"—*mashiach,* in Yiddish—came to him. At first in two syllables, then the entire word. He sensed it in his fingertips, then felt a blow at his temples. His ears rang. He felt himself floating—I/am I/am I/am. Mashiach, he heard. He wished he hadn't heard it but was glad he had.

Days melted. The silent, austere wilderness penetrated his bones. A tamarisk, a salt marsh, broke the monotonous desolation. Nachman slept lightly, without dreams, anxious lest he miss the dawn, the sunrise. The passage from darkness to light was not subtle, but like a candle lit in a cave. Suddenly, the crags of the mountains became pink, as if God had crushed rose petals and scattered their essence on the hills.

The caravan followed an ancient path. The drivers nodded and snoozed; the camels sailed on; they knew their way. Did camels dream, Nachman wondered, as they walked?

Suddenly a shiny, dark blue expanse filled the horizon. Minutes later the Bedouin and he floated in the Dead Sea. The stark mountains bobbed up and down. Once again, like long ago, Nachman was rowing on the river near Bratslav. Defying gravity. But this water brought no essence of hay.

A joy he had never before known coursed through him. Soul energy. Removed from fields and flowers, here in this rainbow-hued wilderness, Nachman felt his spirit expanding, adding measure upon measure of happiness. He had stopped coughing. Reb Avremele was right. The dry air was good for his lungs. He had had no lustful dreams. He stretched his hands, felt his limber muscles. No tiredness. He looked into his body, looked into his soul. Both were pure. Finally, he was ascending the ladder with ease.

Before sunset the Dead Sea was calm, the life of wind removed. Not a surface ripple. The Bedouin hobbled their camels and guided Nachman to caves above the path. They chose one for themselves, pointed out another for him. The floor of the cave was soft; a mixture of fine sand and crumbled limestone. A light breeze blew. Nachman looked down at the water. At sunset waves of lilac light coruscated there like a thin blanket. The Dead Sea came alive with energy. When he could see no more, Nachman lay down to sleep and at once began to dream.

"As of tomorrow morning," he heard a voice, "drink no more and eat no more. Purify yourself for three days. At the end of the sea, past the Pillar of Salt, there will be a cave. Ascend and enter. Speak to no one. Answer no one. React to no pleas. They are tricks of the other forces, who know of your coming. The evil ones will do their best to tempt you. Be strong. Be careful. Do not be afraid, but approach and . . ." The voice faded.

In the morning one of the Bedouin woke him.

Nachman felt refreshed, as if he'd slept for a week.

Later that morning they met another caravan led by a lone Bedouin with one heavily laden camel and four donkeys. Nachman's guides signalled that he would join the new caravan, for they were heading east to Moab, while the other man was going south.

The Bedouin helped Nachman dismount, said farewell, and rode away. The new guide bowed. "*Salaam aleikum.* Mahmud." He pointed to himself, then patted a fine, ivory-colored donkey. Nachman climbed onto the donkey's back unaided. He sat comfortably on a thick layer of blankets. Occasionally, Mahmud said a word or two, to his animal or to himself. The sun grew hotter. The animals hugged the rocky walls, seeking shade. Mahmud talked to himself in two voices.

In a narrow gorge, the guide suddenly dismounted and bent down to his boots. Nachman saw the glitter of a knife and quickly jumped off his donkey. Where could he run? This is my destiny, my punishment. I sinned in water; I die in sand. Man's legs take him where he is destined to go. Mahmud gestured with his knife. He rubbed his fingers: money.

Nachman, searching for coins in his pockets, approached him. He sang, weaving one melody into another. The Bedouin stood on his toes, tense as a spring. A warning flick of his knife shifted sunlight in a quick arc. Nachman looked behind Mahmud and nodded, as if responding to someone standing there. When the wary Bedouin turned, Nachman sprung forward, seized and twisted the man's arm. Mahmud cried out in pain and dropped the knife, which Nachman kicked over a ridge. He applied more pressure and forced Mahmud to the ground. The man grovelled, begged for mercy. "Allah, Allah," he squealed. For good measure, Nachman suddenly raised his hand—Mahmud covered his head and made a ball of his body—then dropped it. Mahmud pressed his head to Nachman's feet.

Nachman signalled the Bedouin to stand. He searched his belongings for other weapons. But Mahmud cried, swore, bent his knees; he had none. He rubbed his forehead on the ground, pleading for forgiveness. It was hot, he said. The heat. The cursed sun that Allah casts upon his servants around Sodom. But they could cool off in David's pool, Eyn Gedi, not far away. He swore friendship, and rubbed his forehead once more in the ash dust of the path.

They took up the journey again. Mahmud rode ahead. He chattered to himself. Another hour passed. Despite the heat, Nachman neither ate nor drank. They rode up to a grove of palm trees and dismounted.

"*Maya, maya,*" said Mahmud.

Flowers grew out of water-fed crevices in the surface of the rocks. Nachman's head felt clear. The shadows were thick and comforting. A rush of water in the distance. Mahmud, smiling now, pointed and made a tumbling motion with his hands. Follow me, he indicated, and jabbered to himself as he walked. Once, he slapped his own face.

Soon Nachman heard a tumultuous roar of water. At the end of the path he saw a hundred-foot waterfall that formed a natural pool.

Mahmud bent down and lapped water from a rivulet. Nachman undressed and stepped into the pure cold water. Here King David bathed; here my ancestor drank when pursued by Saul. Once, twice, and five more times. Seven times did Nachman purify himself in the fresh running water. Then seven times again. How that number haunted him. Thirteen plus one. I shall complete it, Nathan! Do you hear? I shall create a fourteenth tale. Nachman bent down to the pool to see his face in the water. When he had not been complete, when he did not have all the letters, he could not imagine his own face. But now he was complete. He had the letters. Here in the Holy Land the last of the holy letters had been returned to him.

Out of the water, he felt light on his feet. He chose not to fly, for he did not wish to alarm Mahmud. The energy flowed to all his limbs. Nachman went up to a sweet-smelling bush, broke a sprig, and placed it in his pocket.

Riding again. Moving once more. But differently. Now, on the white donkey, the land did not undulate as it had on the camel; it moved forward nervously, with jagged, mincing steps. Late in the afternoon, past the Pillar of Salt, Nachman wondered: how much more?

Overhead, two little birds with white breasts twittered and circled each other.

They flew up to a flat stone on another level. Nachman signalled Mahmud to wait, and followed the birds. Up Nachman climbed alone. The air grew fresher. He looked down at the Sea of Salt, the Sea of Death, shining like polished silver. His heart beat more quickly. The same excitement as—no, he dare not compare it. As when he and—no, he dare not. Nachman pressed the palm of his hand to his heart. He saw a cave. A white ibex with huge curved horns stood before the entrance. Is this where it begins? Nachman breathed deeply, afraid of pain in his chest. But he felt no pain. The ibex bounded into the opening and vanished.

Just before Nachman entered the cave, he saw a ram's horn on the ground and picked it up.

But it was a false cave, for after momentary blackness came light. He stood in the open on a narrow ledge. To his left was an abyss. A drop of hundreds of feet. But an upgrade path circled to the right next to the wall of the hill. A plum-colored dusk settled. Nachman looked down at the silent wilderness. The profile of the hills reminded him of a musical score, notes moving up and down.

On a promontory he saw an old, hand-lettered sign: "No man shall enter this house unless he be a prophet or a king."

I am neither a prophet nor the son of a prophet, Nachman thought. But all the Children of Israel are likened unto kings, for they are the children of the King of Kings. He sensed an acrid smell. Smoke rose from the ground. The earth rumbled and quaked; thunder resounded, lightning flashed. Fire shattered the slabs of rock. Fire split the stones around him. Nachman trembled within, but his hands were steady. He held the sweet sprig in one hand and the ram's horn in the other. Hands outstretched, he said aloud, "I am not afraid." He thought: Once again I am following a dream.

The sudden appearance of an old, long-bearded man blocking the cave made him feel faint. The man held a white stick. Nachman's knees buckled, but he revived as he inhaled the scent of the aromatic plant.

"Son of man, what do you seek here?"

"To bring salvation. Rid the world of evil . . . Let me enter, Elijah!" Nachman tucked the sprig and the ram's horn in his belt.

"My name is not Elijah!" came the curt reply. The old man banged the stick on the stone. "Listen carefully. Speak to no one."

"But the Mess—"

"Not another word. Here is a key. For the final door. I have spoken too much already." He gave Nachman the key and a flat, round stone. Then the old man rounded a corner. His white cloak trailed behind him. Nachman turned the stone over, looked for an inscription. A hint. Something. But found no sign, no word.

Nachman entered the cave. He felt warm; his throat was dry, parched by fires of Sodom. A stream ran by the side of the path. He disregarded the cool running water. Water also dripped from the many inverted cones hanging from the roof of the cave. Nachman wrapped his cloak tighter. Adam disobeyed; I won't.

Heat rose. The floor of the cave was strewn with white-hot coals. Nachman pushed them aside with his stone and hurried into another chamber. Smells of a kitchen on Friday morning. A table set with roast goose, noodle puddling, kasha and onions. Cakes and apples and fruits he had never seen before. Take, take, the dishes seemed to say. This is home. For a moment his childhood flashed before him. The fragrance of the Sabbath. A longing for home, mother, came over him. He clenched his fists. Laughed. I, who was never tempted by such fare at home, do you expect me to succumb here? He bent low through another entrance. The path narrowed. He pressed against the rock wall. Down to his left, a deep pool of swirling water. Ahead, a knot of serpents and scorpions moved toward him. There was no turning back. Joseph survived the pit of scorpions and serpents. But did anyone promise him that he, Nachman, would survive? The mass of snakes moved in a slow swirl, now backward, now forward. Nachman pressed his lids shut and concentrated. The year according to the reckoning of the gentiles is 1800. One hundred times *chai*. Life. Nachman felt himself rising. The air was warm beneath his legs as the snakes, shedding heat and a venomous grey green light, passed beneath him.

In the next chamber, Nachman felt something dripping down his forehead and neck. He feared it was blood, but it was only perspiration, pungent and malodorous. He heard a familiar sound. An old woman dressed in rags stretched out her hand to him and cried in Yiddish: "Help me, young man. Help me. My husband, over there."

About to move from the path, he felt something pulling him away. Do not react. Do not speak. He bit his lips and moved on. Then he heard a roar, a sizzling crack. Four musicians with repugnant faces sat on a platform in an alcove. The music sounded like Mozart, but was not Mozart; it sounded like Beethoven, but was not Beethoven. Still, their music was beautiful. He had not heard such heavenly music since leaving Vienna. He wanted to stop, climb up on the recessed ledge to the quartet. Instead he brought the ram's horn to his lips. It gave out a pure, clear blast. The musicians played discordant notes. He blew again—they vanished. He laughed to himself. Had it been Beethoven himself, I might have stopped. The forces of temptation are not clever at all.

Nachman's heart beat fast as he swung open a stone door and entered the next chamber. Soldiers in red and green uniforms stood guard in an anteroom. They took no notice of Nachman. He entered an even brighter hall. The Sultan again? With an ailing Edirna? A king with a crown sat on a throne. At his side stood a large, detailed portrait of a monarch, but the face was blank. The king raised his hand and pointed. Nachman turned and saw the Sultan's pool. Smelled the hot water, the rising mist; saw the blind eunuch. The naked women stood with outstretched arms; those still in gauze shifts slowly removed them and cast them in the air, where they floated like clouds. Nachman marched straight ahead. The girl who looked like Lizabeta was not there. He blew his ram's horn. Dead, empty sounds. The king now pointed the other way, to a flowing spring. A princess entered, stepped over the spring. She wore a white dress; around her neck was a green kerchief emblazoned with Hebrew letters. A white silk scarf covered her hair.

"Is this my bridegroom?" she asked the king, as a look of pain creased her face.

"No." He winked at her. "You know who we chose for you." And moved his gaze to the unfinished painting.

The princess approached her father. She moved with Lizabeta's grace. But Nachman must press on. Must not stop. He had the key. Behind the king's throne was another door. And beyond that—the door with the key. His goal. He must get through. No one would hinder him. Avoid all temptations. Resist. He walked behind the throne. The king did not turn. The princess followed. She removed the scarf, shook free her long blonde hair. As soon as her hands touched his and he looked at her face, he saw who she was.

"I am imprisoned here," she whispered. "They keep me here by force. I was taken from my Jewish home." She pointed to the Hebrew letters on her scarf. "This is all they've left me," she said, giving him the scarf. Her green eyes glinted. Rowboats and rushes, reeds and hay. "Hold my hand and take me with you."

"Is it really you?" Nachman wanted to say. "Is it really you, princess of my dreams?" he wanted to say aloud. Now I am not dreaming. Perhaps she too was being tested. And just as he sought salvation, so did she. Who could say one salvation was more important than another?

Nachman closed his eyes and considered. Had he loved anyone else in his life? Of whom did he dream, if not of her? Then she appeared. On the path. At the lake. Then three more times. In the carriage to Vienna. In the Sultan's private pool. And here. She filled his dreams. This is the village she'd been exiled to, and she wants to go back home. There could be no doubt: it was Lizabeta. And suppose he withstood temptation and obeyed the order not to listen, not to touch, to pay no heed, but only to proceed? Suppose he did this and when he came to free the Messiah, the Messiah admonished him:

Why didn't you free the girl? *That* was your test, false Reb Nachman! Where is your lifetime of good deeds?

But I was told . . .

You were told! Freeing the girl had nothing to do with temptation—that was a mitzva. Until the ladder of good deeds is completed, nothing can be accomplished. Now it is too late, false Reb Nachman. You should have freed the girl. She is no less bound than I. I seek to be free; she sought to be free. You always preached compassion, Nachman, did you not? Until the essence of a false Reb Nachman seeped into you.

Nachman stood rooted for a moment. Do not stop. Do not look. Do not touch. No other man has been given such a chance. Do not ruin it. Take care. Speak to no one. Answer no one. All the evil forces in the world seek to stop you. Everything here is evil, from the snakes and scorpions to the bearded man and the festive wedding. The woman is Lilith, demon in disguise. Everything is shadow. Seek light. Let no music, no sounds, no singing, no pleading dissuade you from your task.

But if he refused, Nachman thought, she might be trapped forever. Move on, move on, move on, an inner voice counselled. Just another step. He had saved her once, by rushes and river; now he'll save her again. History repeats; private histories too. What we have done before we may do again. Full repentance cannot come until one is placed before the very same temptation—and resists.

He seized her hand. She could not be the demon Lilith. Lilith, said the Kabbala, is the antithesis of joy. But Lizabeta was full of joy. Hence she could not be Lilith, handmaiden to Satan, and there was nothing to fear. The entire world is a very narrow bridge, he told the princess. The main thing is not to fear. Abyss on both sides. But with you, gladly, would I walk this thin line to eternity. Her hand radiated waves of feverish heat. At once his desire rose, as in his dreams. How could this urge, this lust, be contained? Memories were sterile satisfaction. Signals, not clear cut. Did she bring her lips to his, or he to hers? He kissed her with the same ardor that he kissed the soil of the Land. No, with even greater joy. But no tears came, only a laughter that bubbled, burst within. Out of his lips into hers he poured music, herbs, the gathered prayers. Sunbeams and silk. Petals and notes. An *aleph* that flew. How sweet the sensation, as if he were kissed by God. All his life—how long had it been since he saw her by the river, by the rushes, by the reeds?—he had dreamt of love like this. Happy, happily, hand in hand, he walked, ran through the door with Lizabeta. Cries and shouts followed them. The noise of the waterfall, without the gush of water, thundered in his ears. His hands hurt. His heart beat. Coughs wracked his chest. There. There, off to a side, was the door he was looking for. The door he had to open. No, he dare not open it. False Elijah had given him a false key. He would not be falsely tempted. The last chamber. He expected light. The most heavenly light one can hope to see. And then . . . And then . . . Instead of light, there was

Emptiness.

He found himself once again in the open, alone, under morning clouds. A spring beside his feet. Drink, he heard. Now you can. Overwhelmed by thirst, he bent down and gulped. Drank and drank. Could not drink enough of the cold water. When he thought he had slaked his thirst, he put his lips to the spring and drank again. The cold water rushed into the dry gulleys of his mouth. Into the sere channels of his soul. He stood. He could feel the emptiness in his hands. He coughed again; his chest ached. Ashamed, he lowered his eyes. The yetzer ho-reh has defeated me again, he thought. Strong as death is love.

In his hand, no key. No silk scarf, but a grey rag. Threads instead of Hebrew letters. He wished he could utter a plea to God for forgiveness.

He stood with his back to the Dead Sea. The dry, grey red flat-topped hills glimmered. Abyss on his left, abyss on his right. A narrow slab of rock before him. Here, then, Nachman, is your world. What would I have found, he wondered, had I used the key?

Why didn't you use it?

The key was real.

This folk tale follows no laws I've learned, Nachman said bitterly. False Elijah gave it. Therefore, I thought the key too was false.

He closed his eyes, imagining nothing. Drained of thought, emptied of feeling. The sun, the heat, burned his lids, bored into his eyes. Was he delirious? Nachman rubbed his eyes. The heat made him sleepy. Gazing skyward he saw—could not believe, but yes, on a ledge above sat a figure, back turned, hunched over, bound in chains. A depression whose existence Bratslav did not recognize fell over Nachman like a huge wave. If it weren't for the could-have-been that is the mystery of the folk tale, he could have proclaimed himself to the world as the Messiah.

A mist came; or was it Nachman's eyes that misted? The old strength of a leader came back to him, like Samson between the pillars.

"Turn around," Nachman ordered. "I like people to look me in the eye when I talk to them."

The figure turned slowly. Nachman saw the Messiah's face. And Nachman screamed a silent scream. A terrible scream that tore the silence like the rent in a mourner's garment. A scream that moved hills and crags and mountaintops. God's whisper lost. Nachman clapped his hands to his face and looked no more. Where do you look out to see in? the Sultan had asked. A window at night becomes a mirror. Now Nachman had seen that mirror. He had seen the image in the mirror and draped a sheet over it.

Was everything false? The Messiah too? Nachman thought of the Seventh Beggar, hero of the veiled story he had told his Hasidim. Everyone awaited the beggar like an honored guest at a wedding, like a Messiah. But he never came. No one knew who the seventh beggar was. But Nachman knew. So did Reb Leybele and Reb Avremele. It was no accident that they had white canes. White was the Messiah's color. No accident that Mahmud's donkey, reserved for Nachman, was white. It was all predestined in God's whisper. The legend had played out for him. Nachman's sigh came out of him like blood from an open wound. He looked down at his shoes. His feet of their own volition scuffed the dust. What might have been. But for one moment, what might have been. Again he was a false Nachman. And now? Too late. Down to the bottom of the ladder again.

Broken, head down, Nachman did not see the plain, the crags. He did not hear the silent music of the dipping and rising hills. Did not notice the little stones that moved before his feet. Slowly he made his way back to the waiting Mahmud. Once, long ago, the true Nachman had succumbed to a peasant girl named Lizabeta; and now the false Nachman had done the same. He should have known. Losing the Psalms was a portent of what was to come.

You are human, he heard. You are not a god. You are not an angel. You are human. You are human. You are human.

Mahmud waited. When he saw Nachman he seemed startled but said nothing. He kept staring at Nachman's head. Defeat shines out of a man's face, Nachman thought. They mounted their donkeys and rode back. Gloom, like a glove, encased itself around Nachman. At an oasis they stopped to drink. Nachman saw his face in the water. The mirror told the truth. A quiver ran through his body. He understood Mahmud's fright. His hair was white.

Book Six

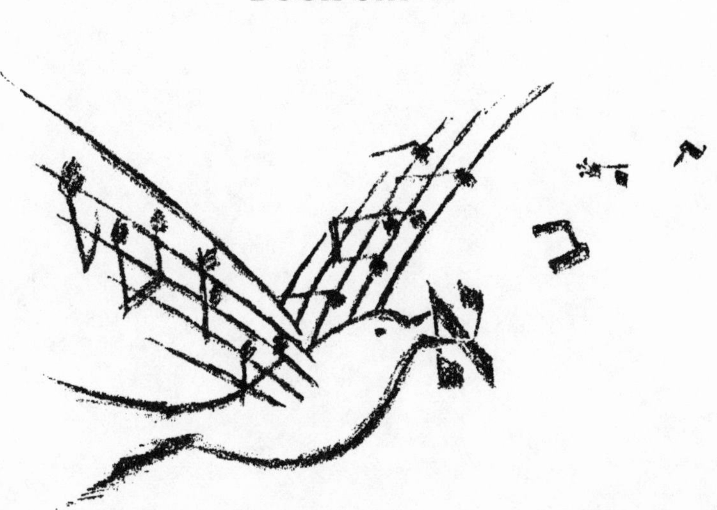

Like a shadow Nachman passed through the Land of Israel to the Port of Jaffa on to Istanbul. Here, beardless again, mute, clad in a blue turban, and affecting a slight nervous tic, he moved safely past Istanbul through the open lands to the north.

Like a mourner, Nachman did not look at a mirror, did not want to see his hair, wanted no reminder of his failure. Should he dye it black? He wanted only to get home. Nothing more. Was that such an earth-shaking desire?

Nachman stubbornly made his way back. In 1800, a hundred times *chai,* the Ukraine was beset by autumn storms, heavy rain, mudslides. He waded through sticky roads, swam around washed-out wooden bridges, bound for home. He coughed every day. Occasionally, he saw blood. The pain that lingered in his heart moved to his chest. What does one do, he wondered, with a fading whisper?

One afternoon the weather cleared. Abated the fatigue that had plagued him and lengthened his journey. Beethoven slipped into his mind. Blink, and he was there. Broad pockmarked face, wide brow, hesitating smile. Dear Beethoven, I'm ashamed to say I've written nothing. I am without music. I had thought that the music that music listens to is in the Land of Israel. But I could not find that either. Can you put your finger on a day, an act, when a man goes astray? Nachman saw Beethoven look up at the sky. It was the sort of day the composer would like, deep blue sky, clouds for decoration, air clean after a long rain, his spirit buoyed by the smell of earth and flowers.

Weak, pale, exhausted, Nachman arrived in Bratslav at night, protected by darkness. Deep in his heart he had dreamt of a different return. His beard, touched with grey, was fully grown. In his room he donned a black, wide-brimmed hat that covered his white hair. He wondered what his Hasidim would say. The next morning, in the bes medresh, the welcome was mute. Did they sense his failure? he wondered. Feel his soul fever? Still, he had just returned from the Land of Israel. That alone deserved a better welcome for him. But the Hasidim were so distant. Why did everything seem so far away?

Bratslav was unchanged. All was in order. As if he were not there. *As if he were not there.* The thought pressed dully against his skull. So that was his hallmark, the Rebbe of Bratslav who is not there. The rebbe with the empty chair. And that's the way it would remain, he decided. Empty. Like the chair in Reb Leybele's floating shul.

Nachman's body was at rest, even-keeled, a ship riding the waves. No bent masts, no storms. No dreams. Long ago, in the midst of prayers she would entice him, sparking a heat in him that blanked out God's words. Once, long ago, he had prayed for temptation and his prayer was answered. Should he now, weak and beaten, pray like Samson for just one more resurge of strength?

On the third day of Nachman's return Nathan came and made his request.

A coal fire warmed the room. Nachman, at his writing desk, wore a sweater and a jacket under his long black gaberdine. He could no longer suffer the cold. No longer tortured himself by being only partially warm. He knew why Nathan had come. The silence became too much for Nathan.

"You promised," Nathan said.

Nachman took a deep breath, released it heavily as if spitting out something bitter. Grimaced and held his hand to his chest for a moment.

"I did . . . But can you go? Think!"

"I know." Nathan's sigh was broken into two sounds. "Just as the Jews can't run away from God, even if I wanted to I couldn't run away." He looked down at his fingers moving rhythmically against his thighs.

Nachman could no longer contain the cough that exploded out of him.

"You should see a doctor," said Nathan. "A good one has moved into Bratslav."

"A Jew?"

"Yes."

"Then why isn't he here?"

"Maybe he prays at the other end of town."

"Maybe he doesn't pray at all."

"Maybe."

"If he hasn't cured himself, how can he cure me? I don't need a doctor. I'm just exhausted from the journey. My soul is tired, coming back from Israel."

One day and then another. Some days he spent half his day in bed, reading and writing.

Nachman closed his eyes. Slept, but did not dream. Thank God, no dreams. My sort of dreams don't come to the weak. He thanked God he was weak. At the edge of sleep, he said: Like a cardplayer, I gambled and lost.

The sequence of events in the cave blurred in Nachman's mind. He looked for the point where he could have done something else, said something else, turned fate around. In his daydreams he tried to reverse destiny. But no matter what scenes he invented, what other paths he imagined, he still emerged from the cave as empty-handed as he had entered.

The next day, as Nathan stood by the door, Nachman began to cough. When he caught his breath, he said: "Ask Natasha . . ."

"Natalya."

". . . Natalya to prepare some warm milk and honey."

When Nathan returned, Nachman asked: "Is she still studying Hebrew?"

"Oh, yes. She reads quite well now."

Nachman shook his head in wonder. He had never considered it before: Natalya in Hebrew means "God has taken."

"Does she still want to become a Jew?"

"She hasn't mentioned it since you left."

"Just as well. We have enough problems . . ." Nachman swung his legs over the side of the bed, reached for his cape.

"What are you doing, Rebbe?" Nathan asked.

"It's Mincha time. I want to pray with the congregation."

"We'll open the door. When you feel better, you'll join us in the bes medresh."

"I feel better now."

And before Nathan could persuade him to stay, Nachman wrapped himself in Beethoven's cape. "Not too long ago I was a meta-magician strolling through the court of the Sultan; now I sit like an old man."

He leaned on Nathan as he walked; felt dizzy but did not want to show it. The blood circled around and around, descending from his head to his feet.

Prayers had not yet begun. Snatches of conversation floated. Among the buzz and hum of talk he heard "Messiah" and "Napoleon." Interesting that the two should fuse, he thought. Both are mysteries. From both too much is expected.

In the middle of the prayers Nachman suddenly stopped. As usual, the prayers flew on without him. Again he was in the same place: the bes medresh. He recognized every bench, every chair. His own big, black, hand-carved mahogany chair, every chip on the lectern, every fleck on the grey walls. They need whitewash, he thought. The faces were the same. The prayers the same. So what had changed? His hair. The hue of his soul.

He pressed his fingers into the prayer stand and, to his surprise, whispered to himself: "Nachman, you are a ladder without rungs." He felt nothing. The words were just shapes and sounds. If all prayer was a request for salvation and he had had his chance and missed, what reason was there to pray? I am Mahmud. Talking to myself in two voices.

Nachman took two strides away from his prayer stand. Felt disoriented. He heard his name. "Nachman ben Simcha." Where did that voice come from? Summoning him where? To judgment?

A Hasid stood at his side, led him to the table.

Nachman sat down. He raised his hand.

"Everything," he addressed the gathered Hasidim. "Everything is . . ." false he was about to say. Everything is false. There is no

Messiah. He is just a man like you and me who sits there, bound in chains, waiting. With your face or mine. Everyone sees his own face in the Messiah's. Everyone can be a Messiah.

Until he fails.

"He who says we can bring the Messiah by denying ourselves, that man lies! Curbing appetite doesn't make a man holier, but madder. Rolling naked in the snow doesn't bring on the Messiah. Do you know what it brings on?"

Nachman looked around the room. A grey gloom was etched into every face.

"Well, do you?"

Silence. No one answered.

"It brings on lung disease."

Nachman heard someone sighing. Perhaps himself.

He rose. Stood by the window that faced the yard. A soft twilight lit the grass and painted the little fence behind his garden gold. Natalya, slightly hunched, walked to the well with an empty bucket. Ha! She is going to fulfill the mitzvas while this Jew breaks them. The world is upside down. The gentile wants to join the convenant that I, the Jew, have broken.

A burst of energy, a powerful sea wave within him, forced the words out. He turned back to the Hasidim.

"There is no Reb Nachman. He is not here. Truth is hard to grasp. The only true things are music and tales. Music cannot lie; tales, even if they lie, tell truth. There is no Reb Nachman. Your Reb Nachman is false. Everything is . . ." And he bit his lip, bit until he tasted blood.

The Hasidim looked at him. He knew they gazed at his white sidelocks, but they could not see his hair, covered by the wide-brimmed hat. Did they wonder if the change went any deeper? White hair comes from within. A man's hair does not change overnight for nothing. Nachman felt empty. He had no more messages. No more words. No more letters. He wished he could be free—oh that look of the Messiah in chains, oh that scream from his own throat—free to return to his room, slam the door, and never face them again.

Before he could ponder his thought or withdraw his wish, Nachman stood, wheeled, strode to the door. He did not want to do it; he wanted to reverse the deed the moment his hands moved, but a hot flash surged like lightning through him, pleasant but quite uncontrollable, and he slammed the door furiously behind him and stood in his room, alone, whispering to those who could not hear, "I am sorry. Forgive me. Forgive me."

A knock on the other door. The old woman came in with the hot, honeyed milk. He thanked her, took it quickly, but sipped slowly so as to avoid speaking to her. She looked at him fondly from behind her red checkered kerchief.

From Nathan's Diary

What can I say? It is four days now that he refuses to see anyone. "Leave the food outside the door," he says. Or, "Go away. I am at peace now." Or, "I do not deserve your attention, your respect, your love." But who is he to say to whom we should offer our love, respect, attention? *That* he cannot command us to deny him. The journey to Israel has sapped his strength. He has become older, weaker. He is forgetful. He rambles. He says things he never said before. And the responsibility on me increases. Has the trip to the Holy Land made him mad? I did not want to say it earlier; but now it must be said. We knew all along he was a holy man. But what happens when a holy man sets foot in the Holy Land? No wonder the Baal Shem Tov was forbidden to go. God knew what He was doing. The world cannot take two such holinesses. Is too much holiness a prelude, a stepping stone, to madness? Has the Rebbe forgotten that I wanted to leave, that I promised to stay only till he returned? Or is it more convenient for him to remain silent? And now I am trapped here. When I mentioned this to him, he looked over my shoulder at someone—something—far away. A dreamy look, which by degrees turned plaintive and sad, as if he were seeing something that distressed him.

"You promised," said Reb Nachman.

Promised what? I thought. I don't remember promising anything beyond staying till he returned.

"You promised," the Rebbe continued, "to stay on till . . ."

But he did not finish.

"Rebbe," I said gently. "You asked me to stay till you came back. When you returned, you said, I could go for as long as I please."

"Have I returned?" he said quickly. There was a sharp edge to his voice that belied the ambiguity of his remark. "Am I really back?"

The Rebbe looked me in the eye. For a moment we understood each other like brothers, without words. He was right. In a way, he had not returned; he was not really back. Before leaving for the Land of Israel, the Rebbe told us, "I am more there than here." He had obviously left most of himself there. He could not wrench himself away from the Land; departing was difficult. Reb Nachman was right. He was not back. And since he has not come back, I cannot go.

If the Rebbe continues his isolation, he will sink deeper and deeper into himself until it will be too late.

Then I had an idea.

On the fifth or sixth day of his isolation, a fine Sabbath morning, Nachman heard singing in the yard. He pushed the curtain aside. His Hasidim had carried out benches and the reader's table. They were praying outside. During the past few days, he had stood on the other side of the closed bes medresh door and followed the congregation's prayers. At night he sat at his desk. With his books at his side, he read and dipped quill into ink. A little wave, a little hook of desire to join them outside swirled through Nachman. He stepped back. Enough. Enough. They can manage without me. Let Nathan lead them. In fact, things were better when I was away.

Then, from afar, he heard his name. Once. Twice. He went to the window.

"*Ya'amod!*"

Summoned to the Torah.

"Rabbenu Nachman ben Simcha."

Instinctively, he stepped back, but he knew he could not stay hidden. One cannot refuse an *aliya* to the Torah. Nachman smiled. His Hasidim had outsmarted him. So this too was destined.

He opened the door, inhaled the fresh air. Remembered the warm moist air in Tiberias, the crisp dry air of the desert. A feeling of freedom, akin to creative joy, warmed his limbs and his cold lungs. What could that sweet feeling be compared to? Had he felt this surge of life when he was with Lizabeta, during his sweet ecstatic sinful dreams? But the dreams had not returned. A holiness from the Land clung to him, the Land flowing with milk and honey. Nachman wanted to break into dance as he walked to the Torah, but he could not. His legs. He looked around. Whose, whose brilliant idea was it to call him to the Torah? Days before he had almost uttered the word "false" to the Hasidim.

Who knows how many spiritual ladders he would have broken by saying that word? Indeed, the only false thing was his reclusion.

As Nachman approached the Torah and held the scroll's wooden rollers he felt a release of joy. With the edge of his prayer shawl he kissed the Torah and chanted the blessing. The Torah reader began reading. The fine, thread-like crenellations on some of the letters were like the antennae of beautiful butterflies. Soundless music, with all of music's hidden art. He recalled his old dictum: I've never met a woman as beautiful as the alphabet. Until . . . until . . . He breathed deeply. I feel better, he thought. I feel better. Perhaps, he thought, perhaps all is not lost after all.

He shook hands with the Hasidim, who gathered happily around him.

"Forgive me," he said. He saw the astonishment in their eyes.

"You've come back to us," said a Hasid. "We missed you. And now you've come back to us."

"We've found you. We've found you," said another Hasid playfully. "You were hiding and we found you."

Nachman laughed. "When I was a child, I played hide and seek with a friend. When my turn came, I hid in the hollow of a tree and peeked out, waiting for my friend to look for me. I waited a long time. But he had changed his mind. Later, I complained to my father. My father of blessed memory said, 'God too is in hiding and no one looks for him.' And he told me a story: 'Once, God wanted to amuse Adam. So He played hide and seek with him in the Garden of Eden. Adam looked and looked and then lost patience. He stopped looking. Since then evil has come into the world. God is still in hiding and no one looks for him.'"

Nachman turned, sought out Nathan. Was he in hiding too? Ah, there he was. He winked at him.

"How is that for a fourteenth tale?"

Nathan's eyes darkened. "You must be joking, Rebbe. That is your father's story."

Nachman nodded, agreeing. "Just to let you know I haven't forgotten."

The Hasidim arranged a celebration for Nachman's return from his inner exile. Wrapped in his cape, he watched the dancing. They infused joy into themselves; but he, his heart was empty. He felt the cold woodenness of his old carved mahogany chair. A sudden chill breezed through him, a gush of icy wind into the room. I'm old King David, who could not be warmed. In all my clothes I'm cold.

Then a chill pierced his soul. Nachman pressed a finger to his lips. Perhaps the Hasidim too are only pretending to enjoy the dancing, hoping to draw inspiration from me. Nachman shifted in his chair. He was uncomfortable. A vacuum rose like dark fog from his stomach to his chest. Nachman smiled for them, his smile a mask. When the black mist swirled up to his head, he fainted.

Days passed. The weather turned colder. Winds from the north brought freezing rain. Soon the snows would follow. Mornings, the taste of frost was in the air. Flocks of honking white geese flew daily overhead. The fatigue of the journey did not abate. Nachman's energy ebbed. He lay in bed more often, a board propped on his knees, books and writing paper beside him. If he felt well enough, he prayed in the bes medresh on the Sabbath; but even then he stayed only an hour.

One morning he had a coughing fit and spat blood. Now he did not hesitate: he told Nathan to summon a doctor.

"Wait. Before you go. You always told me, but I assure you, it hasn't . . . I haven't forgotten."

Nathan shook his head, eyes narrowed. He could not understand what Nachman was saying. What am I saying? Nachman thought. The words aren't coming out right.

"What I mean is: I assure you, Nathan, that the last story . . ."

"Last?"

"The last story I tell will contain all the others. The thirteenth, the seventh, and the first. It will even go beyond the first."

"Last, Rebbe, last?" Nathan screamed, as if in pain.

"I have no more strength."

From Nathan's Diary

The doctor's words brought no comfort. Lungs ravaged, he said. That's why he brings up blood. We asked the doctor not to tell him the severity of his illness. Get fresh air, the doctor told the Rebbe.

Nachman sat outside more often, wrapped in robes and blankets, but the fresh air made him sleepy. With much sleep the days passed quickly. Was he getting better? He could not tell. Perhaps he remained the same.

But he knew it could not be the same because nature does not work that way. Either better or worse. Am I, then, no longer in control of my body? Nachman shook his head in disbelief. He could not imagine his body, which he had commanded to defy gravity, was now stronger than his will.

One night he dreamt of his parents. Both smiled at him, as if welcoming him home. The next morning, a sharp pain in his chest accented the dream's message. He summoned Nathan and spoke in a voice so strong it surprised him.

"Nathan, we must get down to basic truths. Prepare. No more hiding from one another. God can play hide and seek with Adam, but we—we down here must talk honestly. No hiding. No, no, I'm watching your hands, Nathan. Do not, do not begin trembling. Please. Not now. I can't take such an attack of nerves . . . Tell me, how many years ago did I go to Vienna?"

"This year. Late spring. You went to Vienna this year."

Nachman lowered his voice. He spoke softly, afraid of a spell of coughing, afraid of fainting. "This year? And when did I go to Eretz Yisroel?"

"Also this year. After you returned from Vienna. You just came back six weeks ago."

"All this in one year? And Edirna in Istanbul?"

"I don't know Edirna. What's that?"

"Not *that!* Who is she, you are supposed to ask."

"Well, then, who is she?"

"She became a dog and I cured her, the Sultan's daughter in Istanbul, by becoming a dog myself . . ."

"I see," said Nathan flatly, but he did not see at all.

"Edirna, Selim, Prince Lichnowsky," Nachman chanted. "And where was the Rebbe of Bratslav when I went to the Land of Israel?"

"But *you* are the Rebbe of Bratslav."

"No, no. I am the false Reb Nachman, the dark mirror of the real one. How could the Rebbe of Bratslav leave his people so often? Vienna, Istanbul, Israel. True, I went away, but the real Rebbe of Bratslav remained. To tell stories in neighboring towns."

Nathan stepped back, took a deep breath.

Nachman looked at a point above Nathan's head, where the letters used to hang.

"Did he learn from this experience, this travelling, teller of tales who wanted to imitate the Rebbe of Bratslav? I entered the synagogue from a back door. Heard the end of a familiar story. *My* story. But the speaker's back was turned. I couldn't see his face. I suspected . . . but I dismissed the suspicion as unworthy . . ."

Nathan was silent.

"So that is why you were so anxious for me to leave for Vienna, the Land of Israel, anywhere."

"A moment of temptation," Nathan said weakly.

"Say that again?"

"A moment of temptation."

"So you too have moments of temptation? You too are human? Each of us has his downfall in a moment of temptation."

"I was gone for two weeks. For two weeks I was you. I felt what it is like to be you."

"And how did it feel? Did it feel good?"

Nathan glanced at the bedcovers. Nachman's feet spoiled the smoothness, like rough waves in a sea.

"You always wanted to become a rebbe," said Nachman.

Nathan was silent.

"Every man is given his own clock. I know what's happening to me, and I want to talk to you while my head is clear. What's on your mind?"

"But you called *me*."

"Because I know what's on your mind. Be honest. Don't look at me like a golem. It doesn't become you."

Nathan's lips, jaws, moved, clacked as if unglued.

"Everyone is asking, Rebbe . . . They asked me to ask you . . . Please don't think me impudent . . . Who do you . . . ? That is, do you want anyone . . .? Who, Rebbe, will you choose to . . . ?"

From Nathan's Diary

I can dance, I can sing, I can tell stories. The Hasidim like me; I like them. It will be a burden, a responsibility, but I trained myself. All my life I've prepared myself for leadership. I know how to serve. That is why I shall know how to lead.

Nachman shook his head emphatically from side to side. "I had a vision of an empty chair. And that's the way it will remain. *Eyn ish.* No man. No one."

Nathan put his hand to his face, held his chin.

"When I die . . ." Nachman said.

"God forbid!"

"Don't cry! All my life I've been learning how to die. I know how to die. Dying needs as much skill and self-control as living. There was a time when I was so afraid of death that when I read the laws about washing the corpse, I fainted. I couldn't imagine anyone dead, least of all myself. In shul, when someone said Kaddish, I moved away, lest the aura of death that clung to him would rub off on me. And yet, when my parents of blessed memory died and I sat *shiva,* I found that when people came to comfort me, I felt more sorry for them than they felt for me. That was the turning point. I knew my loss; they didn't. They came in, poor souls, hesitant, unsure, ill at ease. And I would calm them by asking questions, by getting them to talk, as if *they* were the mourners." Should I console him now? Nachman wondered.

"So it's your wish that it should be no one." Nathan swallowed. "Perhaps it will be better that way . . . Better for everyone."

"You look too much like me, Nathan. Save yourself from the dangers, the temptations, of being rebbe."

Nathan's face was pale. From his lips the pallor spread, a reverse slap, to his cheeks, eyelids, and forehead. Nachman pitied Nathan. His dream, his hopes, and his ambition were shattered.

"No one," said Nathan. "The chair will remain empty."

At that moment Nachman again saw the dream shul with the empty chair. Prelude. Mystic hint.

"But you will take my writings . . . That will be your responsibility. Call in the people from the bes medresh."

Nathan opened the door.

Nachman saw faces. Only faces. Where were their bodies? Dozens of faces pressed in at the doorway, not daring to set foot in the room, as if a flaming sword held them back.

"Tell them, Nathan."

"The Rebbe says that the chair will remain empty."

"Empty," said the faces.

"*Eyn ish,*" Nachman said.

"*Eyn ish,*" they chanted. Their faces hung forward, ready for more. But Nachman said, "Please excuse me. I want to sleep."

From Nathan's Diary

Daily the Rebbe grows weaker. Still, incredibly, he has strength to study and write. In the bes medresh and at home the Hasidim recite Psalms daily, praying to God for his health. Some people say his illness is a punishment from God. He shouldn't have set out into the world. He had no business studying music in Vienna. One Hasid said: "The Rebbe said that Beethoven may even be descended from Sephardic Jews in Holland. *Beeth—offen:* open house. But *I* say Beeth-*oven,* 'oven' meaning 'sin' in Hebrew. House of sin. The Rebbe should have stayed with us."

The next morning, as if he somehow knew what people were saying, the Rebbe told me:

"Send my regards to the master in Vienna."

"Which master?"

"I once told you. My master of music, my old friend, Beethoven. It has been so long since I've seen him. And give him this melody as a gift . . . Are you listening, with both ears?"

I leaned closer. Reb Nachman clasped his hands and began to hum. He closed his eyes; his voice rose, fell; he seemed to gain strength from the singing. Only the flush on his face showed the strain.

"Do you have it, Nathan?"

"Yes, Rebbe."

"Sing it back to me."

I sang the melody, note for note.

"Almost," Reb Nachman said. He leaned back on the pillow. "But that is why you couldn't really imitate me, for when it comes to the ultimate test, they would test your pitch. Not perfect. Therefore, not Nachman . . . Draw me groups of five thin lines, like this, on a page."

I prepared the lines for him; he sang and wrote down the notes. "Send this to Beethoven in Vienna."

"No address?"

"Beethoven, Vienna, is enough."

The Rebbe closed his eyes for a moment.

"And the fourteenth tale?" I said.

The Rebbe clapped his thin translucent hands and glanced at the ceiling in exasperation. "Are you still hounding me?"

"You spoke about a fourteenth tale. The magic number. Twice seven. Completion."

> "When the time comes," Reb Nachman replied, "you will have it."
> "Tell it, Master," I said. "Everyone is waiting." But I didn't believe my words. He won't tell it. He has been locked too long into silence.
> "I promise," Reb Nachman said.

Just as Nachman said, "I promise," the old caretaker burst into the room. "You promised me too, rabbi."

"Out!" Nathan shouted at Natalya. He walked toward her. "How dare you barge in like this?"

"I serve the rabbi daily. I don't barge."

"Impudent," cried Nathan.

"Shh," Nachman said. "Please!" And to the old woman he said, "Speak!"

"I've waited patiently, rabbi. I've been studying," she said in her old voice. Her arms dangled pathetically at her side. "You told me three or four months. I marked them off on my calendar. Not three months but four. One hundred and twenty days. One day for each year of Moses's life. I've been studying. I read all the Russian books. The histories. I know the laws of kashrus. I know the Bible. Test me. Hear me out. Listen."

From under her arm she took a Siddur, began to read, fervently, fluently, with the intonation and accent of the Jews in Bratslav.

"I've listened outside the bes medresh window. I know all the prayers. Melodies too. I am a Jew in everything but name. Make me a Jew."

"I can't make you a Jew."

"Then tell God to make me a Jew."

"If we could tell God what to do," Nathan snapped, "we'd tell him first to cure the Rebbe."

"Maybe last," Nachman said. "Other things come first." Nachman looked at Nathan. "The woman is right. She has studied. She has shown devotion. She knows."

"It's not a year, Rebbe. She has to be put off three more times for three months."

"No matter. She is an old woman, doing it purely for the sake of faith. A youngster who has marriage in mind, well, that's another issue. We let them cool their blood for a year . . . Tell the wife of one of the Hasidim to take her to bathe in the mikva."

The old woman ran up to Nachman as though to take his hand and kiss it, then stopped suddenly.

"Thank you, rabbi, thank you." Her face glowed. Behind her droopy bandana, despite her stoop, despite her plain peasant's garb, the old woman looked vigorous. Nachman remembered how she had lifted the chair with one hand. Her enthusiasm for life kept her young.

When she left, Nachman told Nathan, "One Jew dies, another is born . . . Did I ever thank you for all that you did for me? No, no, I'm not being sarcastic. No father could find a better son, no son a better father, no man a better brother . . ."

"Please, Rebbe."

"When I first met you, Nathan, I was a young man . . . And now I look like an old man. Hair white. Coughing. Catching my breath . . . Yet for me, time stretched miraculously, like the gap between the two mountains for zayde. I have seen so much, lived so much, that a dozen people in a dozen lands would have to live a dozen lives to fit all of it in . . ."

"You're *still* a young man."

"A man's life can't be judged by the length of his days. But only by the miracles in it. And every hour, every minute is a miracle. That we breathe is a miracle. That we wake in the morning from the near eternal journey of night is a miracle. A little wound that heals is a miracle. Twenty-eight years of daily miracles. What isn't a miracle in our lives? Reading? Singing? Dancing? All miracles. Every letter in the alphabet is a miracle. Did you ever see an *aleph* bird made of music? Twice in my life I learned to read. How many men can say that? In each letter we penetrate mysterious worlds. Making melodies—ah, dear Beethoven!—is a miracle. So don't look sad, Nathan. I've really lived a long life. And thank God I'm still alive. I'm not afraid. I haven't been afraid of living and I'm not afraid of dying."

Nachman began to cough. For a moment, two, his breath stopped. He gasped for air. Held a handkerchief to his mouth. Spots of red appeared. His shoulders shook. Nathan looked helpless.

"Does it hurt you, Rebbe?"

"If the pain gets too bad, I can shut it off when I like, thank God."

Nachman closed his eyes, filled the blank parchment of his mind. I have not achieved what I wanted to achieve. I strived for perfection. I had a chance, and I lost that chance. I could have embraced the entire world; instead, I embraced a branch, a twig, a bit of fleeting nothingness. I could have held an entire forest in the palm of my hand. But I was tempted by a leaf.

He looked at the little table to his right. On it were books and quills and a little copper bell to call for aid. He stretched his hand, then changed his mind. At the foot of the bed another table with towels and a basin of water. If the room were locked, nothing would change. Books and copper and basin would remain in silent stasis.

And Nachman, does he change? Is his prayer the same? Was his mind wandering? His eyes moved over the prayers like greased wheels, without volition, without thought. He remembered how he liked to look through prayer books and straighten the bent corners of pages, for the pages of a Siddur also had a soul. And how he loved to open different Siddurim and see different styles of print. The same prayer took on a different character when the typeface changed. His chest—it wasn't there. An empty floating feeling like hunger hovered in his lungs. He closed his eyes. Where was he? Of what had he thought? For years and years, in his dreams, on most nights after a day's work, in dead tired sleep, a young woman came and stroked his face, limbs and body, and then, like Avishag who warmed the bed of cold King David, she slipped naked into his bed and into his arms. To whom should he have confessed these dreams? To whom could he pour out his soul? *He* was a rebbe, and a rebbe had no rebbe. Was there a doctor who would tell him he was ill? That his mind was wandering? And what if he told this doctor that his ability to read had disappeared and then come back? That he could defy gravity and rise in the air? That in the mountains near Sodom he had seen the face of the doomed Messiah, and that the Messiah was none other than—Wouldn't that doctor pronounce him mad? Wouldn't those charlatans who call themselves doctor consider mad one who preached holiness and lusted in secret?

I only wanted her for a moment, to test my will with temptation. I wanted one image of a beautiful woman, and God pushed a thousand mirrors of her in front of my face, one night after another. The pressure. Hands choking my lungs.

"Nathan, Nathan," he called softly and rang the bell. "Are you there?"

Nathan opened the door from the bes medresh. "Rebbe?" He came to the foot of the bed. "Are you—?"

"I'm fine. But my breathing is heavy." Nachman cocked his head toward the wall. "But he's still waiting." A weak smile. "Let him wait . . ." Nachman gave a little laugh. "I'm serious. He's there. I sense his presence. Over there, by the books . . . But don't be afraid. Now the entire world is not a narrow bridge. It is a wide and spacious roadway."

Nathan looked at the bookcase and then gazed into the basin of water at the foot of the bed, as if seeing his image there. He held onto the edge of the bed. The water sloshed in the basin.

"Nathan?"

"Yes, Rebbe."

"I don't know."

A pause. Nachman heard a crack running down a wall.

"Can I get you something?"

"Yes. Get me some parchment. I want to write . . ."

"Your will?" Nathan blurted and then, too late, could not withdraw the remark.

"My will? No . . ." Nachman took a deep, heavy breath. His chest pained him now. "My will be. My should have been. A man's will is written when he is young."

Nathan, trembled, wept, laughed, did not know which emotion to suppress, which to allow.

"Enough, Nathan," Nachman said sharply. "I can't abide a grown man with eyes wet constantly. Even Natalya doesn't cry as much when she peels onions . . . What were we talking about?"

"I'm to get your parchment. I'll have to go to the scribe's workshop. I'll be back in half an hour, Rebbe."

"Nathan. Wait."

"Yes?"

"I don't know."

Nathan waited.

"Yes, now I remember. You know what the saddest words are? 'I could have been.'" Nachman lowered his voice. Because of pain or something else?

"Oy, Nathan. I could have. I could have been. If I hadn't been such a false Reb Nachman, I could have raised you higher. *You* might have become the true Reb Nachman."

Nathan, hands at his side, clenched and unclenched his fists.

"If I were truly Nachman, I could have brought on salvation. But I became a false Nachman and that false Nachman is going to die. The true one will live on. He'll sit in that old mahogany chair. No, don't worry, Nathan, I don't mean you. You are not a false Reb Nachman.

You are a true Nathan. Now go. The parchment. The finest. I want to write . . ."

Nathan went to the door.

"Wait," Nachman said. "I want to ask . . . "

But where was that question? If he could only put his hand somewhere out there, beyond his mind, and touch the question. It was there, out of reach. Ah! Now he had it.

"Did you send the music to Beethoven?"

Nathan closed the door quietly behind him. Did he say, "Yes"? Nachman hadn't heard. He was alone. Was there someone in the bes medresh? It was daylight. Afternoon. All the Hasidim were at work. Now he was alone with the old caretaker and that Whoever—Nachman turned to look at him—who waited patiently in the shadow. Where was Natalya? On her haunches behind the stove? Warming some milk for his strained throat? Or saying Psalms for him? He did not want to be alone. Not alone with the shadow. He rang the bell furiously.

The door opened. The old woman walked in, stooped slightly over her cane. The red bandana loose around her face as usual. Suddenly, she lifted the cane high over her head. For a moment Nachman blanked out. The stroke of death. So it wasn't a *he* by the wall, but a she. It was she who waited, in the guise of a loyal servant, hovering around him for months. "I do not fear you," he whispered in her language. But then why had she bothered becoming a Jew? The black angel has no religion. I do not fear you. I am ready. The entire world is a very narrow bridge. The main thing is not to fear.

Nachman opened his eyes, waited for the blow. Sought the words for the *Shema*. But she cast the cane behind her. It slid on the wooden floor with a long, shiny sound. Natalya bent over the basin, took the hand towel, dipped it, and wiped her forehead. The black streaks of age disappeared. Dipped again and washed her cheeks, eyes, chin. Nachman's eyes clouded. Why had the Angel thrown away the cane? To postpone the final stroke? To torture him? Natalya rubbed her face. What miracle was this? Is she, perhaps, the Angel of Life? Am I to be cured? Nachman closed his eyes. What is happening? Am I in the cave again? The woman removed her floppy bandana and shook out her hair. Oh, that feeling. Like a cool breeze in the heat of Sodom. Like the waterfall at Eyn Gedi. Like breathing without pain. Like the dreams. Her blonde hair floated slowly. She removed her black rags. Beneath them she wore a white short-sleeved open blouse, the one she had worn that time, long ago, at the river.

Standing straight, she smiled at him. Although the room was darkened, her hair glowed.

He felt a cough coming, like a sneeze building up, but it went away.

"You?"

She nodded.

"I don't understand."

"Think. Understand. You are Rabbi Nachman who makes everyone else think and understand."

"All along? All this time?"

"Yes," she whispered. "This is my village. My exile."

"Why?" he said softly.

"Think. I love you. When I first saw you dancing, alone in the forest, that's when I began to love you. I heard your songs."

"So it was not a dream. I am not mad." Nachman laughed. Shook his head slowly.

"You became an old woman for all these years, just to be with me?"

"The Song of Songs says: 'Floods cannot quench love, nor can river drown it.'"

"You didn't drown in the river."

"Love never dies." She gazed at him, closed her eyes, opened th again. "And you? Did you, do you love me too?"

"My princess," Nachman said. "Lizabeta. *Alpha beta*. Lovelier t all the letters."

"At the mikva I chose the name Rachel."

What an ending to the tale, Nachman thought.

"Nathan is coming back," he said. "If they find you, if ey notice . . . "

"I passed through the slowly moving hours of the day to be with you at night. Night after night."

A sensation, an old sensation wound slowly, weakly, through him. Was it desire again? He remembered the Yiddish saying: In dreams it is not the dreamer who sins but his dreams. But if his lovemaking was not a dream, who was the sinner?

"I cast a spell into your milk and honey, the spell of Yadwiga the witch, the same spell she cast on me, Yadwiga who put the curse of heat for a man into a young woman's bones."

"Yadwiga? Witch? But . . . you're a Jew."

"When I studied and learned, I threw all that away. I posed as an old woman, but now I am a Jew."

It was her fault. Hers. He could have done, he could have achieved, he could have won, if not for the fire she had stirred in him. His desire for her had followed him everywhere. At home, on the road, in Istanbul. Even in the Land of Israel. A vague memory of a cave filled his mind.

"Why were you in the cave? I saw you there. With your long blonde hair and the silk scarf with the Hebrew letters. Why did you stop me? Do you know what I could have accomplished? Who I could have been?"

She stared at him, looked past him, uncomprehending.

"A man's feet take him where he is destined to go."

Who said that? Nachman wondered. Could she quote the Jerusalem Talmud? His head sank back onto the pillow.

"Look what I gave up because of you."

Did he say that? Nachman thought. Or did she?

Nachman could not tell who said what anymore.

"Give me your blessing," she said.

He wasn't going to bless her. She was his Eve, his serpent. Because of her . . . because of her.

"I've never given blessings. I'm not that sort of rebbe. If a person deserves it, he calls blessings down upon himself."

Suddenly she covered her face with her hands and burst into tears.

"I've sinned, I've sinned. If I'm not blessed it means I'll be cursed. Give me something, give me something."

What could he give her? What could he do for her? For her, he wanted to levitate now, but he could not. He barely raised his chest in a shallow breath and let it fall with a heavy sigh.

"I wanted to teach you the language of the birds, the petals and leaves, the song of the hay. I wanted to teach you the language of the trees, of fire, of stone. But I had no time. No time. Once, yes once, I knew these languages. Tongues unlike any others. Their grammar defies gravity. . . . Go back to your father."

"No. I am a Jew."

"I lost my letters because of you."

"But you found me. Lovelier than all the letters. And I gained mine because of you."

"But you—"

"Stop blaming me for everything," she shouted. "You made your choice too, you know."

But it *is* your fault, he wanted to say. Why were you in the cave? I told you to stay in Bratslav. You didn't listen. You spoiled everything. Do you know who I could have been?

Instead, he said, "Where will you stay?"

She took a deep breath. Her chest expanded. He imagined her by the rushes. Remembered the smell of hay. She shrugged one shoulder. "Maybe here."

A swirl of desire flared in him. "Milk and honey," Nachman said.

She left the room, assuming he wanted to drink.

The rooms were empty. A void. My princess. My princess who became a Jew. At least one dream come true. But too late? He gazed at the utter emptiness, the emptiness after sadness, after tears. Ay ay, what could have been. He wanted to say the *Shema,* but could only remember the first word.

"Here is the parchment. Berel sent the finest he had . . . Master, Master, are you all right?"

Nachman opened his eyes. He pushed himself up on the bed. "Even Moses didn't want to die. He chased away the angel at least three times. Finally, the soul said it wouldn't leave. God himself had to kiss Moses. Even the Angel of Death couldn't do the job."

"Please, Rebbe, don't speak of death."

"Do you think we can cheat him by silence? Do you think he'll close his eyes rather than mine? Strange. My body tells me soon, and yet my soul feels serene. I can almost say I feel well . . ."

Nachman bent for his handkerchief. A cough came up from his depth. He gagged, turned red in the face, fell back on the pillow. Nathan daubed his forehead and cheeks with a wet towel.

"I can suppress the pain. . . . But it is . . . getting . . . more and more difficult. . . . I think you should call everyone in," Nachman whispered.

"Now?"

"No. Not now. I'll tell you."

Nachman closed his eyes for a moment. "Are you still here?"

"Yes, Rebbe."

"You know I was a rebbe?"

"Am, not was."

"But I've also been a dog. I have been a ladder. I have been an angel. I have been a piano string. I have been a prayer, a song, a sheaf of rushes, an oar. I have been a lover, a field of flowers, a spray of sea. I have been on the back of the *aleph* bird. She gave me her song. I have been . . . have been . . . have been. But what I *could* have been, alas, I am not and will never be."

Nathan looked at the murky water in the basin, black with Lizabeta's charcoal.

"Nathan, do you know the Baal Shem's melody?"

"No."

"I'll teach it to you. Put music lines on the parchment. And give me five minutes by myself. In precisely five minutes come back and then call in the Hasidim."

Nachman floated into a tunnel. At the end of the tunnel there was a white light. Not a light like a candle. Not a light like a sun. But a soft white velvety light. It drew him on, this light, and seemed to say: Come, come, come. Yet at the other end of the tunnel Hasidim called him to come to them. He felt he was free of himself, looking down at them, looking out at the light. Like a speck of dust, a sunbeam, a grain of gold, he stood balanced, not knowing which way to go. To that calm, beckoning light, or to the people who wanted him. But he wanted, he so much wanted to go toward that light that was not moon or sun but shed a light unlike any light he had seen before.

Nachman felt his soul fluttering, beating its wings against the flower petals out There. But he still had strength to hold his pen. He wished he could have thought as did zeyde as he lay dying, whispering, "Get away from me, foolish, empty pride. Off with you. Even during my last moments you come to me and whisper, 'Think of the wonderful funeral you're going to have!' Begone! Away!" But he was not like the Baal Shem Tov. It was a different time. He was different too. What went wrong? He knew. But the thought was out of reach. In the clouds somewhere, the clouds by the bookcase, kissing the walls, clutching with airy fingers. Eluding him like a tiny, zero-shaped speck floating before his eyes in sunlight. She . . . she . . . the princess. He had chosen her instead of salvation. The wrong path. The error. Zayde. Oh strength! Oh God, just a few moments more. The melody. Not struggling anymore. It was sweet, this feeling, this soul hovering, this fog coming, this ecstatic separating, this sleepy feeling of peace and exaltation. Oh,

God! To die with a kiss, like Moses. The blessed death that is sleep so sweet and overpowering, like sleeping in the sun, like sleeping in the sun of the sun, a weariness so inviting, blissful sleep, hovering soul wanting rest, rest, and the tilt of the light of the sun, now full blaze into him, the ecstasy, the music, the lightness of sunlight. Then it came, in a wave, a tremor, a tremble, a vibration, a joyous lambent pulsation: into eternal sleep, prelude to eternal waking, the f

i

n

a

l

o

r

From Nathan's Diary

When I came back, the Master's precious soul had departed. Too late for the Besht's holy melody. The pen had fallen from our beloved Rebbe's hand. The remnant of a soft sigh, as if the struggle were no struggle at all, but a kiss of God, hung on his lips. Under his pillow, a sheaf of papers. Reb Nachman's face was turned to them, for me to notice. I picked up the pages he wrote and placed it among his papers.

After the period of mourning—no children to say Kaddish; no relatives to sit shiva; only the Hasidim—I looked at his writings. Over my sorrow, over our loss, my heart leaped with joy. With gratitude, ecstasy. I pressed his manuscript fervently to my lips. The Rebbe had kept his promise. To complete the cycle. Twice perfect seven. A tale that, in his words, would contain all the tales and even go beyond the first.

As I read his manuscript, night fell. And strangely, though I did not light a candle, the pages themselves seemed to light up the darkness.

This is how it began. . . .

During that mystery-laden time of day when, in the words of the Passover song, it was "neither day nor night," and the milk-white no-light might have been dawn or dusk, so tenuous, so precarious, was the silver balance between light and darkness, Nachman of Bratslav, the great-grandson of the holy Baal Shem Tov, walked to the river, alone in the world. He walked to the river, alone in the world, and that was his undoing; he walked to the river, alone in the world, and that was his uniqueness; he always walked alone in the world, for that, he knew, was his choice, his destiny. He walked alone with his thoughts, humming songs of his own creation as he looked at firs and up at tops of swaying hills, rounded like carefully scribed Hebrew letters. He marvelled at the wonders of God, who daily renews His acts of creation and garbs Himself in light